The Man on the Box

Henry E. Dixey in " The Man on the Box."

The Man on the Box

By

Harold Mac Grath

Author of
The Grey Cloak
The Puppet Crown

Illustrated by scenes from Walter N. Lawrence's beautiful production of the play as seen for 123 nights at the Madison Square Theatre, New York

Grosset & Dunlap
Publishers, New York

THE QUINN & BODEN CO. PRESS
RAHWAY, N. J.

To Miss Louise Everts

Contents

He either fears his fate too much,
Or his deserts are small,
Who dares not put it to the touch
To win or lose it all.

Dramatis Personae

Colonel George Annesley	A retired Army Officer
Miss Betty Annesley	His daughter
Lieutenant Robert Warburton	Lately resigned
Mr. John Warburton	His elder brother, of the War Department
Mrs. John Warburton	The elder brother's wife
Miss Nancy Warburton	The Lieutenant's sister
Mr. Charles Henderson	Her fiancè
Count Karloff	An unattached diplomat
Colonel Frank Raleigh	The Lieutenant's Regimental Colonel
Mrs. Chadwick	A product of Washington life
Monsieur Pierre	A chef
Mademoiselle Celeste	A lady's maid
Jane	Mrs. Warburton's maid
The Hopeful	A baby
William	A stable-boy
Fashionable People	Necessary for a dinner party
Celebrities	Also necessary for a dinner party
Unfashionables	Police, cabbies, grooms, clerks, etc.

TIME—Within the past ten years.

SCENE—Washington, D. C., and its environs.

The Man on the Box

THE MAN ON THE BOX

I

If you will carefully observe any map of the world that is divided into inches at so many miles to the inch, you will be surprised as you calculate the distance between that enchanting Paris of France and the third-precinct police-station of Washington, D. C., which is not enchanting. It is several thousand miles. Again, if you will take the pains to run your glance, no doubt discerning, over the police-blotter at the court (and frankly, I refuse to tell you the exact date of this whimsical adventure), you will note with even greater surprise that all this hubbub was caused by no crime against the commonwealth of the Republic or against the person of any of its conglomerate people. The blotter reads, in heavy simple fist, "disorderly conduct," a phrase which is almost as embracing as the word diplomacy, or society, or respectability.

So far as my knowledge goes, there is no such
a person as James Osborne. If, by any unhappy
chance, he *does* exist, I trust that he will pardon
the civil law of Washington, my own measure of
familiarity, and the questionable taste on the part
of my hero—hero, because, from the rise to the
fall of the curtain, he occupies the center of the
stage in this little comedy-drama, and because
authors have yet to find a happy synonym for the
word. The name James Osborne was given for
the simple reason that it was the first that occurred to the culprit's mind, so desperate an effort did he make to hide his identity. Supposing,
for the sake of an argument in his favor, supposing he had said John Smith or William Jones or
John Brown? To this very day he would have
been hiring lawyers to extricate him from libel
and false-representation suits. Besides, had he
given any of these names, would not that hound-
like scent of the ever suspicious police have been
aroused?

To move round and round in the circle of com-
monplace, and then to pop out of it like a tailed
comet!. Such is the history of many a man's life.
I have a near friend who went away from town

one fall, happy and contented with his lot. And
what do you suppose he found when he returned
home? He had been nominated for alderman.
It is too early to predict the fate of this unhappy
man. And what tools Fate uses with which to
carve out her devious peculiar patterns! An
Apache Indian, besmeared with brilliant greases
and smelling of the water that never freezes, an
understudy to Cupid? Fudge! you will say, or
Pshaw! or whatever slang phrase is handy and
prevalent at the moment you read and run.

I personally warn you that this is a really-truly
story, though I do not undertake to force you to
believe it; neither do I purvey many grains of salt.
If Truth went about her affairs laughing, how
many more persons would turn and listen! For
my part, I believe it all nonsense the way artists
have pictured Truth. The idea is pretty enough,
but so far as hitting things, it recalls the woman,
the stone, and the hen. I am convinced that
Truth goes about dressed in the dowdiest of
clothes, with black-lisle gloves worn at the fingers,
and shoes run down in the heels, an exact portrait
of one of Phil May's lydies. Thus it is that we
pass her by, for the artistic sense in every being

is repelled at the sight of a dowdy with weeping eyes and a nose that has been rubbed till it is as red as a winter apple. Anyhow, if she *does* go about in beautiful nudity, she ought at least to clothe herself with smiles and laughter. There are sorry enough things in the world as it is, without a lachrymal, hypochondriacal Truth poking her face in everywhere.

Not many months ago, while seated on the stone veranda in the rear of the Metropolitan Club in Washington (I believe we were discussing the merits of some very old product), I recounted some of the lighter chapters of this adventure.

"Eempossible!" murmured the Russian attaché, just as if the matter had not come under his notice semi-officially.

I presume that this exclamation disclosed another side to diplomacy, which, stripped of its fine clothes, means dexterity in hiding secrets and in negotiating lies. When one diplomat believes what another says, it is time for the former's government to send him packing. However, the Englishman at my right gazed smiling into his partly emptied glass and gently stirred the ice. I admire the English diplomat; he never wastes a lie. He is frugal and saving.

"But the newspapers!" cried the journalist. "They never ran a line; and an exploit like this would scarce have escaped them."

"If I remember rightly, it was reported in the regular police items of the day," said I.

"Strange that the boys didn't look behind the scenes."

"Oh, I don't know," remarked the congressman; "lots of things happen of which you are all ignorant. The public mustn't know everything."

"But what's the hero's name?" asked the journalist.

"That's a secret," I answered. "Besides, when it comes to the bottom of the matter, I had something to do with the suppressing of the police news. In a case like this, suppression becomes a law not excelled by that which governs self-preservation. My friend has a brother in the War Department; and together we worked wonders."

"It's a jolly droll story, however you look at it," the Englishman admitted.

"Nevertheless, it had its tragic side; but that is even more than ever a secret."

The Englishman looked at me sharply, even

gravely; but the veranda is only dimly illuminated at night, and his scrutiny went unrewarded.

"Eh, well!" said the Russian; "your philosopher has observed that all mankind loves a lover."

"As all womankind loves a love-story," the Englishman added. "You ought to be very successful with the ladies,"—turning to me.

"Not inordinately; but I shall not fail to repeat your epigram,"—and I rose.

My watch told me that it was half after eight; and one does not receive every day an invitation to a dinner-dance at the Chevy Chase Club.

I dislike exceedingly to intrude my own personality into this narrative, but as I was passively concerned, I do not see how I can avoid it. Besides, being a public man, I am not wholly averse to publicity; first person, singular, perpendicular, as Thackeray had it, in type looks rather agreeable to the eye. And I rather believe that I have a moral to point out and a parable to expound.

My appointment in Washington at that time was extraordinary; that is to say, I was a member of one of those committees that are born frequently and suddenly in Washington, and which die almost immediately after registration in the vital statistics of national politics. I had been sent to Congress, a dazzling halo over my head, the pride and hope of my little country town; I had been defeated for second term; had been recommended to serve on the committee afore-said; served with honor, got my name in the great newspapers, and was sent back to Congress, where I am still to-day, waiting patiently for a discern-ing president and a vacancy in the legal depart-ment of the cabinet. That's about all I am willing to say about myself.

As for this hero of mine, he was the handsom-est, liveliest rascal you would expect to meet in a day's ride. By handsome I do not mean perfect features, red cheeks, Byronic eyes, and so forth. That style of beauty belongs to the department of lady novelists. I mean that peculiar manly beauty which attracts men almost as powerfully as it does women. For the sake of a name I shall call him Warburton. His given name in actual life is Robert. But I am afraid that nobody but his mother and one other woman ever called him Robert. The world at large dubbed him Bob, and such he will remain up to that day (and may it be many years hence!) when recourse will be had

· to Robert, because "Bob" would certainly look very silly on a marble shaft.

What a friendly sign is a nickname! It is always a good fellow who is.called Bob or Bill, Jack or Jim, Tom, Dick or Harry. Even out of Theodore there comes a Teddy. I know in my own case the boys used to call me Chuck, simply because I was named Charles. (I haven't the slightest doubt that I was named Charles because my good mother thought I looked something like Vandyke's *Charles I,* though at the time of my baptism I wore no beard whatever.) And how I hated a boy with a high-sounding, unnicknamable given name!—with his round white collar and his long glossy curls! I dare say he hated the name, the collar, and the curls even more than I did. Whenever you run across a name carded in this stilted fashion, "A. Thingumy Soandso", you may make up your mind at once that the owner is ashamed of his first name and is trying manfully to live it down and eventually forgive his parents.

Warburton was graduated from West Point, ticketed to a desolate frontier post, and would have worn out his existence there but for his guiding star, which was always making frantic efforts to bolt its established orbit. One day he was doing scout duty, perhaps half a mile in advance of the pay-train, as they called the picturesque caravan which, consisting of a canopied wagon and a small troop of cavalry in dingy blue, made progress across the desert-like plains of Arizona. The troop was some ten miles from the post, and as there had been no sign of Red Eagle all that day, they concluded that the rumor of his being on a drunken rampage with half a dozen braves was only a rumor. Warburton had just passed over a roll of earth, and for a moment the pay-train had dropped out of sight. It was twilight; opalescent waves of heat rolled above the blistered sands. A pale yellow sky, like an inverted bowl rimmed with delicate blue and crimson hues, encompassed the world. The bliss of solitude fell on him, and, being something of a poet, he rose to the stars. The smoke of his corncob pipe trailed lazily behind him. The horse under him was loping along easily. Suddenly the animal lifted his head, and his brown ears went forward.

At Warburton's left, some hundred yards distant, was a clump of osage brush. Even as he looked, there came a puff of smoke, followed by the evil song of a bullet. My hero's hat was carried away. He wheeled, dug his heels into his horse, and cut back over the trail. There came a second flash, a shock, and then a terrible pain in the calf of his left leg. He fell over the neck of his horse to escape the third bullet. He could see the Apache as he stood out from behind the bush. Warburton yanked out his Colt and let fly. He heard a yell. It was very comforting. That was all he remembered of the skirmish.

For five weeks he languished in the hospital. During that time he came to the conclusion that he had had enough of military life in the West. He applied for his discharge, as the compulsory term of service was at an end. When his papers came he was able to get about with the aid of a crutch. One morning his colonel entered his subaltern's bachelor quarters.

"Wouldn't you rather have a year's leave of absence, than quit altogether, Warburton?"

"A year's leave of absence?" cried the invalid. "I am likely to get that, I am."

"If you held a responsible position I dare say it would be difficult. As it is, I may say that I can obtain it for you. It will be months before you can ride a horse with that leg."

"I thank you, Colonel Raleigh, but I think I'll resign. In fact, I have resigned."

"We can withdraw that, if you but say the word. I don't want to lose you, lad. You're the only man around here who likes a joke as well as I do. And you will have a company if you'll only stick to it a little longer."

"I have decided, Colonel. I'm sorry you feel like this about it. You see, I have something like twenty-five thousand laid away. I want to see at least five thousand dollars' worth of new scenery before I shuffle off this mortal coil. The scenery around here palls on me. My throat and eyes are always full of sand. I am off to Europe. Some day, perhaps, the bee will buzz again; and when it does, I'll have you go personally to the president."

"As you please, Warburton."

"Besides, Colonel, I have been reading *Treasure Island* again, and I've got the fever in my veins to hunt for adventure, even a treasure. It's in my blood to wander and do strange things, and here I've been hampered all these years with routine. I shouldn't care if we had a good fight once in a while. My poor old dad traveled around

the world three times, and I haven't seen anything of it but the maps."

"Go ahead, then.   Only, talking about *Treasure Island,* don't you and your twenty-five thousand run into some old Long John Silver."

"I'll take care."

And Mr. Robert packed up his kit and sailed
away.   Not many months passed ere he met his
colonel again, and under rather embarrassing circumstances.

II

Let me begin at the beginning. The boat had been two days out of Southampton before the fog cleared away. On the afternoon of the third day, Warburton curled up in his steamer-chair and lazily viewed the blue October seas as they met and merged with the blue October skies. I do not recollect the popular novel of that summer, but at any rate it lay flapping at the side of his chair, forgotten. It never entered my hero's mind that some poor devil of an author had sweated and labored with infinite pains over every line, and paragraph, and page—labored with all the care and love his heart and mind were capable of, to produce this finished child of fancy; or that this same author, even at this very moment, might be seated on the veranda of his beautiful summer villa, figuring out royalties on the backs of stray envelopes. No, he never thought of these things. What with the wind and the soft, ceaseless jar

of the throbbing engines, half a dream hovered
above his head, and touched him with a gentle,
insistent caress. If you had passed by him this
afternoon, and had been anything of a mathematician who could straighten out geometrical
angles, you would have come close to his height
had you stopped at five feet nine. Indeed, had
you clipped off the heels of his low shoes, you
would have been exact. But all your nice calcu-
lations would not have solved his weight. He was
slender, but he was hard and compact. These
hard, slender fellows sometimes weigh more than
your men of greater bulk. He tipped the scales
at one hundred sixty-two, and he looked twenty
pounds less. He was twenty-eight; a casual
glance at him, and you would have been willing
to wager that the joy of casting his first vote was
yet to be his.

The princess commands that I describe in detail
the charms of this Army Adonis. Far be it that
I should disobey so august a command, being, as
I am, the prime minister in this her principality
of Domestic Felicity. Her brother has never
ceased to be among the first in her dear regard.
He possessed the merriest black eyes : his mother's
eyes, as I, a boy, remember them. No matter how

immobile his features might be, these eyes of his were ever ready for laughter. His nose was clean-cut and shapely. A phrenologist would have said that his head did not lack the bump of caution; but I know better. At present he wore a beard; so this is as large an inventory of his personal attractions as I am able to give. When he shaves off his beard, I shall be pleased to add further particulars. I often marvel that the women did not turn his head. They were always sending him notes and invitations and cutting dances for him. Perhaps his devil-may-care air had something to do with the enchantment. I have yet to see his equal as a horseman. He would have made it interesting for that pair of milk-whites which our old friend, Ulysses (or was it Diomedes?) had such ado about.

Every man has some vice or other, even if it is only being good. Warburton had perhaps two: poker and tobacco. He would get out of bed at any hour if some congenial spirit knocked at the door and whispered that a little game was in progress, and that his money was needed to keep it going. I dare say that you know all about these little games. But what would you? What is a man to do in a country where you may buy a whole village for ten dollars? Warburton seldom drank, and, like the author of this precious volume, only special vintages.

At this particular moment this hero of mine was going over the monotony of the old days in Arizona, the sand-deserts, the unlovely landscapes, the dull routine, the indifferent skirmishes with cattle-men and Indians; the pagan bullet which had plowed through his leg. And now it was all over; he had surrendered his straps; he was a private citizen, with an income sufficient for his needs. It will go a long way, forty-five hundred a year, if one does not attempt to cover the distance in a five-thousand motor-car; and he hated all locomotion that was not horse-flesh.

For nine months he had been wandering over Europe, if not happy, at least in a satisfied frame of mind. Four of these months had been delightfully passed in Paris; and, as his nomad excursions had invariably terminated in that queen of cities, I make Paris the starting point of his somewhat remarkable adventures. Besides, it was in Paris that he first saw Her. And now, here he was at last, homeward-bound. That phrase had a mighty pleasant sound; it was to the ear what honey is to the tongue. Still, he might yet have been in Paris but for one thing: She was on board this very boat.

Suddenly his eyes opened full wide, bright with eagerness.

"It is She!" he murmured.   He closed his eyes again, the hypocrite!

Permit me to introduce you to my heroine. Mind you, she is not *my* creation; only Heaven may produce her like, and but once.   She is well worth turning around to gaze at.   Indeed I know more than one fine gentleman who forgot the time of day, the important engagement, or the trend of his thought, when she passed by.

She was coming forward, leaning against the wind and inclining to the uncertain roll of the ship.   A gray raincoat fitted snugly the youthful rounded figure.   Her hands were plunged into the pockets.   You may be sure that Mr. Robert noted through his half-closed eyelids these inconsequent details.   A tourist hat sat jauntily on the fine light brown hair, that color which has no appropriate metaphor.   (At least, I have never found one, and I am *not* in love with her and *never* was.)   Warburton has described to me her eyes, so I am positive that they were as heavenly blue as a rajah's sapphire.   Her height is of no moment. What man ever troubled himself about the height of a woman, so long as he wasn't undersized himself? What pleased Warburton was the exquisite skin. He was always happy with his comparisons, and particularly when he likened her skin to the bloomy olive pallor of a young peach. The independent stride was distinguishingly American. Ah, the charm of these women who are my countrywomen! They come, they go, alone, unattended, courageous without being bold, self-reliant without being rude; inimitable. In what an amiable frame of mind Nature must have been on the day she cast these molds! But I proceed. The young woman's chin was tilted, and Warburton could tell by the dilated nostrils that she was breathing in the gale with all the joy of living, filling her healthy lungs with it as that rare daughter of the Cyprian Isle might have done as she sprang that morn from the jeweled Mediterranean spray, that beggar's brooch of Neptune's.

Warburton's heart hadn't thrilled so since the day when he first donned cadet gray. There was scarce any room for her to pass between his chair and the rail; and this knowledge filled the rascal with exultation. Nearer and nearer she came.

He drew in his breath sharply as the corner of his foot-rest (aided by the sly wind) caught her raincoat.

"I beg your pardon!" he said, sitting up.

She quickly released her coat, smiled faintly, and passed on.

Sometimes the most lasting impressions are those which are printed most lightly on the memory. Mr. Robert says that he never will forget that first smile. And he didn't even know her name then.

I was about to engage your attention with a description of the villain, but on second thought I have decided that it would be rather unfair. For at that moment he was at a disadvantage. Nature was punishing him for a few shortcomings. The steward that night informed Warburton, in answer to his inquiries, that he, the villain, was dreadfully seasick, and was begging him, the steward, to scuttle the ship and have done with it. I have my doubts regarding this. Mr. Robert is inclined to flippancy at times. It wasn't seasickness; and after all is said and done, it is putting it harshly to call this man a villain. I recant. True villainy is always based upon selfishness. Remember this, my wise ones.

Warburton was somewhat subdued when he learned that the suffering gentleman was *her* father.

"What did you say the name was?" he asked innocently. Until now he hadn't had the courage to put the question to any one, or to prowl around the purser's books.

"Annesley; Colonel Annesley and daughter," answered the unsuspecting steward.

Warburton knew nothing then of the mental tragedy going on behind the colonel's state-room door. How should he have known? On the contrary, he believed that the father of such a girl must be a most knightly and courtly gentleman. He *was*, in all outward appearance. There had been a time, not long since, when he had been knightly and courtly in all things.

Surrounding every upright man there is a mire, and if he step not wisely, he is lost. There is no coming back; step by step he must go on and on, till he vanishes and a bubble rises over where he but lately stood. That he misstepped innocently does not matter; mire and evil have neither pity nor reason. To spend what is not ours and then to try to recover it, to hide the guilty step: this is futility. From the alpha men have made this step; to the omega they will make it, with the same unchanging futility.   After all, it *is* money.   Money *is* the root of all evil; let him laugh who will, in his heart of hearts he knows it.

Money! Have you never heard that siren call to you, call seductively from her ragged isle, where lurk the reefs of greed and selfishness? Money! What has this siren not to offer? Power, ease, glory, luxury; aye, I had almost said love! But, no; love is the gift of God, money is the invention of man: all the good, all the evil, in the heart of this great humanity.

III

It was only when the ship was less than a day's journey off Sandy Hook that the colonel came on deck, once more to resume his interest in human affairs. How the girl hovered about him! She tucked the shawl more snugly around his feet; she arranged and rearranged the pillows back of his head; she fed him from a bowl of soup; she read from some favorite book; she smoothed the fur= rowed brow; she stilled the long, white, nervous fingers with her own small, firm, brown ones; she was mother and daughter in one. Wherever she moved, the parent eye followed her, and there lay in its deeps a strange mixture of fear, and trouble, and questioning love. All the while he drummed ceaselessly on the arms of his chair.

And Mr. Robert, watching all these things from afar, Mr. Robert sighed dolorously. The residue air in his lungs was renewed more fre= quently than nature originally intended it should be. Love has its beneficences as well as its pangs, only they are not wholly appreciable by the recipient. For what is better than a good pair of lungs constantly filled and refilled with pure air? Mr. Robert even felt a twinge of remorse besides. He was brother to a girl almost as beautiful as yonder one (to my mind far more beautiful!) and he recalled that in two years he had not seen her nor made strenuous efforts to keep up the correspondence. Another good point added to the score of love! And, alas! he might never see this charming girl again, this daughter so full of filial love and care. He had sought the captain, but that hale and hearty old sea-dog had politely rebuffed him.

"My dear young man," he said, "I do all I possibly can for the entertainment and comfort of my passengers, but in this case I must refuse your request."

"And pray, why, sir?" demanded Mr. Robert, with dignity.

"For the one and simple reason that Colonel Annesley expressed the desire to be the recipient of no ship introductions."

"What the deuce is he, a billionaire?"

"You have me there, sir. I confess that I know

nothing whatever about him. This is the first time he has ever sailed on my deck."

All of which perfectly accounts for Mr. Robert's sighs in what musicians call the *doloroso*. If only he knew some one who knew the colonel! How simple it would be! Certainly, a West Point graduate would find some consideration. But the colonel spoke to no one save his daughter, and his daughter to none but her parent, her maid, and the stewardess. Would they remain in New York, or would they seek their far-off southern home? Oh, the thousands of questions which surged through his brain! From time to time he glanced sympathetically at the colonel, whose fingers drummed and drummed and drummed.

"Poor wretch! his stomach must be in bad shape. Or maybe he has the palsy." Warburton mused upon the curious incertitude of the human anatomy.

But Colonel Annesley did not have the palsy. What he had is at once the greatest blessing and the greatest curse of God—remembrance, or conscience, if you will.

What a beautiful color her hair was, dappled with sunshine and shadow! . . . Pshaw!

Mr. Robert threw aside his shawl and book (it is of no real importance, but I may as well add that he never completed the reading of that summer's most popular novel) and sought the smoking-room, where, with the aid of a fat perfecto and a liberal stack of blues, he proceeded to divert himself till the boat reached quarantine. I shall not say that he left any of his patrimony at the mahogany table with its green-baize covering and its little brass disks for cigar ashes, but I am certain that he did not make one of those stupendous winnings we often read about and never witness. This much, however: he made the acquaintance of a very important personage, who was presently to add no insignificant weight on the scales of Mr. Robert's destiny.

He was a Russian, young, handsome, suave, of what the newspapers insist on calling distinguished bearing. He spoke English pleasantly but imperfectly. He possessed a capital fund of anecdote, and Warburton, being an Army man, loved a good droll story. It was a revelation to see the way he dipped the end of his cigar into his coffee, a stimulant which he drank with Balzacian frequency and relish. Besides these accomplishments, he played a very smooth hand at the great American game. While Mr. Robert's admiration was not aroused, it was surely awakened.

My hero had no trouble with the customs offi-- cials. A brace of old French dueling pistols and a Turkish simitar were the only articles which might possibly have been dutiable. The inspector looked hard, but he was finally convinced that Mr. Robert was *not* a professional curio-collector. Warburton, never having returned from abroad before, found a deal of amusement and food for thought in the ensuing scenes. There was one man, a prim, irascible old fellow, who was not allowed to pass in two dozen fine German razors. There was a time of it, angry words, threats, pro- testations. The inspector stood firm. The old gentleman, in a fine burst of passion, tossed the razors into the water. Then they were going to arrest him for smuggling. A friend extricated him. The old gentleman went away, saying something about the tariff and an unreasonably warm place which has as many synonyms as an octopus has tentacles.

Another man, his mouth covered by an enor- mous black mustache which must have received a bath every morning in coffee or something stronger, came forward pompously. I don't know to this day what magic word he said, but the inspectors took never a peep into his belongings. Doubtless they knew him, and that his word was as good as his bond.

Here a woman wept because the necklace she brought trustingly from Rotterdam must be paid for once again; and here another, who clenched her fists (do women have fists?) and if looks could have killed there would have been a vacancy in customs forthwith. All her choicest linen strewn about on the dirty boards, all soiled and rumpled and useless!

When the colonel's turn came, Warburton moved within hearing distance. How glorious she looked in that smart gray traveling habit! With what well-bred indifference she gazed upon the scene! Calmly her glance passed among the circles of strange faces, and ever and anon returned to the great ship which had safely brought her back to her native land. There were other women who were just as well-bred and indifferent, only Warburton had but one pair of eyes. Sighs in the *doloroso* again. Ha! if only one of these meddling jackasses would show her some disrespect and give him the opportunity of avenging the affront!

(Come, now; let me be your confessor. Have you never thought and acted like this hero of mine? Haven't you been just as melodramatic and ridiculous? It is nothing to be ashamed of. For my part, I should confess to it with the same equanimity as I should to the mumps or the measles. It comes with, and is part and parcel of, all that strange medley we find in the Pandora box of life. Love has no diagnosis, so the doctors say. 'Tis all in the angle of vision.)

But nothing happened. Colonel Annesley and his daughter were old hands; they had gone through all this before. Scarce an article in their trunks was disturbed. There was a slight duty of some twelve dollars (Warburton's memory is marvelous), and their luggage was free. But alas, for the perspicacity of the inspectors! I can very well imagine the god of irony in no better or more fitting place than in the United States Customs House.

Once outside, the colonel caught the eye of a cabby, and he and his daughter stepped in.

"Holland House, sir, did you say?" asked the cabby.

The colonel nodded. The cabby cracked his whip, and away they rolled over the pavement.

Warburton's heart gave a great bound. She had actually leaned out of the cab, and for one brief moment their glances had met. Scarce knowing what he did, he jumped into another cab and went pounding after. It was easily ten blocks from the pier when the cabby raised the lid and peered down at his fare.

"Do you want t' folly them ahead?" he cried.

"No, no!" Warburton was startled out of his wild dream. "Drive to the Holland House—no —to the Waldorf. Yes, the Waldorf; and keep your nag going."

"Waldorf it is, sir!" The lid above closed.

Clouds had gathered in the heavens. It was beginning to rain. But Warburton neither saw the clouds nor felt the first few drops of rain. All the way up-town he planned and planned—as many plans as there were drops of rain; the rain wet him, but the plans drowned him—he became submerged. If I were an expert at analysis, which I am not, I should say that Mr. Robert was

not violently in love; rather I should observe that
he was fascinated with the first really fine face he
had seen in several years. Let him never see Miss
Annesley again, and in two weeks he would entirely forget her. I know enough of the race to
be able to put forward this statement. Of course,
it is understood that he would have to mingle for
the time among other handsome women. Now,
strive as he would, he could not think out a feasi-
ble plan. One plan might have given him light,
but the thousand that came to him simply over-
whelmed him fathoms deep. If he could find
some one he knew at the Holland House, some
one who would strike up a smoking-room acquaintance with the colonel, the rest would be
simple enough. Annesley—Annesley; he couldn't
place the name. Was he a regular, retired, or a
veteran of the Civil War? And yet, the name
was not totally unfamiliar. Certainly, he was a
fine-looking old fellow, with his white hair and
Alexandrian nose. And here he was, he, Robert
Warburton, in New York, simply because he happened to be in the booking office of the *Gare du
Nord* one morning and overheard a very beautiful girl say: "Then we shall sail from Southamp-

ton day after to-morrow." Of a truth, it is the infinitesimal things that count heaviest.

So deep was he in the maze of his tentative romance that when the cab finally stopped abruptly, he was totally unaware of the transition from activity to passivity.

"Hotel, sir!"

"Ah, yes!" Warburton leaped out, fumbled in his pocket, and brought forth a five-dollar note, which he gave to the cabby. He did not realize it, but this was the only piece of American money he had on his person. Nor did he wait for the change. Mr. Robert was exceedingly careless with his money at this stage of his infatuation; being a soldier, he never knew the real value of legal tender. I know that *I* should never have been guilty of such liberality, not even if Mister Cabby had bowled me from Harlem to Brooklyn. And you may take my word for it, the gentleman in the ancient plug-hat did not wait to see if his fare had made a mistake, but trotted away good and hearty. The cab system is one of the most pleasing and amiable phases of metropolitan life.

Warburton rushed into the noisy, gorgeous lobby, and wandered about till he espied the desk.

Here he turned over his luggage checks to the clerk and said that these accessories of travel must be in his room before eight o'clock that night, or there would be trouble. It was now half after five. The clerk eagerly scanned the register. Warburton, Robert Warburton; it was not a name with which *he* was familiar. A thin film of icy hauteur spread over his face.

"Very well, sir. Do you wish a bath with your room?"

"Certainly." Warburton glanced at his watch again.

"The price—"

"Hang the price! A room, a room with a bath —that's what I want. Have you got it?" This was said with a deal of real impatience and a hauteur that overtopped the clerk's.

The film of ice melted into a gracious smile. Some new millionaire from Pittsburg, thought the clerk. He swung the book around.

"You have forgotten your place of residence, sir," he said.

"Place of residence!"

Warburton looked at the clerk in blank astonishment. Place of residence? Why, heaven help him, he had none, none! For the first time since he left the Army the knowledge came home to him, and it struck rather deep. He caught up the pen, poised it an indecisive moment, then hastily scribbled Paris: as well Paris as anywhere. Then he took out his wallet, comfortably packed with English and French bank-notes, and a second wave of astonishment rolled over him. Altogether, it was a rare good chance that he ever came to the surface again. No plan, no place of residence, no American money!

"Good Lord! I forgot all about exchanging it on shipboard!" he exclaimed.

"Don't let that trouble you, sir," said the clerk, with real affability. "Our own bank will exchange your money in the morning."

"But I haven't a penny of American money on my person!"

"How much will you need for the evening, sir?"

"Not more than fifty."

The clerk brought forth a slip of paper, wrote something on it, and handed it to Warburton.

"Sign here," he said, indicating a blank space.

And presently Mr. Robert, having deposited his foreign money in the safe, pocketed the receipt for its deposit along with five crisp American notes. There is nothing lacking in these modern hostelries, excepting it be a church.

Our homeless young gentleman lighted a cigar and went out under the portico. An early darkness had settled over the city, and a heavy steady rain was falling. The asphalt pavements glistened and twinkled as far as the eye's range could reach. A thousand lights gleamed down on him, and he seemed to be standing in a cañon dappled with fireflies. Place of residence! Neither the fig-tree nor the vine! Did he lose his money to-morrow, the source of his small income, he would be without a roof over his head. True, his brother's roof would always welcome him: but a roof-tree of his own! And he could lay claim to no city, either, having had the good fortune to be born in a healthy country town. Place of residence! Truly he had none; a melancholy fact which he had not appreciated till now. And all this had slipped his mind because of a pair of eyes as heavenly blue as a rajah's sapphire!

Hang it, what should he do, now that he was no longer traveling, now that his time was no longer Uncle Sam's? He had never till now known idleness, and the thought of it did not run smoothly with the grain. He was essentially a man of ac-

tion. There might be some good sport for a
soldier in Venezuela, but that was far away and
uncertain. It was quite possible Jack, his brother,
might find him a post as military attaché, perhaps in France, perhaps in Belgium, perhaps in
Vienna. That was the goal of more than one
subaltern. The English novelist is to be blamed
for this ambition. But Warburton could speak
French with a certain fluency, and his German
was good enough to swear by; so it will be seen
that he had some ground upon which to build this
ambition.

Heigho! The old homestead was gone; his sister dwelt under the elder brother's roof; the
prodigal was alone.

"But there's always a fatted calf waiting in
Washington," he laughed aloud. "Once a soldier,
always a soldier. I suppose I'll be begging the
colonel to have a chat with the president. There
doesn't seem to be any way of getting out of it.
I'll have to don the old togs again. I ought to
write a letter to Nancy, but it will be finer to drop
in on 'em unexpectedly. Bless her heart! (So
say I!) And Jack's, too, and his little wife's!
And I haven't written a line in eight weeks. But
I'll make it all up in ten minutes. And if I haven't

a roof-tree, at least I've got the ready cash and
can buy one any day." All of which proves that
Mr. Robert possessed a buoyant spirit, and refused to be downcast for more than one minute
at a time.

He threw away his cigar and reëntered the
hotel, and threaded his way through the appalling
labyrinths of corridors till he found some one to
guide him to the barber shop, where he could
have his hair cut and his beard trimmed in the
good old American way, money no object. For a
plan had at last come to him; and it wasn't at all
bad. He determined to dine at the Holland House
at eight-thirty. It was quite possible that he
would see Her.

My only wish is that, when I put on evening
clothes (in my humble opinion, the homeliest
and most uncomfortable garb that man ever invented!) I might look one-quarter as handsome
and elegant as Mr. Robert looked, as he came
down stairs at eight-ten that night. He wasn't
to be blamed if the women glanced in his direction, and then whispered and whispered, and nodded and nodded. Ordinarily he would have observed these signs of feminine approval, for there
was warm blood in his veins, and it is proverbial

that the Army man is gallant. But to-night Diana
and her white huntresses might have passed him
by and not aroused even a flicker of interest or
surprise on his face. There was only one pair of
eyes, one face, and to see these he would have
gladly gone to the ends of the earth, travel-weary
though he was.

He smoked feverishly, and was somewhat troubled to find that he hadn't quite got his land legs,
as they say. The floor swayed at intervals, and
the throbbing of the engines came back. He left
the hotel, hailed a cab, and was driven down
Fifth Avenue. He stopped before the fortress of
privileges. From the cab it looked very formidable. Worldly as he was, he was somewhat innocent. He did not know that New York hotels
are formidable only when your money gives out.
To get past all these brass-buttoned lackeys and
to go on as though he really had business
within took no small quantity of nerve. However, he slipped by the outpost without any challenge and boldly approached the desk. A quick
glance at the register told him that they had indeed put up at this hotel. He could not explain
why he felt so happy over his discovery. There
are certain exultations which are inexplicable.

As he turned away from the desk, he bumped into
a gentleman almost as elegantly attired as himself.

"I beg your pardon!" he cried, stepping aside.

"What? Mr. *Warrr*burton?"

Mr. Robert, greatly surprised and confused,
found himself shaking hands with his ship acquaintance, the Russian.

"I am very glad to see you again, Count," said
Warburton, recovering.

"A great pleasure! It is wonderful how small
a city is. I had never expect' to see you again.
Are you stopping here?" I had intended to try
to reproduce the Russian's dialect, but one dialect
in a book is enough; and we haven't reached the
period of its activity.

"No, I am at the Waldorf."

"Eh? I have heard all about you millionaires."

"Oh, we are not all of us millionaires who stop
there," laughed Warburton. "There are some of
us who try to make others believe that we are."
Then, dropping into passable French, he added:
"I came here to-night with the purpose of dining.
Will you do me the honor of sharing my table?"

"You speak French?"—delighted. "It is wonderful. This English has so many words that

mean so many things, that of all languages I
speak it with the least fluency. But it is my deep
regret, Monsieur, to refuse your kind invitation.
I am dining with friends."

"Well, then, breakfast to-morrow at eleven,"
Warburton urged, for he had taken a fancy to
this affable Russian.

"Alas! See how I am placed. I am forced to
leave for Washington early in the morning. We
poor diplomats, we earn our honors. But my
business is purely personal in this case, neither
political nor diplomatic." The count drew his
gloves thoughtfully through his fingers. "I shall
of course pay my respects to my ambassador. Do
I recollect your saying that you belonged to the
United States Army?"

"I recently resigned. My post was in a wild
country, with little or nothing to do; monotony
and routine."

"You limp slightly?"

"A trifling mishap,"—modestly.

"Eh, you do wrong. You may soon be at war
with England, and having resigned your commission, you would lose all you had waited these
years for."

Warburton smiled. "We shall not go to war with England."

"This Army of yours is small."

"Well, yes; but made of pretty good material—fighting machines with brains."

"Ha!" The count laughed softly. "Bah! how I detest all these cars and ships! Will you believe me, I had rather my little château, my vineyard, and my wheat fields, than all the orders. . . . Eh, well, *my country:* there must be some magic in that phrase. Of all loves, that of country is the most lasting. Is that Balzac? I do not recall. Only once in a century do we find a man who is willing to betray his country, and even then he may have for his purpose neither hate, revenge, nor love of power." A peculiar gravity sat on his mobile face, caused, perhaps, by some disagreeable inward thought.

"How long shall you be in Washington?" asked Warburton.

The count shrugged. "Who can say?"

"I go to Washington myself within a few days."

"Till we meet again, then, Monsieur."

The count lifted his hat, a courtesy which was gracefully acknowledged by the American; while

the clerks at the desk eyed with tolerant amusement these polite but rather unfamiliar cere-
monies of departure. These foreigners were odd
duffers.

"A very decent chap," mused Warburton, "and
a mighty shrewd hand at poker—for a foreigner.
He is going to Washington: we shall meet again.
I wonder if she's in the restaurant now."

Meet again? Decidedly; and had clairvoyance
shown my hero that night how he and the count
were to meet again, certainly he would have
laughed.

If I dared, I should like to say a good deal
more about this Russian. But I have no desire
to lose my head, politically or physically. Even
the newsboys are familiar with this great young
man's name; and if I should disclose it, you
would learn a great many things which I have
no desire that you should. One day he is in
Paris, another in Berlin, then off to Vienna, to
Belgrade, or St. Petersburg, or Washington, or
London, or Rome. A few months ago, previous
to this writing, he was in Manchuria; and to this
very day England and Japan are wondering how
it happened; not his being there, mind you, but
the result. Rich, that is to say independent; un-

married, that is to say unattached; free to come
and go, he stood high up in that great army of
the czar's, which I call the uncredited diplomatic
corps, because the phrase "secret service" always
puts into my mind a picture of the wild-eyed,
bearded anarchist, whom I most heartily detest.

What this remarkable diplomatic free-lance did
in Washington was honestly done in the interests
of his country. A Russ understands honor in
the rough, but he lacks all those delicate shadings
which make the word honor the highest of all
words in the vocabularies of the Gaul and the
Saxon. And while I do not uphold him in what
he did, I can not place much blame at the count's
door. Doubtless, in his place, and given his cast
of mind, I might have done exactly as he did.
Russia never asks how a thing is done, but why
it is *not* done. Ah, these Aspasias, these Circes,
these Calypsos, these Cleopatras, with their blue,
their gray, their amber eyes! I have my doubts
concerning Jonah, but, being a man, I am fully
convinced as to the history of Eve. And yet, the
woman in this case was absolutely innocent of any
guile, unless a pair of eyes as heavenly blue as a
rajah's sapphire may be called guile.

Pardon me this long parenthesis. By this time,

no doubt, Mr. Robert has entered the restaurant.
We shall follow him rather than this aimless train
of thought.

Mr. Robert's appetite, for a healthy young
man, was strangely incurious. He searched the
menu from top to bottom, and then from bottom
to top; nothing excited his palate. Whenever
persons entered, he would glance up eagerly, only
to feel his heart sink lower and lower. I don't
know how many times he was disappointed. The
waiter ahemmed politely. Warburton, in order
to have an excuse to remain, at length hit upon a
partridge and a pint of Chablis.

Nine o'clock. Was it possible that the colonel
and his daughter were dining in their rooms?
Perish the possibility! And he looked in vain
for the count. A quarter-past nine. Mr. Robert's anxiety was becoming almost unendurable.
Nine-thirty. He was about to surrender in despair. His partridge lay smoking on his plate,
and he was on the point of demolishing it, when,
behold! they came. The colonel entered first,
then his daughter, her hand—on—the—arm—
of—the—count! Warburton never fully described to me his feelings at that moment; but,
knowing him as I do, I can put together a very

respectable picture of the chagrin and consterna-
tion that sat on his countenance.

"To think of being nearly six days aboard,"
Mr. Robert once bawled at me, wrathfully, "and
not to know that that Russian chap knew her!"
It *was* almost incredible that such a thing should
happen.

The three sat down at a table seven times removed from Warburton's. He could see only an
adorable profile and the colonel's handsome but
care-worn face. The count sat with his back
turned. In that black evening gown she was simply beyond the power of adjectives. What shoulders, what an incomparable throat! Mr. Robert's
bird grew cold; the bouquet from his glass fainted
and died away. How her face lighted when she
laughed, and she laughed frequently! What a
delicious curve ran from her lips to her young
bosom! But never once did she look in his direction. Who invented mirrors, the Egyptians?
I can not say. There were mirrors in the room,
but Mr. Robert did not realize it. He has since
confessed to me that he hadn't the slightest idea
how much his bird and bottle cost. Of such is
love's young dream! (Do I worry you with all
these repetitious details? I am sorry.)

'At ten o'clock Miss Annesley rose, and the count escorted her to the elevator, returning almost immediately. He and the colonel drew their heads together. From time to time the count shrugged, or the colonel shook his head. Again and again the Russian dipped the end of his cigar into his coffee-cup, which he frequently replenished.

But for Mr. Robert the gold had turned to gilt, the gorgeous to the gaudy. She was gone. The imagination moves as swiftly as light, leaping from one castle in air to another, and still another. Mr. Robert was the architect of some fine ones, I may safely assure you. And he didn't mind in the least that they tumbled down as rapidly as they builded: only, the incentive was gone. What the colonel had to say to the count, or the count to the colonel, was of no interest to him; so he made an orderly retreat.

I am not so old as not to appreciate his sleeplessness that night. Some beds are hard, even when made of the softest down.

In the morning he telephoned to the Holland House. The Annesleys, he was informed, had departed for parts unknown. The count had left directions to forward any possible mail to the

Russian Embassy, Washington. Sighs in the *doloroso;* the morning papers and numerous cigars; a whisky and soda; a game of indifferent billiards with an affable stranger; another whisky and soda; and a gradual reclamation of Mr. Robert's interest in worldly affairs.

She was gone.

IV

Warburton had not been in the city of Washington within twelve years. In the past his furloughs had been spent at his brother's country home in Larchmont, out of New York City. Thus, when he left the train at the Baltimore and Potomac station, he hadn't the slightest idea where Scott Circle was. He looked around in vain for the smart cab of the northern metropolis. All he saw was a line of omnibuses and a few ramshackle vehicles that twenty years back might very well have passed for victorias. A grizzled old negro, in command of one of these sea-going conveyances, caught Warburton's eye and hailed jovially. Our hero (as the good novelists of the past generation would say, taking their readers into their innermost confidences) handed him his traveling case and stepped in.

"Whar to, suh?" asked the commodore.

"Scott Circle, and don't pommel that old nag's

47

bones in trying to get there. I've plenty of time."
"I reckon I won't pommel him, suh. Skt! skt!"
And the vehicle rattled out into broad Pennsylvania Avenue, but for the confusion and absurdity of its architectural structures, the handsomest
· thoroughfare in America. (Some day I am going to carry a bill into Congress and read it, and
become famous as having been the means of making Pennsylvania Avenue the handsomest highway in the world.)

Warburton leaned back luxuriously against the
faded horse-hair cushion and lighted a cigar,
which he smoked with relish, having had a hearty
breakfast on the train. It was not quite nine
o'clock, and a warm October haze lay on the
peaceful city. Here were people who did not
rush madly about in the pursuit of riches. Rather
they proceeded along soberly, even leisurely, as
if they knew what the day's work was and the
rewards attendant, and were content. Trucks,
those formidable engines of commerce, neither
rumbled nor thundered along the pavements, nor
congested the thoroughfares. Nobody hurried
into the shops, nobody hurried out. There were
no scampering, yelling newsboys. Instead, along
the curbs of the market, sat barelegged negro

boys, some of them selling papers to those who wanted them, and some sandwiched in between baskets of popcorn and peanuts. There was a marked scarcity of the progressive, intrusive white boy. Old negro mammies passed to and fro with the day's provisions.

Glancing over his shoulder, Warburton saw the Capitol, shining in the sun like some enchanted palace out of Wonderland. He touched his cap, conscious of a thrill in his spine. And there, far to his left, loomed the Washington monument, glittering like a shaft of opals. Some orderlies dashed by on handsome bays. How splendid they looked, with their blue trousers and broad yellow stripes! This was before the Army adopted the comfortable but shabby brown duck. How he longed to throw a leg over the back of a good horse and gallop away into the great green country beyond!

In every extraordinary looking gentleman he saw some famed senator or congressman or diplomat. He was almost positive that he saw the secretary of war drive by in a neat brougham. The only things which moved with the hustling spirit of the times were the cables, and doubtless these would have gone slower but for the invisi-

ble and immutable power which propelled them.
On arriving in New York, one's first thought is
of riches; in Washington, of glory. What a difference between this capital and those he had seen
abroad! There was no militarism here, no con-
scription, no governmental oppression, no signs
of discontent, no officers treading on the rights
and the toes of civilians.

But now he was passing the huge and dingy
magic Treasury Building, round past the Executive Mansion with its spotless white stone, its
stately portico and its plush lawns.

"Go slow, uncle; I haven't seen this place since
I was a boy."

"Yes, suh. How d' y' like it? Wouldn' y'
like t' live in dat house, suh?"—the commodore
grinned.

"One can't stay there long enough to please
me, uncle. It takes four years to get used to it;
and then, when you begin to like it, you have to
pack up and clear out."

"It's de way dey goes, suh. We go eroun'
Lafayette, er do yuh want t' see de Wa' Depa't-
ment, suh?"

"Never mind now, uncle; Scott Circle."

"Scott Circle she am, suh."

The old ark wheeled round Lafayette Square and finally rolled into Sixteenth Street. When at length it came to a stand in front of a beautiful house, Warburton evinced his surprise openly. He knew that his brother's wife had plenty of money, but not such a plenty as to afford a house like this.

"Are you sure, uncle, that this is the place?"

"Dere's de Circle, suh, an' yuh can see de num-buh fo' y'se'f, suh."

"How much do I owe you?"

"I reckon 'bout fifty cents 'll make it, suh."

Warburton gave him a dollar, marveling at the difference between the cab hire here and in New York. He grasped his case and leaped up the steps two at a bound, and pressed the bell. A prim little maid answered the call.

"Does Mr. John Warburton live here?" he asked breathlessly.

"Yes, sir."

"Fortunate John!" he cried, pushing past the maid and standing in the hall of his brother's household, unheralded and unannounced. "Jack!" he bawled.

The maid eyed the handsome intruder, her face
expressing the utmost astonishment. She touched
his arm.

"Sir!—" she began.

"It's all right, my dear," he interrupted.

She stepped back, wondering whether to scream
or run.

"Hi, Jack! I say, you old henpecked, where
are you?"

The dining-room door slid back and a tall,
studious-looking gentleman, rather plain than
otherwise, stood on the threshold.

"Jane, what is all this— Why, Bob, you
scalawag!"—and in a moment they were pump-
ing hands at a great rate. The little maid leaned
weakly against the balustrade.

"Kit, Kit! I say, Kit, come and see who's
here!" cried John.

An extraordinarily pretty little woman, whose
pallor any woman would have understood, but
no man on earth, and who was dressed in a
charming pink negligée morning-gown, hurried
into the hall.

"Why, it's Bob!" She flung her arms around
the prodigal and kissed him heartily, held him
away at arm's length, and hugged and kissed him

again. I'm not sure that Mr. Robert didn't like it.

Suddenly there was a swish of starched skirts on the stairs, and the most beautiful woman in all the world (and I am always ready to back this statement with abundant proofs!) rushed down and literally threw herself into Mr. Robert's eager, outstretched arms.

"Nancy!"

"Bob! Bob! you wicked boy! You almost break our hearts. Not a line in two months!—How could you!— You might have been dead and we not know it!"—and she cried on his shoulder.

"Come now, Nancy; nonsense! You'll start the color running out of this tie of mine!" But for all his jesting tone, Mr. Robert felt an embarrassing lump wriggle up and down in his throat.

"Had your breakfast?" asked the humane and practical brother.

"Yep. But I shouldn't mind another cup of coffee."

And thereupon he was hustled into the dining-room and pushed into the best chair. How the dear women fussed over him, pressed this upon him and that; fondled and caressed him, just as

if the beggar was worth all this trouble and love
and affection!

"Hang it, girls, it's worth being an outlaw to
come to this," he cried. He reached over and
patted Nancy on the cheek, and pressed the young
wife's hand, and smiled pleasantly at his brother.
"Jack, you lucky pup, you!"

"Two years," murmured Nancy; "and we
haven't had a glimpse of you in two long years."

"Only in photograph," said the homeless one,
putting three lumps of sugar into his coffee because he was so happy he didn't know what he
was about.

"And you have turned twenty-eight," said Kit,
counting on her fingers.

"That makes you twenty-four, Nan," Jack
laughed.

"And much I care!" replied Nancy, shaking
her head defiantly. I've a sneaking idea that she
was thinking of me when she made this declara-
tion. For if *I* didn't care, why should she?

"A handsome, stunning girl like you, Nan,
ought to be getting married," observed the prodigal. "What's the matter with all these dukes and
lords and princes, anyhow?"

An embarrassed smile ran around the table, but Mr. Robert missed it by some several inches.

Jack threw a cigar across the table. "Now," said he, "where the deuce did you come from?"

"Indirectly from Arizona, which is a synonym, once removed, for war."

Jack looked at his plate and laughed; but Mrs. Jack wanted to know what Bob meant by that.

"It's a word used instead of war, as applied by the late General Sherman," Jack replied. "And I am surprised that a brother-in-law of yours should so far forget himself as to hint it, even."

Knowing that she could put him through the inquisition later, she asked my hero how his leg was.

"It aches a little when it rains; that's about all."

"And you never let us know anything about it till the thing was all over," was Nancy's reproach.

"What's the use of scaring you women?" Robert demanded. "You would have had hysterics and all that."

"We heard of it quick enough through the newspapers," said Jack. "Come, give us your own version of the rumpus."

"Well, the truth is,"—and the prodigal told them his tale.

"Why, you are a hero!" cried Mrs. Jack, clasp-
ing her hands.

"Hero nothing," sniffed the elder brother.
"He was probably star-gazing or he wouldn't
have poked his nose into an ambush."

"Right you are, brother John," Robert acknowledged, laughing.

"And how handsome he has grown, Nancy,"
Mrs. Jack added, with an oblique glance at her
husband.

"He does look 'distangy'," that individual admitted. A handsome face always went through
John's cuirass. It was all nonsense, for his wife
could not have adored him more openly had he
been the twin to Adonis. But, there you are; a
man always wants something he can not have.
John wasn't satisfied to be one of the most brilliant young men in Washington; he also wanted
to be classed among the handsomest.

"By the way, Jack," said my hero, lighting the
cigar and blowing the first puff toward the ceiling,
his face admirably set with nonchalance, "do you
know of a family named Annesley—Colonel Annesley?" I knew it would take only a certain
length of time for this question to arrive.

"Colonel Annesley? Why, yes. He was in the War Department until a year or so ago. A fine strategist; knows every in and out of the coast defenses, and is something of an inventor; lots of money, too. Tall, handsome old fellow?"

"That's the man. A war volunteer?"

"No, a regular. Crippled his gun-fingers in some petty Indian war, and was transferred to the Department. He was a widower, if my recollection of him is correct; and had a lovely daughter."

"Ah!" There was great satisfaction evident in this syllable. "Do you know where the colonel is now?"

"Not the faintest idea. He lived somewhere in Virginia. But he's been on the travel for several years."

Robert stirred his coffee and took a spoonful— and dropped the spoon. "Pah! I must have put in a quart of sugar. Can you spare me another cup?"

"Annesley?" Nancy's face brightened. "Colonel Annesley? Why, I know Betty Annesley. She was my room-mate at Smith one year. She was in my graduating class. I'll show you her picture later. She was the dearest girl! How she loved horses! But why are you so interested?"—slyly.

"I ran across them coming home."

"Then you met Betty! Isn't she just the loveliest girl you ever saw?"

"I'm for her, one and indivisible. But hang my luck, I never came within a mile of an introduction."

"What? You, and on shipboard where she couldn't get away?" John threw up his hands as a sign that this information had overcome him.

"Even the captain shied when I approached him," said Robert, gloomily.

"I begin to see," said the brother.

"See what?"

"Have a match; your cigar has gone out."

Robert relighted his cigar and puffed like a threshing-machine engine.

John leaned toward Nancy. "Shall I tell him, Nan?"

Nancy blushed. "I suppose he'll have to know sooner or later."

"Know what?" asked the third person singular.

"Your charming sister is about to bring you a brother-in-law."

"What?" You could have heard this across the street.

"Yes, Bobby dear. And don't look so hurt. You don't want me to become an old maid, do you?"

"When did it happen?"—helplessly. How the thought of his sister's marrying horrifies a brother! I believe I can tell you why. Every brother knows that no man is good enough for a good woman. "When did it happen?" Mr. Robert repeated, with a look at his brother, which said that *he* should be held responsible.

"Last week."

Robert took in a long breath, as one does who expects to receive a blow of some sort which can not be warded off, and asked: "Who is it?" Nancy married? What was the world coming to, anyhow?

"Charlie Henderson,"—timidly.

Then Robert, who had been expecting nothing less than an English duke, let loose the flaming ions of his righteous wrath.

"Chuck Henderson?—that duffer?" (Oh, Mr. Robert, Mr. Robert; and after all I've done for you!)

"He's not a duffer!" remonstrated Nancy, with

a flare in her mild eyes. (How I wish I might have seen her as she defended me!) "He's the dearest fellow in the world, and I love him with all my heart!" (How do you like that, Mr. Robert? Bravo, Nancy! I may be a duffer, true enough, but I rather object to its being called out from the housetops.) And Nancy added: "I want you to understand distinctly, Robert, that in my selection of a husband you are not to be consulted."

This was moving him around some.

"Hold on, Nan! Drat it, don't look like that! I meant nothing, dearie; only I'm a heap surprised. Chuck *is* a good fellow, I'll admit; but I've been dreaming of your marrying a prince or an ambassador, and Henderson comes like a jolt. Besides, Chuck will never be anything but a first-rate politician. You'll have to get used to cheap cigars and four-ply whisky. When is it going to happen?"

"In June. I have always loved him, Bob. And he wants you to be his best man."

Robert appeared a bit mollified at this knowledge. "But what shall I do after that?" he wailed. "You're the only person I can order

about, and now you're going the other side of
the range."

"Bob, why don't you get married yourself?"
asked Mrs. Warburton. "With your looks you
won't have to go far nor begging for a wife."

"There's the rub, sister mine by law and the
admirable foresight of my only brother. What
am I good for but ordering rookies about? I've
no business head. And it's my belief that an
Army man ought never to wed."

"Marry, my boy, and I'll see what can be done
for you in the diplomatic way. The new adminis-
tration will doubtless be Republican, and my influence will have some weight,"—and John
smiled affectionately across the table. He loved
this gay lad opposite, loved him for his own self
and because he could always see the mother's eyes
and lips. "You have reached the age of discretion. You are now traveled and a fairly good
linguist. You've an income of forty-five hundred,
and to this I may be able to add a berth worth
two or three thousand. Find the girl, lad; find
the girl."

"Honestly, I'll think it over, Jack."

"Oh!"

Three of the quartet turned wonderingly toward Mrs. Jack.

"What's the matter?" asked Jack.

"We have forgotten to show Bob the baby!"

"Merciful heavens!" bawled Robert. "A baby? This is the first time I've heard anything about a baby,"—looking with renewed interest at the young mother.

"Do you mean to tell me, John Warburton, that you failed to mention the fact in any of your letters?" indignantly demanded Mrs. John.

"Why—er—didn't I mention it?" asked the perturbed father.

"Nary a word, nary a word!" Robert got up. "Now, where is this wonderful he?—or is it a she?"

"Boy, Bob; greatest kid ever."

And they all trooped up the stairs to the nursery, where Mr. Robert was forced to admit that, as regarded a three-months-old, this was the handsomest little colt he had ever laid eyes on! Mr. Robert even ventured to take the boy up in his arms.

"How d'ye hold him?" he asked.

Mrs. John took the smiling cherub, and the manner in which she folded that infant across her young breast was a true revelation to the prodigal, who felt his loneliness more than ever. He was a rank outsider.

"Jack, you get me that diplomatic post, and I'll see to it that the only bachelor in the Warburton family shall sleep in yonder cradle."

"Done!"

"How long is your furlough?" asked Nancy.

"Whom do you think the baby resembles?" asked the mother.

"One at a time, one at a time! The baby at present doesn't resemble any one."

"There's your diplomat!" cried John, with a laugh.

"And my furlough is for several years, if not longer."

"What?" This query was general and simultaneous.

"Yes, I've disbanded. The Army will now go to rack and ruin. I am a plain citizen of the United States. I expect to spend the winter in Washington."

"The winter!" echoed Jack, mockingly dejected.

"John!" said his wife. John assumed a meek expression; and Mrs. John, putting the baby in the cradle, turned to her brother-in-law. "I thought the Army was a hobby with you."

"It was. I've saved up quite a sum, and I'm going to see a lot of fine scenery if my leg doesn't give-out."

"Or your bank account," supplemented John.

"Well, or my bank account."

"Draw on me whenever you want passage out West," went on the statesman in chrysalis.

Whereupon they all laughed; not because John had said anything particularly funny, but because there was a good and generous measure of happiness in each heart.

"Bob, there's a ball at the British embassy tonight. You must go with us."

"Impossible!" said Robert. "Remember my leg."

"That will not matter," said Mrs. John; "you need not dance."

"What, not dance? I should die of intermittent fever. And if I did dance, my leg might give out."

"You can ride a horse all right," said John, in the way of argument.

"I can do that easily with my knees. But I

can't dance with my knees. No, I shall stay at home. I couldn't stand it to see all those famous beauties, and with me posing as a wall-flower."

"But what will you do here all alone?"

"Play with the kid, smoke and read; make myself at home. You still smoke that Louisiana, Jack?"

"Yes,"—dubiously.

"So. Now, don't let me interfere with your plans for to-night. I haven't been in a home in so long that it will take more than one night for the novelty to wear off. Besides, that nurse of yours, Kit, is good to look at,"—a bit of the rogue in his eye.

"Bob!"—from both women.

"I promise not to look at her; I promise."

"Well, I must be off," said John. "I'm late now. I've a dozen plans for coast defenses to go over with an inventor of a new carriage-gun. Will you go with me, while I put you up at the Metropolitan, or will you take a shopping trip with the women?"

"I'll take the shopping trip. It will be a sensation. Have you any horses?"

"Six."

"Six! You *are* a lucky pup: a handsome wife, a bouncing boy, and six horses! Where's the stable?"

"In the rear. I keep only two stablemen; one to take care of the horses and one to act as groom. I'm off. I've a cracking good hunter, if you'd like a leg up. We'll all ride out to Chevy Chase Sunday. By-by, till lunch."

Mr. Robert immediately betook himself to the stables, where he soon became intimately acquainted with the English groom. He fussed about the harness-room, deplored the lack of a McClelland saddle, admired the English curbs, and complimented the men on the cleanliness of the stables. The men exchanged sly smiles at first, but these smiles soon turned into grins of admiration. Here was a man who knew a horse from his oiled hoofs to his curried forelock.

"This fellow ought to jump well," he said, patting the sleek neck of the hunter.

"He does that, sir," replied the groom. "He has never taken less than a red ribbon. Only one horse beat him at the bars last winter in New York. It was Mr. Warburton's fault that he did not take first prize. He rode him in the park the

day before the contest, and the animal caught a
· bad cold, sir."

And then it was that this hero of mine conceived his great (not to say young and salad)
idea. It appealed to him as being so rich an idea
that the stables rang with his laughter.

"Sir?" politely inquired the groom.

"I'm not laughing at your statement, my good
fellow; rather at an idea which just occurred to
me. In fact, I believe that I shall need your assistance."

"In what way, sir?"

"Come with me."

The groom followed Warburton into the yard.
A conversation began in low tones.

"It's as much as my place is worth, sir. I
couldn't do it, sir," declared the groom, shaking
his head negatively.

"I'll guarantee that you will not suffer in the
least. My brother will not discharge you. He
likes a joke as well as I do. You are not handed
twenty dollars every day for a simple thing like
this."

"Very well, sir. I dare say that no harm will
come of it. But I am an inch or two shorter than
you."

"We'll tide that over."

"I am at your orders, sir." But the groom returned to the stables, shaking his head dubiously.
He was not thoroughly convinced.

During the morning ride down-town the two
women were vastly puzzled over their brother's
frequent and inexplicable peals of laughter.

"For mercy's sake, what do you see that is so
funny?" asked Nancy.

"I'm thinking, my dears; only thinking."

"Tell us, that we may laugh, too. I'll wager
that you are up to some mischief, Master Robert.
Please tell," Nancy urged.

"Later, later; at present you would fail to appreciate the joke. In fact, you might make it
miscarry; and that wouldn't do at all. Have a
little patience. It's a good joke, and you'll be in
it when the time comes."

And nothing more could they worm out of
him.

I shall be pleased to recount to you the quality
of this joke, this madcap idea. You will find it
lacking neither amusement nor dénouement. Already I have put forth the casual observation that
from Paris to the third-precinct police-station in
Washington is several thousand miles.

V

THE PLOT THICKENS

At dinner that night I met my hero face to face for the first time in eight years, and for all his calling me a duffer (I learned of this only recently), he was mighty glad to see me, slapped me on the back and threw his arm across my shoulder. And why shouldn't he have been glad? We had been boys together, played hooky many a school-time afternoon, gone over the same fishing grounds, plunged into the same swimming-holes, and smoked our first cigar in the rear of my father's barn; and it is the recollection of such things that cements all the more strongly friendship in man and man. We recalled a thousand episodes and escapades, the lickings we got, and the lickings others got in our stead, the pretty school-teacher whom we swore to wed when we grew up. Nobody else had a chance to get a word in edgewise. But Nancy laughed aloud at times. She had been a witness to many of these long-ago pranks.

"What! you are not going to the ball?" I asked, observing that he wore only a dinner-coat and a pair of morocco slippers.

"No ball for me. Just as soon as you people hie forth, off comes this b'iled shirt, and I shall probably meander around the house in my new silk pajamas. I shall read a little from Homer —Jack, let me have the key to that locked case; I've an idea that there must be some robust old, merry old tales hidden there—and smoke a few pipes."

"But you are not going to leave Mrs. Warburton and your sister to come home without escort?" I expostulated.

"Where the deuce are you two men going?" Robert asked, surprised. Somehow, I seemed to catch a joyful rather than a sorrowful note in his tones.

"An important conference at midnight, and heaven only knows how long it may last," said Jack. "I wish you would go along, Bob."

"He can't go now, anyhow," said the pretty little wife. "He has got to stay now, whether he will or no. William will see to it that we women get home all right,"—and she busied herself with the salad dishes.

Suddenly I caught Robert's eye, and we stared hard at each other.

"Chuck, you old pirate," he said presently, "what do you mean by coming around and making love to my sister, and getting her to promise to marry you? You know you aren't good enough for her."

I confess to no small embarrassment. "I—I know it!"

"What do you mean by it, then?"

"Why—er—that is— Confound you, Bob, *I* couldn't help it, and besides, I didn't *want* to help it! And if you want to have it out—"

"Oh, pshaw! You know just as well as I do that it is against the law to hit a man that wears glasses. We'll call it quits if you'll promise that in the days to come you'll let me hang around your hymeneal shack once in a while."

"Why, if you put it that way!"—and we were laughing and shaking hands again across the table, much to the relief of all concerned.

Dear Nan! I'm not afraid to let the whole world see how much I love you. For where exists man's strength if not in the pride of his love?

"What time does the kid get to sleep?" asked Robert.

"He ought to be asleep now," said Mrs. W. "We shall not reach the embassy until after ten. We have a reception first, and we must leave cards there. Won't you be lonesome here, Bobby?"

"Not the least in the world;"—and Bobby began to laugh.

"What's the joke?" I asked.

He looked at me sharply, then shook his head. "I'll tell you all about it to-morrow, Chuck. It's the kind of joke that has to boil a long time before it gets tender enough to serve."

"I'd give a good deal to know what is going on behind those eyes of yours, Bob." Nancy's eyes searched him ruthlessly, but she might just as well have tried to pierce a stone wall. "You have been laughing all day about something, and I'd like to know what about. It's mischief. I haven't known you all these years for nothing. Now, don't do anything silly, Bob."

"Nancy,"—reproachfully—"I am a man almost thirty; I have passed the Rubicon of cutting up tricks. Go to the ball, you beauty, dance and revel to your heart's content; your brother Robert will manage to pass away the evening. Don't forget the key to that private case, Jack,"—as the women left the table to put the finishing touches to their toilets.

"Here you are," said Jack. "But mind, you must put those books back just as you found them, and lock the case. They are rare editions."

"With the accent on the *rare*, no doubt."

"I am a student, pure and simple," said Jack, lowering his eyes.

"I wouldn't swear to those adjectives," returned the scalawag. "If I remember, you had the reputation of being a high-jinks man in your class at Princeton."

"Sh! Don't you dare to drag forth any of those fool corpses of college, or out you go, bag and baggage." Jack glanced nervously around the room and toward the hall.

"My dear fellow, your wife wouldn't believe me, no matter what I said against your character. Isn't that right, Chuck? Jack, you are a lucky dog, if there ever was one. A handsome wife who loves you, a kid, a fine home, and plenty of horses. I wonder if you married her for her money?"

Jack's eyes narrowed. He seemed to muse. "Yes, I believe I can do it as easily as I did fifteen years ago."

"Do what?" I asked.

"Wallop that kid brother of mine. Bob, I hope you'll fall desperately in love some day, and that you will have a devil of a time winning the girl. You need something to stir up your vitals. By George! and I hope she won't have a cent of money."

"Lovable brother, that!" Bob knocked the ash from his cigar and essayed at laughter which wasn't particularly felicitous. "Supposing I was in love, now, and that the girl had heaps of money, and all that?"

"*And all that,*" mimicked the elder brother. "What does 'and all that' mean?"

"Oh, shut up!"

"Well, I hope you *are* in love. It serves you right. You've made more than one girl's heart ache, you good-looking ruffian!"

Then we switched over to politics, and Robert became an interested listener. Quarter of an hour later the women returned, and certainly they made a picture which was most satisfactory to the masculine eye. Ah, thou eager-fingered Time, that shall, in days to come, wither the roses in my beauty's cheeks, dim the fire in my beauty's eyes, draw my beauty's bow-lips inward, tarnish the golden hair, and gnarl the slender, shapely fingers, little shall I heed you in your passing if you but leave the heart untouched!

Rob jumped to his feet and kissed them both, a thing I lacked the courage to do. How pleased they looked! How a woman loves flattery from those she loves!

Well, William is in front with the carriage; the women are putting on their cloaks, and I am admiring the luxurious crimson fur-lined garment which brother Robert had sent to Nancy from Paris. You will see by this that he was not altogether a thoughtless lad. Good-by, Mr. Robert; I leave you and your guiding-star to bolt the established orbit; for after this night the world will never be the same careless, happy-go-lucky world. The farce has its tragedy, and what tragedy is free of the ludificatory? Youth must run its course, even as the gay, wild brook must riot on its way to join the sober river.

I dare say that we hadn't been gone twenty minutes before Robert stole out to the stables, only to return immediately with a bundle under his arm and a white felt hat perched rakishly on his head. He was chuckling audibly to himself.

"It will frighten the girls half to death. A gray

horse and a bay; oh, I won't make any mistake. Let me see; I'll start about twelve o'clock. That'll get me on the spot just as the boys leave. This is the richest yet. I'll wager that there will be some tall screaming." He continued chuckling as he helped himself to his brother's perfectos and fine old Scotch. I don't know what book he found in the private case; some old rascal's merry tales, no doubt; for my hero's face was never in repose.

We had left Mrs. Secretary-of-the-Interior's and were entering the red brick mansion on Connecticut Avenue. Carriages lined both sides of the street, and mounted police patrolled up and down.

"I do hope Bob will not wake up the baby," said Mrs. W.

"Probably he won't even take the trouble to look at him," replied Jack; "not if he gets into that private case of mine."

"I can't understand what you men see in those horrid chronicles," Nancy declared.

"My dear girl," said Jack, "in those days there were no historians; they were simply story-tellers, and we get our history from these tales. The tales themselves are not very lofty, I am willing to admit; but they give us a general idea of the times in which the characters lived. This is called literature by the wise critics."

"Critics!" said I; "humph! Criticism is always a lazy man's job. When no two critics think alike, of what use is criticism?"

"Ah, yes; I forgot. That book of essays you wrote got several sound drubbings. Nevertheless," continued Jack, "what you offer is in the main true. Time alone is the true critic. Let him put his mark of approval on your work, and not all the critical words can bury it or hinder its light. But Time does not pass his opinion till long after one is dead. The first waltz, dearest, if you think you can stand it. You mustn't get tired, little mother."

"I am wonderfully strong to-night," said the little mother. "How beautifully it is arranged!"

"What?" we men asked, looking over the rooms.

"The figures on Mrs. Secretary-of-State's gown. The lace is beautiful. Your brother, Nan, has very good taste for a man. That cloak of yours is by far the handsomest thing I have seen to-night; and that bit of scarf he sent me isn't to be matched."

"Poor boy!" sighed Nancy. "I wonder if he'll be lonely. It's a shame to leave him home the very first night."

"Why didn't he come, then?" Mrs W. shrugged her polished shoulders.

"Oh, my cigars and Scotch are fairly comforting," put in Jack, complacently. "Besides, Jane isn't at all bad looking,"—winking at me. "What do you say, Charlie?"

But Charlie had no time to answer. The gray-haired, gray-whiskered ambassador was bowing pleasantly to us. A dozen notable military and naval attachés nodded; and we passed on to the ball-room, where the orchestra was playing *A Summer Night in Munich*. In a moment Jack and his wife were lost in the maze of gleaming shoulders and white linen. It was a picture such as few men, once having witnessed it, can forget. Here were the great men in the great world: this man was an old rear-admiral, destined to become the nation's hero soon; there, a famous general, of long and splendid service; celebrated statesmen, diplomats, financiers; a noted English duke;

a scion of the Hapsburg family; an intimate of
the German kaiser; a swart Jap; a Chinaman with
his peacock feather; tens of men whose lightest
word was listened to by the four ends of the
world; representatives of all the great kingdoms
and states. The President and his handsome
wife had just left as we came, so we missed that
formality, which detracts from the pleasures of
the ball-room.

"Who is that handsome young fellow over
there, standing at the side of the Russian ambassador's wife?" asked Nancy, pressing my arm.

"Where? Oh, he's Count Karloff (or something which sounds like it), a wealthy Russian, in
some way connected with the Russian government; a diplomat and a capital fellow, they say.
I have never met him. . . . Hello! there's a
stunning girl right next to him that I haven't seen
before. . . . Where are you going?"

Nancy had dropped my arm and was gliding,
kitty-corner fashion, across the floor. Presently
she and the stunning girl had saluted each other
after the impulsive fashion of American girls,
and were playing cat-in-the-cradle, to the amusement of those foreigners nearest. A nod, and I
was threading my way to Nancy's side.

"Isn't it glorious?" she began. "This is Miss
'Annesley, Charlie; Betty, Mr. Henderson." Miss
'Annesley looked mildly curious at Nan, who suddenly flushed. "We are to be married in the
spring," she explained shyly; and I dare say that
there was a diffident expression on my own face.

Miss Annesley gave me her hand, smiling.
"You are a very fortunate man, Mr. Henderson."

"Not the shadow of a doubt!" Miss Annesley,
I frankly admitted on the spot, was, next to
Nancy, the handsomest girl I ever saw; and as I
thought of Mr. Robert in his den at home, I sin-
cerely pitied him. I was willing to advance the
statement that had he known, a pair of crutches
would not have kept him away from No. 1300
Connecticut Avenue.

I found three chairs, and we sat down. There
was, for me, very little opportunity to talk.
Women always have so much to say to each
other, even when they haven't seen each other
within twenty-four hours. From time to time
Miss Annesley glanced at me, and I am positive
that Nancy was extolling my charms. It was
rather embarrassing, and I was balling my gloves
up in a most dreadful fashion. As they seldom
addressed a word to me, I soon became absorbed

in the passing scene. I was presently aroused, however.

"Mr. Henderson, Count Karloff," Miss Annesley was saying. (Karloff is a name of my own choosing. I haven't the remotest idea if it means anything in the Russian language. I hope not.)

"Charmed!" The count's r's were very pleasantly rolled. I could see by the way his gaze roved from Miss Annesley to Nancy that he was puzzled to decide which came the nearer to his ideal of womanhood.

I found him a most engaging fellow, surprisingly well-informed on American topics. I credit myself with being a fairly good reader of faces, and, reading his as he bent it in Miss Annesley's direction, I began to worry about Mr. Robert's course of true love. Here was a man who possessed a title, was handsome, rich, and of assured social position: it would take an extraordinary American girl to look coldly upon his attentions. By and by the two left us, Miss Annesley promising to call on Nancy.

"And where are you staying, Betty?"

"Father and I have taken Senator Blank's house in Chevy Chase for the winter. My horses are already in the stables. Do you ride?"

"I do."

"Then we shall have some great times together."

"Be sure to call. I want you to meet my brother."

"I believe I have," replied Miss Annesley.

"I mean my younger brother, a lieutenant in the Army."

"Oh, then you have two brothers?"

"Yes," said Nancy.

"The dance is dying, Mademoiselle," said the count in French.

"Your arm, Monsieur. *Au revoir,* Nancy."

"Poor Bobby!" Nancy folded her hands and sighed mournfully. "It appears to me that his love affair is not going to run very smooth. But isn't she just beautiful, Charlie? What color, what style!"

"She's a stunner, I'm forced to admit. Bob'll never stand a ghost of a show against that Russian. He's a great social catch, and is backed by many kopecks."

"How unfortunate we did not know that she would be here! Bobby would have met her at his best, and his best is more to my liking than the count's. He has a way about him that the

" What were you doing off your own box?" "Getting on the wrong box."—ACT I.

women like. He's no laggard. But money ought not to count with Betty. She is worth at least a quarter of a million. Her mother left all her property to her, and her father acts only as trustee. Senator Blank's house rents for eight thousand the season. It's ready furnished, you know, and one of the handsomest homes in Washington. Besides, I do not trust those foreigners," —taking a remarkably abrupt curve, as it were.

"There's two Bs in your bonnet, Nancy," I laughed.

"Never mind the Bs; let us have the last of this waltz."

This is not my own true story; so I shall bow off and permit my hero to follow the course of true love, which is about as rough-going a thoroughfare as the many roads of life have to offer.

VI

THE MAN ON THE BOX

At eleven-thirty he locked up his book and took to his room the mysterious bundle which he had purloined from the stables. It contained the complete livery of a groom. The clothes fitted rather snugly, especially across the shoulders. He stood before the pier-glass, and a complacent (not to say roguish) smile flitted across his face. The black half-boots, the white doeskin breeches, the brown brass-buttoned frock, and the white hat with the brown cockade. . . . Well, my word for it, he was the handsomest jehu Washington ever turned out. With a grin he touched his hat to the reflection in the glass, and burst out laughing. His face was as smooth as a baby's, for he had generously sacrificed his beard.

I can hear him saying to himself: "Lord, but this is a lark! I'll have to take another Scotch to screw up the edge of my nerve. Won't the boys laugh when they hear how I stirred the girls' frizzes! We'll have a little party here when they all get home. It's a good joke."

Mr. Robert did not prove much of a prophet. Many days were to pass ere he reëntered his brother's house.

He stole quietly from the place. He hadn't proceeded more than a block when he became aware of the fact that he hadn't a penny in his clothes. This discovery disquieted him, and he half turned about to go back. He couldn't go back. He had no key.

"Pshaw! I won't need any money;"—and he started off again toward Connecticut Avenue. He dared not hail a car, and he would not have dared had he possessed the fare. Some one might recognize him. He walked briskly for ten minutes. The humor of the escapade appealed to him greatly, and he had all he could do to smother the frequent bursts of laughter which surged to his lips. He reached absently for his cigar-case. No money, no cigars.

"That's bad. Without a cigar I'm likely to get nervous. Scraping off that beard made me forgetful. Jove! with these fleshings I feel as self-conscious as an untried chorus girl. These togs can't be very warm in winter. Ha! that must be the embassy where all those lights are; carriages. *Allons!"*

To make positive, he stopped a pedestrian.

"Pardon me, sir," he said, touching his hat, "but will you be so kind as to inform me if yonder is the British embassy?"

"It is, my man," replied the gentleman.

"Thank you, sir."

And each passed on to his affairs.

"Now for William; we must find William, or the joke will be on Robert."

He manœuvred his way through the congested thoroughfare, searching the faces of the grooms and footmen. He dodged hither and thither, and was once brought to a halt by the mounted police.

"Here, you! What d'ye mean by runnin' around like this? Lost yer carriage, hey? I've a mind to run ye in. Y' know th' rules relatin' th' leavin' of yer box in times like these. Been takin' a sly nip, probably, an' they've sent yer hack down a peg. Get a gait on y', now."

Warburton laughed silently as he made for the sidewalk. The first man he plumped into was William—a very much worried William, too.

Robert could have fallen on his neck for joy. All was plain sailing now.

"I'm very glad to see you, sir," said William. "I was afraid you could not get them clothes on, sir. I was getting a trifle worried, too. Here's the carriage number."

Warburton glanced hastily at it and stuffed it into a convenient pocket.

"It's sixteen carriages up, sir; a bay and a gray. You can't miss them. The bay, being a saddle-horse, is a bit restive in the harness; but all you have to do is to touch him with the whip. And don't try to push ahead of your turn or you will get into trouble with the police. They are very strict. And don't let them confuse you, sir. The numbers won't be in rotation. You'll hear one hundred and fifteen, and the next moment thirty-five, like as not. It's all according as to how the guests are leaving. Good luck to you, sir, and don't forget to explain it all thoroughly to Mr. Warburton, sir."

"Don't you worry, William; we'll come out of this with colors flying."

"Very well, sir. I shall hang around till you are safely off,"—and William disappeared.

Warburton could occasionally hear the faint strains of music. From time to time the carriage-caller bawled out a number, and the carriage would roll up under the porte-cochère. Warburton concluded that it would be a good plan to hunt up his rig. His search did not last long. The bay and the gray stood only a little way from the gate. The box was vacant, and he climbed up and gathered the reins. He sat there for some time, longing intensely for a cigar, a good cigar, such as gentlemen smoked.

"Seventeen!" came hoarsely along on the wings of the night. "Number seventeen, and lively there!"

Warburton's pulse doubled its beat. His number!

"Skt!" The gray and the bay started forward, took the half-circle and stopped under the porte-cochère. Warburton recollected that a fashionable groom never turned his head unless spoken to; so he leveled his gaze at his horses' ears and waited. But from the very corner of his eye he caught the glimpse of two women, one of whom was enveloped in a crimson cloak. He thrilled with exultation. What a joke it was! He felt the carriage list as the women stepped in. The door slammed to, and the rare good joke was on the way.

"Off with you!" cried the pompous footman, with an imperious wave of the hand. "Number ninety-nine!"

"Ninety-nine! Ninety-nine!" bawled the carriage man.

Our jehu turned into the avenue, holding a tolerable rein. He clucked and lightly touched the horses with the lash. *This* was true sport; *this* was humor, genuine, initiative, unforced. He could imagine the girls and their fright when he finally slowed down, opened the door, and kissed them both. Wouldn't they let out a yell, though? His plan was to drive furiously for half a dozen blocks, zigzag from one side of the street to the other, taking the corners sharply, and then make for Scott Circle.

Now, a lad of six can tell the difference between seventeen and seventy-one. But this astonishing jehu of mine had been conspicuous as the worst mathematician and the best soldier in his class at West Point. No more did he remember that he was not in the wild West, and that here in the East there were laws prohibiting reckless driving.

He drove decently enough till he struck Dupont Circle. From here he turned into New Hampshire, thinking it to be Rhode Island. Mistake number two. He had studied the city map, but he was conscious of not knowing it as well as he should have known it; but, true to his nature, he trusted to luck.

Aside from all this, he forgot that a woman might appreciate this joke only when she heard it recounted. To live through it was altogether a different matter. In an episode like this, a woman's imagination, given the darkness such as usually fills a carriage at night, becomes a round of terrors. Every moment is freighted with death or disfigurement. Her nerves are like the taut strings of a harp in a wintry wind, ready to snap at any moment; and then, hysteria. With man the play, and only the play, is the thing.

Snap-crack! The surprised horses, sensitive and quick-tempered as all highly organized beings are, nearly leaped out of the harness. Never before had their flanks received a more unwarranted stroke of the lash. They reared and plunged, and broke into a mad gallop, which was exactly what the rascal on the box desired. An expert horseman, he gauged the strength of the animals the moment they bolted, and he knew that they were his. Once the rubber-tired vehicle slid sidewise on the wet asphalt, and he heard a stifled scream.

He laughed, and let forth a sounding "whoop," which nowise allayed the fright of the women inside the carriage. He wheeled into S Street, scraping the curb as he did so. Pedestrians stopped and stared after him. A policeman waved his club helplessly, even hopelessly. On, on: to Warburton's mind this ride was as wild as that which the Bishop of Vannes took from Belle-Isle to Paris in the useless effort to save Fouquet from the wrath of Louis XIV, and to anticipate the pregnant discoveries of one D'Artagnan. The screams were renewed. A hand beat against the forward window and a muffled but wrathful voice called forth a command to stop. This voice was immediately drowned by another's prolonged scream. Our jehu began to find all this very interesting, very exciting.

"I'll wager a dollar that Nan isn't doing that screaming. The Warburtons never cry out when they are frightened. Hang it!"—suddenly; "this street doesn't look familiar. I ought to have reached Scott Circle by this time. Ah! here's a

broader street,"—going lickety-clip into Vermont.
A glass went jingling to the pavement.
"Oho! Nancy will be jumping out the next
thing. This will never do." He began to draw
in.

Hark! His trained trooper's ear heard other
hoofs beating on the iron-like surface of the pavement. Worriedly he turned his head. Five blocks
away there flashed under one of the arc-lights,
only to disappear in the shadow again, two
mounted policemen.

"By George! it looks as if the girls were going
to have their fun, too!" He laughed, but there
was a nervous catch in his voice. He hadn't
counted on any policeman taking part in the comedy. "Where the devil *is* Scott Circle, anyhow?"
—fretfully. He tugged at the reins. "Best draw
up at the next corner. I'll be hanged if *I* know
where I am."

He braced himself, sawed with the reins, and
presently the frightened and somewhat wearied
horses slowed down into a trot. This he finally
brought to a walk. One more pull, and they came
to a stand. It would be hard to say which
breathed the heaviest, the man or the horses.
Warburton leaped from the box; opened the door

and waited. He recognized the necessity of finishing the play before the mounted police arrived
on the scene.

There was a commotion inside the carriage,
then a woman in a crimson cloak stepped (no,
jumped!) out. Mr. Robert threw his arms around
her and kissed her cheek.

"You . . . vile . . . wretch!"

Warburton sprang back, his hands applied to
his stinging face.

"You drunken wretch, how dare you!"

"Nan, it's only I—" he stammered.

"Nan!" exclaimed the young woman, as her
companion joined her. The light from the corner
disclosed the speaker's wrathful features, disdain-
ful lips, palpitating nostrils, eyes darting terrible
glances. "Nan! Do you think, ruffian, that you
are driving serving-maids?"

"Good Lord!" Warburton stepped back still
farther; stepped back speechless, benumbed, ter-
ror-struck. The woman he was gazing at was
anybody in the world but his sister Nancy!

VII

"Officers, arrest this fellow!" commanded the
young woman. Her gesture was Didoesque in
its wrath.

"That we will, ma'am!" cried one of the policemen, flinging himself from his horse. "So
it's you, me gay buck? Thirty days fer you, an'
mebbe more. I didn't like yer looks from th'
start. You're working some kind of a trick.
What complaint, ma'am?"

"Drunkenness and abduction,"—rubbing the
burning spot on her cheek.

"That'll be rather serious. Ye'll have to appear against him in th' mornin', ma'am."

"I certainly shall do so." She promptly gave
her name, address and telephone number.

"Bill, you drive th' ladies home an' I'll see this
bucko to th' station. Here, you!"—to Warburton, who was still dumb with astonishment at
the extraordinary dénouement to his innocent

94

joke. "Git on that horse, an' lively, too, or I'll rap ye with th' club."

"It's all a mistake, officer—"

"Close yer face an' git on that horse. Y' can tell th' judge all that in th' mornin'. *I* ain't got no time t' listen. Bill, report just as soon as ye see th' ladies home. Now, off with ye. Th' ladies'll be wantin' somethin' t' quiet their nerves. Git on that horse, me frisky groom; hustle!" Warburton mechanically climbed into the saddle. It never occurred to him to parley, to say that he couldn't ride a horse. The inventive cells of his usually fertile brain lay passive. "Now," went on the officer, mounting his own nag, "will ye go quietly? If ye don't I'll plug ye in th' leg with a chunk o' lead. I won't stan' no nonsense."

"What are you going to do with me?" asked Warburton, with a desperate effort to collect his energies.

"Lock ye up; mebbe throw a pail of water on that overheated cocoanut of yours."

"But if you'll only let me explain to you! It's all a joke; I got the wrong carriage—"

"Marines, marines! D' ye think I was born yestiddy? Ye wanted th' ladies' sparklers, or I'm

a doughhead." The police are the same all over
the world; the original idea sticks to them, and
truth in voice or presence is but sign of deeper
cunning and villainy. "Anyhow, ye can't run
around Washington like ye do in England, me
cockney. Ye can't drive more 'n a hundred miles
an hour on these pavements."

"But, I tell you—" Warburton, realizing
where his escapade was about to lead him,
grew desperate. The ignominy of it! He would
be the laughing-stock of all the town on the mor-
row. The papers would teem with it. "You'll
find that you are making a great mistake. If you
will only take me to—Scott Circle—"

"Where ye have a pal with a gun, eh? Git
ahead!" And the two made off toward the west.

Once or twice the officer found himself admiring the easy seat of his prisoner; and if the horse
had been anything but a trained animal, he would
have worried some regarding the ultimate arrival
at the third-precinct.

Half a dozen times Warburton was of a mind
to make a bolt for it, but he did not dare trust the
horse or his knowledge of the streets. He had
already two counts against him, disorderly conduct and abduction, and he had no desire to add

uselessly a third, that of resisting an officer, which seems the greatest possible crime a man can commit and escape hanging. Oh, for a mettlesome nag! There would be no police-station for him, then. Police-station! Heavens, what should he do? His brother, his sister; their dismay, their shame; not counting that he himself would be laughed at from one end of the continent to the other. What an ass he had made of himself! He wondered how much money it would take to clear himself, and at the same moment recollected that he hadn't a cent in his clothes. A sweat of terror moistened his brow.

"What were ye up to, anyway?" asked the policeman. "What kind of booze have ye been samplin'?"

"I've nothing to say."

"Ye speak clear enough. So much th' worse, if ye ain't drunk. Was ye crazy t' ride like that? Ye might have killed th' women an' had a bill of manslaughter brought against ye."

"I have nothing to say; it is all a mistake. I got the wrong number and the wrong carriage."

"Th' devil ye did! An' where was ye goin' t' drive th' other carriage at that thunderin' rate?

It won't wash. His honor'll be stone-deaf when ye tell him that. You're drunk, or have been."

"Not to-night."

"Well, I'd give me night off t' know what ye were up to. Don't ye know nothin' about ordinances an' laws? An' I wouldn't mind havin' ye tell me why ye threw yer arms around th' lady an' kissed her,"—shrewdly.

Warburton started in his saddle. He had forgotten all about that part of the episode. His blood warmed suddenly and his cheeks burned. He had kissed her, kissed her soundly, too, the most radiantly beautiful woman in all the world. Why, come to think of it, it was easily worth a night in jail. Yes, by George, he *had* kissed her, kissed that blooming cheek, and but for this policeman, would have forgotten! Whatever happened to him, she wouldn't forget in a hurry. He laughed. The policeman gazed at him in pained surprise.

"Well, ye seem t' take it good an' hearty."

"If you could only see the humor in it, my friend, you'd laugh, too."

"Oh, I would, hey? All I got t' say is that yer nerve gits me. An' ye stand a pretty good show of bein' rounded up for more'n thirty days, too.

Well, ye've had yer joke; mebbe ye have th' price
t' pay th' fiddler. Turn here."

The rest of the ride was in silence, Warburton
gazing callously ahead and the officer watching
him with a wary eye to observe any suggestive
movement. He couldn't make out this chap.
There was something wrong, some deep-dyed villainy—of this he hadn't the slightest doubt. It
was them high-toned swells that was the crafti-
est an' most daring. Handsome is that handsome does. A quarter of an hour later they arrived at the third precinct, where our jehu was
registered for the night under the name of James
Osborne. He was hustled into a small cell and
left to himself.

He had kissed her! Glory of glories! He had
pressed her to his very heart, besides. After all,
they couldn't do anything very serious to him.
They could not prove the charge of abduction.
He stretched himself on the cot, smiled, arranged
his legs comfortably, wondered what she was
thinking of at this moment, and fell asleep. It
was a sign of a good constitution and a decently
white conscience. And thus they found him in
the morning. They touched his arm, and he

awoke with a smile, the truest indication of a man's amiability. At first he was puzzled as he looked blinkingly from his jailers to his surroundings and then back at his jailers. Then it all returned to him, and he laughed. Now the law, as represented and upheld by its petty officers, possesses a dignity that is instantly ruffled by the sound of laughter from a prisoner; and Mr. Robert was roughly told to shut up, and that he'd soon laugh on the other side of his mouth.

"All right, officers, all right; only make allowances for a man who sees the funny side of things." Warburton stood up and shook himself, and picked up his white hat. They eyed him intelligently. In the morning light the young fellow didn't appear to be such a rascal. It was plainly evident that he had *not* been drunk the preceding night; for his eyes were not shot with red veins nor did his lips lack their usual healthy moisture. The officer who had taken him in charge, being a shrewd and trained observer, noted the white hands, soft and well-kept. He shook his head.

"Look here, me lad, you're no groom, not by several years. Now, what th' devil was ye up to, anyway?"

"I'm not saying a word, sir," smiled Warburton. "All I want to know is, am I to have any breakfast? I shouldn't mind some peaches and cream or grapes to start with, and a small steak and coffee."

"Ye wouldn't mind, hey?" mimicked the officer. "What d'ye think this place is, th' Metropolitan Club? Ye'll have yer bacon an' coffee, an' be glad t' git it. They'll feed ye in th' mess-room. Come along."

Warburton took his time over the coffee and bacon. He wanted to think out a reasonable defense without unmasking himself. He was thinking how he could get word to me, too. The "duffer" might prove a friend in need.

"Now where?" asked Warburton, wiping his mouth.

"T' th' court. It'll go hard with ye if ye're handed over t' th' grand jury on th' charge of abduction. Ye'd better make a clean breast of it. I'll speak a word for yer behavior."

"Aren't you a little curious?"

"It's a part of me business,"—gruffly.

"I'll have my say to the judge," said Warburton.

"That's yer own affair. Come."

Once outside, Warburton lost color and a large part of his nonchalance; for an open patrol stood at the curb.

"Have I got to ride in that?"—disgustedly.

"As true as life; an' if ye make any disturbance, so much th' worse."

Warburton climbed in, his face red with shame and anger. He tied his handkerchief around his chin and tilted his hat far down over his eyes.

"'Fraid of meetin' some of yer swell friends, hey? Ten t' one, yer a swell an' was runnin' away with th' wrong woman. Mind, I have an eye on ye."

The patrol rumbled over the asphalt on the way down-town. Warburton buried his face in his hands. Several times they passed a cigar-store, and his mouth watered for a good cigar, the taste of a clear Havana.

He entered the police-court, not lacking in curiosity. It was his first experience with this arm of the civil law. He wasn't sure that he liked it. It wasn't an inviting place with its bare benches and its motley, tawdry throng. He was plumped into a seat between some ladies of irregular habits, and the stale odor of intoxicants, mingling with cheap perfumery, took away the edge of his curiosity.

"Hello, pretty boy; jag?" asked one of these faded beauties, in an undertone. She nudged him with her elbow.

"No, sweetheart," he replied, smiling in spite of himself.

"Ah gowan! Been pinching some one's wad?"

"Nope!"

"What are you here for, then?"

"Having a good time without anybody's consent. If you will listen, you will soon hear all about it."

"Silence there, on the bench!" bawled the clerk, whacking the desk.

"Say, Marie," whispered the woman to her nearest neighbor, "here's a boy been selling his master's harness and got pinched."

"But look at the sweet things coming in, will you! Ain't they swell, though?" whispered Marie, nodding a skinny feather toward the door.

Warburton glanced indifferently in the direction indicated, and received a shock. Two women —and both wore very heavy black veils. The smaller of the two inclined her body, and he was sure that her scrutiny was for him. He saw her say something into the ear of the companion, and repeat it to one of the court lawyers. The lawyer approached the desk, and in his turn whispered a few words into the judge's ear. The magistrate nodded. Warburton was conscious of a blush of shame. This was a nice position for any respectable woman to see him in!

"James Osborne!" called the clerk.

An officer beckoned to James, and he made his way to the prisoner's box. His honor looked him over coldly.

"Name?"

"James Osborne."

"Born here?"

"No."

"Say 'sir'."

"No, sir."

"Where were you born?"

"In New York State."

"How old are you? And don't forget to say 'sir' when you reply to my questions."

"I am twenty-eight, sir."

"Married?"

"No, sir."

"How long have you been engaged as a groom?"

"Not very long, sir."

"How long?"

"Less than twenty-four hours, sir."

Surprise rippled over the faces of the audience on the benches.

"Humph! You are charged with disorderly conduct, reckless driving, and attempted abduction. The last charge has been withdrawn, fortunately for you, sir. Have you ever been up before?"

"Up, sir?"

"A prisoner in a police-court."

"No, sir."

"Twenty-five for reckless driving and ten for disorderly conduct; or thirty days."

"Your Honor, the horses ran away."

"Yes, urged by your whip."

"I was not disorderly, sir."

"The officer declares that you had been drinking."

"Your Honor, I got the wrong carriage. My number was seventeen and I answered to number seventy-one." He wondered if *she* would believe this statement.

"I suppose that fully explains why you made a race-track of one of our main thoroughfares?"—sarcastically. "You were on the wrong carriage to begin with."

"All I can say, sir, is that it was a mistake."

"The mistake came in when you left your carriage to get a drink. You broke the law right then. Well, if a man makes mistakes, he must pay for them, here or elsewhere. This mistake will cost you thirty-five."

"I haven't a penny in my clothes, sir."

"Officer, lock him up, and keep him locked up till the fine is paid. I can not see my way to remit it. Not another word,"—as Warburton started to protest.

"Marie Johnson, Mabel Tynner, Belle Lisle!" cried the clerk.

The two veiled ladies left the court precipitately.

James, having been ushered into a cell, hurriedly called for pen and ink and paper. At half after ten that morning the following note reached me:

"Dear Chuck: Am in a devil of a scrape at the police-court. Tried to play a joke on the girls last night by dressing up in the groom's clothes. Got the wrong outfit, and was arrested. Bring thirty-five and a suit of clothes the quickest ever. And, for mercy's sake, say nothing to any one, least of all the folks. I have given the name of James Osborne. Now, hustle.   Bob."

I hustled.

VIII

When they found him missing, his bed un-touched, his hat and coat on the rack, his insep-arable walking-stick in the umbrella-stand, they were mightily worried. They questioned Jane, but she knew nothing. Jack went out to the stables; no news there. William, having driven the girls home himself, dared say nothing. Then Jack wisely telephoned for me, and I hurried over to the house.

"Maybe he hunted up some friends last night," I suggested.

"But here's his hat!" cried Nancy.

"Oh, he's all right; don't worry. I'll take a tour around the city. I'll find him. He may be at one of the clubs."

Fortunately for Mr. James Osborne I returned home first, and there found his note awaiting me. I was at the court by noon, armed with thirty-five and a suit of clothes of my own. I found the clerk.

"A young man, dressed as a groom, and locked up overnight," I said cautiously. "I wish to pay his fine."

"James Osborne?"

"Yes, that's the name; James Osborne,"— reaching down into my pocket.

"Fine's just been paid. We were about to release him. Here, officer, show this gentleman to James Osborne's cell, and tell him to pack up and get out."

So his fine was paid! Found the money in his clothes, doubtless. On the way to the cells I wondered what the deuce the rascal had been doing to get locked up overnight. I was vastly angry, but at the sight of him all my anger melted into a prolonged shout of laughter.

"That's right; laugh, you old pirate! I wish you had been in my boots a few hours ago. Lord!"

I laughed again.

"Have you got that thirty-five?" he asked.

"Why, your fine has been paid," I replied, rather surprised.

"And didn't you pay it?"

"Not I! The clerk told me that it had just been paid."

Warburton's jaw sank limply. "Just been paid?— Who the deuce could have paid it, or known?"

"First, tell me what you've been up to."

He told me snatches of the exploit as he changed his clothes, and it was a question which of us laughed the more. But he didn't say a word about the stolen kiss, for which I think none the less of him.

"Who were the women?" I asked.

He looked at me for a space, as if deciding. Finally he made a negative sign.

"Don't know who they were, eh?"—incredulously.

He shrugged, laughed, and drew on his shoes.

"I always knew that I was the jackass of the family, Chuck, but I never expected to do it so well. Let's get out of this hole. I wonder who can have paid that fine? . . . No, that would not be possible!"

"What would not be?"

"Nothing, nothing,"—laughing.

But I could see that his spirits had gone up several degrees.

"The whole thing is likely to be in the evening

papers," I said. He needed a little worrying. And I knew his horror of publicity.

"The newspapers? In the newspapers? Oh, I say, Chuck, can't you use your influence to suppress the thing? Think of the girls."

"I'll do the best I can. And there's only one thing for you to do, and that is to cut out of town till your beard has grown. It would serve you right, however, if the reporters got the true facts."

"I'm for getting out of town, Chuck; and on the next train but one."

Here our conversation was interrupted by the entrance of a policeman.

"A note for *Mister* Osborne,"—ironically. He tossed the letter to Warburton and withdrew.

Mister Osborne eagerly tore open an end of the envelope—a very aristocratic envelope, as I could readily discern—and extracted the letter. I closely watched his facial expressions. First, there was interest, then surprise, to be succeeded by amusement and a certain exultation. He slapped his thigh.

"By George, Chuck, I'll do it!"

"Do it? Now what?"

"Listen to this." He cleared his throat, sniffed of the faintly scented paper and cleared his throat again. He looked up at me drolly.

·"Well?" said I, impatiently. I was as eager to hear it as he had been to read it. I believed that the mystery was about to be solved.

"'James Osborne, Sir: I have been thinking the matter over seriously, and have come to the conclusion that there may have been a mistake. Undoubtedly my groom was primarily to blame. I have discharged him for neglecting his post of duty. I distinctly recall the manner in which you handled the horses last night. It may be possible that they ran away with you. However that may be, I find myself in need of a groom. Your horsemanship saved us from a serious accident. If you will promise to let whisky alone, besides bringing me a recommendation, and are without engagement, call at the inclosed address this afternoon at three o'clock. I should be willing to pay as much as forty dollars a month. You would be expected to accompany me on my morning rides.'"

"She must have paid the fine," said I. "Well, it beats anything I ever heard of. Had you arrested, and now wants to employ you! What name did you say?" I asked carelessly.

"I didn't say any name, Chuck,"—smiling. "And I'm not going to give any, you old duffer."

"And why not?"

"For the one and simple reason that I am going to accept the position,"—with a coolness that staggered me.

"What?" I bawled.

"Sure as life, as the policeman said last night."

"You silly ass, you! Do you want to make the family a laughing-stock all over town?" I was really angry.

"Neither the family nor the town will know anything about it,"—imperturbably.

"But you will be recognized!" I remonstrated. "It's a clear case of insanity, after what has just happened to you."

"I promise not to drink any whisky,"—soberly.

"Bob, you are fooling me."

"Not the littlest bit, Chuck. I've worn a beard for two years. No one would recognize me. Besides, being a groom, no one would pay any particular attention to me. Get the point?"

"But what under the sun is your object?" I demanded. "There's something back of all this. It's not a simple lark like last night's."

"Perspicacious man!"—railingly. "Possibly you may be right. Chuck, you know that I've just got to be doing something. I've been inactive too long. I am ashamed to say that I should tire of the house in a week or less. Change, change, of air, of place, of occupation; change—I must have it. It's food and drink."

"You've met this woman before, somewhere."

"I neither acknowledge nor deny. It will be very novel. I shall be busy from morning till night. Think of the fun of meeting persons whom you know, but who do not know you. I wouldn't give up this chance for any amount of money."

"Forty dollars a month," said I, wrathfully.

"Cigar money,"—tranquilly.

"Look here, Bob; be reasonable. You can't go about as a groom in Washington. If the newspapers ever get hold of it, you would be disgraced. They wouldn't take you as a clerk in a third-rate consulate. Supposing you should run into Jack or his wife or Nancy; do you think they wouldn't know you at once?"

"I'll take the risk. I'd deny that I knew them;

they'd tumble and leave me alone. Chuck, I've got to do this. Some day you'll understand."

"But the woman's name, Bob; only her name."

"Oh, yes! And have you slide around and show me up within twenty-four hours. No, I thank you. I am determined on this. You ought to know me by this time. I never back down; it isn't in the blood. And when all is said, where's the harm in this escapade? I can see none. It may not last the day through."

"I trust not,"—savagely.

"I am determined upon answering this letter in person and finding out, if possible, what induced her to pay my fine. Jackass or not, I'm going to see the thing through." Then he stretched an appealing hand out toward me, and said wheedlingly: "Chuck, give me your word to keep perfectly quiet. I'll drop you a line once in a while, just to let you know how I stand. I shall be at the house to-night. I'll find an excuse. I'm to go up North on a hunting expedition; a hurry call. Do you catch on?"

"I shall never be able to look Nancy in the face," I declared. "Come, Bob; forget it. It sounds merry enough, but my word for it, you'll regret it inside of twenty-four hours. You are a graduate of the proudest military school in the world, and you are going to make a groom of yourself!"

"I've already done that and been locked up overnight. You are wasting your breath, Chuck."

"Well, hang you for a jackass, sure enough! I promise; but if you get into any such scrape as this, you needn't send for me. I refuse to help you again."

"I can't exactly see that you did. Let's get out. Got a cigar in your pocket? I am positively dying for a smoke."

Suddenly a brilliant idea came to me.

"Did you know that Miss Annesley, the girl you saw on shipboard, is in Washington and was at the embassy last night?"

"No! You don't say!" He was too clever for me. "When I get through with this exploit, Nancy'll have to introduce me. Did you see her?"

"Yes, and talked to her. You see what you missed by not going last night."

"Yes, I missed a good night's rest and a cold bath in the morning."

"Where shall I say you were last night?" I asked presently.

Mister James scratched his chin disconcertedly.

"I hadn't thought of that. Say that I met some of the boys and got mixed up in a little game of poker."

"You left your hat on the rack and your cane in the stand. You are supposed to have left the house without any hat."

"Hat!" He jumped up from the cot on which he had been sitting and picked up the groom's tile. "Didn't you bring me a hat?"—dismayed.

"You said nothing about it,"—and I roared with laughter.

"How shall I get out of here? I can't wear this thing through the streets."

"I've a mind to make you wear it. And, by Jove, you shall! You'll wear it to the hatter's, or stay here. That's final. I never back down, either."

"I'll wear it; only, mark me, I'll get even with you. I always did."

"*I* am not a boy any longer,"—with an inflection on the personal pronoun. "Well, to continue about that excuse. You left the house without a hat, and you met the boys and played poker all night. That hitches wonderfully. You didn't feel well enough to go to the embassy, but you could go and play poker. That sounds as if you cared

a lot for your sister. And you wanted to stay at
home the first night, because you had almost forgotten how the inside of a private dwelling
looked. Very good; very coherent."

"Cut it, Chuck. What the deuce excuse *can* I
give?"—worriedly lighting the cigar I had given
him.

"My boy, I'm not making up your excuses;
you'll have to invent those. I'll be silent, but I
refuse to lie to Nancy on your account. Poker is
the only excuse that would carry any weight with
it. You will have to let them believe you're a
heartless wretch; which you are, if you persist in
this idiotic exploit."

"You don't understand, Chuck. I wish I could
tell you; honestly, I do. The girls will have to
think mean things of me till the farce is over. I
couldn't escape if I wanted to."

"Is it Miss Annesley, Bob? Was it she whom
you ran away with? Come, make a clean breast
of it. If it's she, why, that altogether alters the
face of things."

He walked the length of the cell and returned.
"I give up. You've hit it. You understand now,
I simply can't back away; I couldn't if I tried."

"Are you in love with the girl?"

"That's just what I want to find out, Chuck. I'm not sure. I've been thinking of her night and day. I never had any affair; I don't know what love is. But if it's shaking in your boots at the sound of her name, if it's getting red in the face when you only just think of her, if it's having a wild desire to pick her up and run away with her when you see her, then I've got it. When she stepped out of that confounded carriage last night, you could have knocked me over with a paper-wad. Come, let's go out. Hang the hat! Let them all laugh if they will. It's only a couple of blocks to the hatter's."

He bravely put the white hat on his head, and together we marched out of the police-office into the street. We entered the nearest hatter's together. He took what they call a drop-kick out of the hat, sending it far to the rear of the establishment. I purchased a suitable derby for him, gave him ten dollars for emergencies, and we parted.

He proceeded to a telegraph office and sent a despatch to a friend up North, asking him to telegraph him to come at once, taking his chances of getting a reply. After this he boarded a north-going car, and was rolled out to Chevy Chase. He had no difficulty in finding the house of which he was in search. It was a fine example of colonial architecture, well back from the road, and fields beyond it. It was of red brick and white stone, with a wide veranda supported by great white pillars. There was a modern portico at one side. A fine lawn surrounded the whole, and white-pebble walks wound in and out. All around were thickly wooded hills, gashed here and there by the familiar yet peculiar red clay of the country. Warburton walked up the driveway and knocked deliberately at the servants' door, which was presently opened. (I learned all these things afterward, which accounts for my accurate knowledge of events.)

"Please inform Miss Annesley that Mr. Osborne has come in reply to her letter," he said to the little black-eyed French maid.

"Ees Meestaire Osborrrrne zee new groom?"

"Yes."

"I go thees minute!" *Hein!* what a fine-looking young man to make eyes at on cold nights in the kitchen!

Warburton sat down and twirled his hat. Several times he repressed the desire to laugh. He gazed curiously about him. From where he sat he could see into the kitchen. The French chef was hanging up his polished pans in a glistening row back of the range, and he was humming a little *chanson* which Warburton had often heard in the restaurants of the provincial cities of France. He even found himself catching up the refrain where the chef left off. Presently he heard footsteps sounding on the hardwood floor, which announced that the maid was returning with her mistress.

He stood up, rested first on one foot, then on the other, and awkwardly shifted his new hat from one hand to the other, then suddenly put the hat under his arm, recollecting that the label was not such as servants wore inside their hats.

There was something disquieting in those magnetic sapphire eyes looking so serenely into his.

IX

THE HEROINE HIRES A GROOM

Remarkable as it may read, his first impression was of her gown—a gown such as women wear on those afternoons when they are free of social obligations, a gown to walk in or to lounge in. The skirt, which barely reached to the top of her low shoes, was of some blue stuff (stuff, because to a man's mind the word covers feminine dress-goods generally, liberally, and handily), overshot with gray. Above this she had put on a white golfing-sweater, a garment which at that time was just beginning to find vogue among women who loved the fields and the road. Only men who own to stylish sisters appreciate these things, and Warburton possessed rather observant eyes. She held a bunch of freshly plucked poppies in her hand. It was the second time that their glances had met and held. In the previous episode (on the day she had leaned out of the cab) hers had been first to fall. Now it was his turn. He studied the tips of his shoes. There were three causes why he lowered his eyes: First, she was mistress here and he was an applicant for employment; second, he loved her; third, he was committing the first bold dishonesty in his life. Once, it was on the very tip of his tongue to confess everything, apologize, and take himself off. But his curiosity was of greater weight than his desire. He remained silent and waited for her to speak.

"Celeste, you may leave us," said Miss Annesley.

Celeste courtesied, shot a killing glance at the tentative groom, and departed the scene.

"You have driven horses for some length of time?" the girl began.

If only he might look as calmly and fearlessly at her! What a voice, now that he heard it in its normal tone! "Yes, Madam; I have ridden and driven something like ten years."

"Where?"

"In the West, mostly."

"You are English?"

"No, Madam." He wondered how much she had heard at the police-court that morning. "I am American born."

"Are you addicted to the use of intoxicants?"
—mentally noting the clearness of the whites of
his eyes.

The barest flicker of a smile stirred his lips.
"No, Madam. I had not been drinking last
night—that is, not in the sense the officers declared I had. It is true that I take a drink once
in a while, when I have been riding or driving
all day, or when I am cold. I have absolutely no
appetite."

She brushed her cheeks with the poppies, and
for a brief second the flowers threw a most beautiful color over her face and neck.

"What was your object in climbing on the
box of my carriage and running away with it?"

Quick as a flash of light he conceived his answer. "Madam, it was a jest between me and
some maids." He had almost said serving-
maids, but the thought of Nancy checked this
libel.

"Between you and some maids?"—faintly contemptuous. "Explain, for I believe an explanation is due me."

His gaze was forced to rove again. "Well,
Madam, it is truly embarrassing. Two maids
were to enter a carriage and I was to drive them

away from the embassy, and once I had them in
the carriage I thought it would be an admirable
chance to play them a trick."

"Pray, since when have serving-maids been
allowed exit from the main hall of the British
embassy?"

Mr. Robert was positive that the shadow of a
sarcastic smile rested for a moment on her lips.
But it was instantly hidden under the poppies.

"That is something of which I have no intimate knowledge. A groom is not supposed to
turn his head when on the box unless spoken to.
You will readily understand that, Madam. I
made a mistake in the number. Mine was seventy-one, and I answered number seventeen. I
was confused."

"I dare say. Seventy-one," she mused. "It
will be easy to verify this, to find out whose carriage that was."

Mr. Robert recognized his mistake, but he saw
no way to rectify it. She stood silently gazing
over his shoulder, into the fields beyond.

"Perhaps you can explain to me that remarkable episode at the carriage door? I should be
pleased to hear your explanation."

It had come,—the very thing he had dreaded

had come. He had hoped that she would ignore it. "Madam, I can see that you have sent for me out of curiosity only. If I offered any disrespect to you last night, I pray you to forgive me. For, on my word of honor, it was innocently done." He bowed, and even placed his hand on the knob of the door.

"Have a little patience. I prefer myself to forget that disagreeable incident." The truth is, "on my word of honor," coming from a groom, sounded strange in her ears; and she wanted to learn more about this fellow. "Mr. Osborne, what were you before you became a groom?"

"I have not always been a groom, it is true, Madam. My past I prefer to leave in obscurity. There is nothing in that past, however, of which I need be ashamed;"—and unconsciously his figure became more erect.

"Is your name Osborne?"

"No, Madam, it is not. For my family's sake, I have tried to forget my own name." (I'll wager the rascal never felt a qualm in the region of his conscience.)

It was this truth which was not truth that won his battle.

"You were doubtless discharged last night?"

"I did not return to ascertain, Madam. I merely sent for my belongings."

"You have recommendations?"—presently.

"I have no recommendations whatever, Madam. If you employ me, it must be done on your own responsibility and trust in human nature. I can only say, Madam, that I am honest, that I am willing, that I possess a thorough knowledge of horse-flesh."

"It is very unusual," she said, searching him to the very heart with her deep blue eyes. "For all I know you may be the greatest rascal, or you may be the honestest man, in the world." His smile was so frank and engaging that she was forced to smile herself. But she thought of something, and frowned. "If you have told me the truth, so much the better; for I can easily verify all you have told me. I will give you a week's trial. After all,"—indifferently—"what I desire is a capable servant. You will have to put up with a good deal. There are days when I am not at all amiable, and on those days I do not like to find a speck of rust on the metals or a blanket that has not been thoroughly brushed. As for the animals, they must always shine like satin. This last is unconditional. Besides all this, our

force of servants is small. Do you know anything about serving?"

"Very little." What was coming now?

"The chef will coach you. I entertain some,
and there will be times when you will be called
upon to wait on the table. Come with me and I
will show you the horses. We have only five,
but my father takes great pride in them. They
are all thoroughbreds."

"Like their mistress," was Warburton's mental
supplementary.

"Father hasn't ridden for years, however.
The groom I discharged this morning was capable enough on the box, but he was worse than
useless to me in my morning rides. I ride from
nine till eleven, even Sundays sometimes. Remain here till I return."

As she disappeared Warburton drew in an exceedingly long breath and released it slowly.
Heavens, what an ordeal! He drew the back of
his hand across his forehead and found it moist.
Not a word about the fine: he must broach it and
thank her. Ah, to ride with her every morning,
to adjust her stirrup, to obey every command to
which she might give voice, to feel her small
boot repulse his palm as she mounted! Heaven

could hold nothing greater than this. And how easily a woman may be imposed upon! Decidedly, Mr. Robert was violently in love.

When she returned there was a sunbonnet on her head, and she had pinned the poppies on her breast. (Why? I couldn't tell you, unless when all is said and done, be he king or valet, a man is always a man; and if perchance he is blessed with good looks, a little more than a man. You will understand that in this instance I am trying to view things through a woman's eyes.) With a nod she bade him precede her, and they went out toward the stables. She noted the flat back, the square shoulders, the easy, graceful swing of the legs.

"Have you been a soldier?" she asked suddenly.

He wheeled. His astonishment could not be disguised quickly enough to escape her vigilant eyes. Once more he had recourse to the truth.

"Yes, Madam. It was as a trooper that I learned horsemanship."

"What regiment?"

"I prefer not to say,"—quietly.

"I do not like mysteries,"—briefly.

"Madam, you have only to dismiss me, to permit me to thank you for paying my fine and to reimburse you at the earliest opportunity."

She closed her lips tightly. No one but herself knew what had been on the verge of passing across them.

"Let us proceed to the stables," was all she said. "If you prove yourself a capable horseman, that is all I desire."

The stable-boy slid back the door, and the two entered. Warburton glanced quickly about; all was neatness. There was light and ventilation, too, and the box-stalls were roomy. The girl stopped before a handsome bay mare, which whinnied when it saw her. She laid her cheek against the animal's nose and talked that soft jargon so embarrassing to man and so intelligible to babies and pet animals. Lucky horse! he thought; but his face expressed nothing.

"This is Jane, my own horse, and there are few living things I love so well. Remember this. She is a thoroughbred, a first-class hunter; and I have done more than five feet on her at home."

She moved on, Warburton following soberly and thoughtfully. There was a good deal to think of just now. The more he saw of this girl, the less he understood her purpose in hiring him.

She couldn't possibly know anything about him, who or what he was. With his beard gone he defied her to recognize in him the man who had traveled across the Atlantic with her. A high-bred woman, such as she was, would scarcely harbor any kind feelings toward a man who had acted as he was acting. If any man had kissed Nancy the way he had kissed her, he would have broken every bone in his body or hired some one to do it. And she had paid his fine at the police-station and had hired him on probation! Truly he was in the woods, and there wasn't a sign of a blazed trail. (It will be seen that my hero hadn't had much experience with women. She knew nothing of him whatever. She was simply curious, and brave enough to attempt to have this curiosity gratified. Of course, I do not venture to say that, had he been coarse in appearance, she would have had anything to do with him.)

"This is Dick, my father's horse,"—nodding toward a sorrel, large and well set-up. "He will be your mount. The animal in the next stall is Pirate."

Pirate was the handsomest black gelding Warburton had ever laid eyes on.

"What a beauty!" he exclaimed enthusiastic-

ally, forgetting that grooms should be utterly
without enthusiasm. He reached out his hand
to pat the black nose, when a warning cry re-
strained him. Pirate's ears lay flat.

"Take care! He is a bad-tempered animal.
No one rides him, and we keep him only to ex-
hibit at the shows. Only half a dozen men have
ridden him with any success. He won't take a
curb in his mouth, and he always runs away. It
takes a very strong man to hold him in. I really
don't believe that he's vicious, only terribly mischievous, like a bullying boy."

"I should like to ride him."

The girl looked at her new groom in a manner
which expressed frank astonishment. Was he in
earnest, or was it mere bravado? An idea came
to her, a mischievous idea.

"If you can sit on Pirate's back for ten minutes, there will not be any question of probation.
I promise to engage you on the spot, recommendation or no recommendation." Would he
back down?

"Where are the saddles, Madam?" he asked
calmly, though his blood moved faster.

"On the pegs behind you,"—becoming interested. "Do you really intend to ride him?"

"With your permission."

"I warn you that the risk you are running is great."

"I am not afraid of Pirate, Madam," in a tone which implied that he was not afraid of any horse living. The spirit of antagonism rose up in him, that spirit of antagonism of the human against the animal, that eternal ambition of the one to master the other. And besides, I'm not sure that James didn't want to show. off before the girl—another very human trait in mankind. For my part, I wouldn't give yesterday's rose for a man who wouldn't show off once in a while, when his best girl is around and looking on.

"On your head be it, then,"—a sudden nervousness seizing her. Yet she was as eager to witness the encounter as he was to court it. "William!" she called. The stable-boy entered, setting aside his broom. "This is James, the new groom. Help him to saddle Pirate."

"Saddle Pirate, Miss Annesley!" cried the boy, his mouth open and his eyes wide.

"You see?" said the girl to Warburton.

"Take down that saddle with the hooded stirrups," said Warburton, briefly. He would ride Pirate now, even if Pirate had been sired in Beelzebub's stables. He carefully inspected the saddle, the stirrup-straps and the girth. "Very good, indeed. Buckles on saddles are always a hidden menace and a constant danger. Now, bring out Pirate, William."

William brought out the horse, who snorted when he saw the saddle on the floor and the curb on Warburton's arm.

"There hasn't been anybody on his back for a year, sir; not since last winter. He's likely to give you trouble," said the boy. "You can't put that curb on him, sir; he won't stand for it a moment. Miss Annesley, hadn't you better step outside? He may start to kicking. That heavy English snaffle is the best thing I know of. Try that, sir. And don't let him get his head down, or he'll do you. Whoa!" as Pirate suddenly took it into his head to leave the barn without any one's permission.

The girl sprang lightly into one of the empty stalls and waited. She was greatly excited, and the color in her cheeks was not borrowed from the poppies. She saw the new groom take Pirate by the forelock, and, quicker than words can tell, Mr. Pirate was angrily champing the cold bit. He reared. Warburton caught him by the nose and the neck. Pirate came down, trembling with rage.

"Here, boy; catch him here," cried Warburton. William knew his business, and he grasped the bridle close under Pirate's jaws. "That's it. Now hold him."

Warburton picked up the saddle and threw it over Pirate's glossy back. Pirate waltzed from side to side, and shook his head wickedly. But the man that was to mount him knew all these signs. Swiftly he gathered up the end of the belly-band strap and ran it through the iron ring. In and out he threaded it, drawing it tighter and tighter. He leaped into the saddle and adjusted the stirrups, then dismounted.

"I'll take him now, William," said James, smiling.

"All right, sir," said William, glad enough to be relieved of all further responsibility.

James led Pirate into the small court and waited for Miss Annesley, who appeared in the doorway presently.

"James, I regret that I urged you to ride him. You will be hurt," she said. Her worry was plainly visible on her face.

James smiled his pleasantest and touched his hat.

"Very well, then; I have warned you. If he bolts, head him for a tree. That's the only way to stop him."

James shortened the bridle-rein to the required length, took a firm grip on Pirate's mane, and vaulted into the saddle. Pirate stood perfectly still. He shook his head. James talked to him and patted his sleek neck, and touched him gently with his heel. Then things livened up a bit. Pirate waltzed, reared, plunged, and started to do the *pas seul* on the flower-beds. Then he immediately changed his mind. He decided to re-enter the stables.

"Don't let him get his head down!" yelled William, nimbly jumping over a bed of poppies and taking his position beside his mistress.

"The gates, William! The gates!" cried the girl, excitedly. "Only one is open. He will not be able to get through."

William scampered down the driveway and swung back the iron barrier. None too soon! Like a black shadow, Pirate flashed by, his rider's new derby rolling in the dust.

The girl stood in the doorway, her hands pressed against her heart. She was as white as the clouds that sailed overhead.

X

On the opposite side of the road there was a stone wall about five feet in height; beyond this was a broad, rolling field, and farther on, a barbwire fence and a boggy stream which oozed its way down toward the Potomac. Far away across the valley the wooded hills were drying and withering and thinning, with splashes of yellow and red. A flock of birds speckled the fleecy October clouds, and a mild breeze sent the grasses shivering.

Toward the wall Pirate directed his course. Warburton threw back his full weight. The effort had little or no effect on Pirate's mouth. His rider remembered about the tree, but the nearest was many yards away. Over the wall they went, and down the field. Pirate tried to get his head down, but he received a check. Score one for the man. Warburton, his legs stiffened in the stirrups, his hands well down, his breath coming in gasps, wondered where they would finally land. He began to use his knees, and Pirate felt the pressure. He didn't like it at all. Oddly enough, Warburton's leg did not bother him as he expected it would, and this gave him confidence. On, on; the dull pounding of Pirate's feet, the flying sod, the wind in his face: and when he saw the barb-wire fence, fear entered into him. An inch too low, a stumble, and serious injuries might result. He must break Pirate's gait.

He began to saw cow-boy fashion. Pirate grew very indignant: he was being hurt. His speed slackened none, however; he was determined to make that fence if it was the last thing he ever did. He'd like to see any man stop him. He took the deadly fence as with the wings of a bird. But he found that the man was still on his back. He couldn't understand it. He grew worried. And then he struck the red-brown muck bordering the stream. The muck flew, but at every bound Pirate sank deeper, and the knees of his rider were beginning to tell. Warburton, full of rage, yet not unreasonable rage, quickly saw his chance. Once more he threw back his weight; this time to the left. Pirate's head came stub-

"He's a newspaper man and makes his living by telling lies."—Act II.

bornly around; his gait was broken, he was floun-
dering in the stream. Now Warburton used his
heels savagely. He shortened the reins and
whacked Mr. Pirate soundly across the ears. Pirate plunged and reared and, after devious evo-
lutions, reached solid ground. This time his
head was high in the air, and, try as he would,
he could not lower his neck a solitary inch.

Warburton knew that the animal could not
make the barb-wire fence again, so he waltzed
him along till he found a break in the wire. Over
this Pirate bounded, snorting. But he had met
a master. Whether he reared or plunged, waltzed
or ran, he could not make those ruthless knees
relent in their pressure. He began to understand
what all beasts understand, sooner or later—the
inevitable mastery of man. There was blood in
his nostrils. A hand touched his neck caressing-
ly. He shook his head; he refused to conciliate.
A voice, kindly but rather breathless, addressed
him. Again Pirate shook his head; but he did
not run, he cantered. Warburton gave a sigh of
relief. Over the field they went. A pull to the
left, and Pirate wheeled; a pull to the right, and
again Pirate answered, and cantered in a circle.
But he still shook his head discontentedly, and

the froth that spattered Warburton's legs was flecked with blood. The stirrup-strap began to press sharply and hurtfully against Warburton's injured leg. He tugged, and Pirate fell into a trot. He was mastered.

After this Warburton did as he pleased; Pirate had learned his lesson. His master put him through a dozen manœuvers, and he was vastly satisfied with the victory. In the heat of the battle Warburton had forgotten all about where and what he was; and it was only when he discerned far away a sunbonnet with fluttering strings peering over the stone wall, and a boy in leggings standing on top of the wall, that he recollected. A wave of exhilaration swept through his veins. He had conquered the horse before the eyes of the one woman.

He guided Pirate close to the wall, and stopped him, looked down into the girl's wonder-lit eyes and smiled cheerfully. And what is more, she smiled faintly in acknowledgment. He had gained, in the guise of a groom, what he might never have gained in any other condition of life, the girl's respect and admiration. Though a thorough woman of the world, high-bred, well-born, she forgot for the moment to control her features; and as I have remarked elsewhere, Warburton was a shrewd observer.

"Bully, Mr. Osborne!" shouted William, leaping down. "It was simply great!"

"There are some bars farther down," said the girl, quietly. "William, run and open them."

Warburton flushed slightly. He could not tell how she had accomplished it, whether it was the tone or the gesture, but she had calmly reëstablished the barrier between mistress and servant.

"I think I'll put him to the wall again," said the hero, seized by a rebel spirit.

He wheeled Pirate about and sent him back at a run. Pirate balked. Round he went again, down the field and back. This time he cleared the wall with a good foot to spare. The victory was complete.

When it was all over, and Pirate was impatiently munching an extra supply of oats, the girl bade Mr. James to report early the following morning.

"I hope I shall please you, Madam."

"Address me as Miss Annesley from now on," she said; and nodding shortly, she entered the house.

To Warburton, half the pleasure of the victory

was gone; for not a word of praise had she given him. Yet, she had answered his smile. Well, he had made a lackey out of himself; he had no right to expect anything but forty dollars a month and orders.

He broke his word with me. He did not return to the house that night for dinner. In fact, he deliberately sent for his things, explaining that he was called North and wouldn't have time to see them before he left. It took all my persuasive oratory to smooth the troubled waters, and then there were areas upon which my oil had no effect whatever.

"He is perfectly heartless!" cried Nancy. "He couldn't go to the embassy, but he could steal away and play poker all night with a lot of idling Army officers. And now he is going off to Canada without even seeing us to say good-by. Charlie, there is something back of all this."

"I'll bet it's a woman," said Jack, throwing a scrutinizing glance at me. But I was something of a diplomat myself, and he didn't catch me napping. "Here's a telegram for him, too."

"I think I'll take the liberty of opening it," said I. I knew its contents. It was the reply Warburton had depended on. I read it aloud.

It is good to have friends of this sort. No question was asked. It was a bald order: "Come up at once and shoot caribou. Take first train."

"Bob's a jackass," was Jack's commentary. I had heard something like it before, that day. "He'll turn up all right;"—and Jack lit a cigar and picked up his paper.

"And Betty Annesley is going to call to-morrow night," said Nancy, her voice overflowing with reproach. Her eyes even sparkled with tears. "I did so want them to meet."

I called myself a villain. But I had given my promise; and I was in love myself.

"I don't see what we can do. When Bob makes up his mind to do anything, he generally does it." Jack, believing he had demolished the subject, opened his *Morning Post* and fell to studying the latest phases of the Venezuelan muddle.

Nancy began to cry softly; she loved the scalawag as only sisters know how to love. And I became possessed with two desires; to console her and to punch Mr. Robert's head.

"It has always been this way with him," Nancy went on, dabbing her eyes with her two-by-four handkerchief. "We never dreamed that he was going into the Army till he came home one night and announced that he had successfully passed his examinations for West Point. He goes and gets shot, and we never know anything about it till we read the papers. Next, he resigns and goes abroad without a word or coming to see us. I don't know what to make of Bobby; I really don't."

I took her hand in mine and kissed it, and told her the rascal would turn up in due time, that they hadn't heard the last of him for that winter.

"He's only thoughtless and single-purposed," interposed Jack.

"Single-purposed!" I echoed.

"Why, yes. He gets one thing at a time in his brain, and thinks of nothing else till that idea is worn out. I know him."

I recalled my useless persuasion of the morning. "I believe you are right."

"Of course I'm right," replied Jack, turning a page of his paper. "Do *you* know where he has gone?"

"I think the telegram explains everything,"— evasively.

"Humph! Don't you worry about him, Nan.

I'll wager he's up to some of his old-time devil-
try."

These and other little observations Jack let fall
made it plain to me that he was a natural student
of men and their impulses, and that his insight
and judgment, unerring and anticipatory, had
put him where he is to-day, at the head of a department.

I left the house about ten o'clock, went down-
town and found the prodigal at a cheap hotel on
Pennsylvania. He was looking over some boots
and leggings and ready-made riding breeches.

"Aha, Chuck, so here you are!"

"Look here, Bob, this will never do at all," I
began.

"I thought we had threshed all that out thoroughly this morning."

"I left Nancy crying over your blamed callous-
ness."

"Nancy? Hang it, I don't want Nancy to
waste any tears over me; I'm not worth it."

"Precious little you care! If it wasn't for the
fact that you have told me the true state of
things, I should have exposed you to-night. Why
didn't you turn up to dinner as you promised?

You might at least have gone through the pre-
tense of saying good-by to them."

"My dear boy, I'll admit that my conduct is
nefarious. But look; Nancy knows Miss Annesley, and they will be calling on each other. The
truth is, I dare not let the girls see me without
a beard. And I'm too far gone into the thing to
back out now."

"I honestly hope that some one recognizes you
and gives you away," I declared indignantly.

"Thanks. You're in love with Nancy, aren't
you? To be sure. Well, wouldn't you do anything to keep around where she is, to serve her,
to hear her voice, to touch her hand occasionally,
to ride with her; in fact, always to be within the
magic circle of her presence? Well, I love this
girl; I know it now, it is positive, doubtless. Her
presence is as necessary to me as the air I breathe.
Had I met her in the conventional way, she
would have looked upon me as one of the pillars
of convention, and mildly ignored me. As I am,
she does not know what I am, or who I am; I
am a mystery, I represent a secret, and she desires to find out what this secret is. Besides all
this, something impels me to act this part, something aside from love. It is inexplicable; fate,

maybe." He paused, went to the window, and looked down into the street. It was after-theater time and carriages were rolling to and fro.

"Bob, I apologize. You know a great deal more about feminine nature than I had given you credit for. But how can you win her this way?"

He raised his shoulders. "Time and chance."

"Well, whate'er betide, I can't help wishing you luck."

We shook hands silently, and then I left him.

"Father," said Betty Annesley at the dinner-table that same night, "I have engaged a new groom. He rode Pirate to-day and thoroughly mastered him."

"Pirate? You don't say! Well, I'm glad of that. Pirate will make a capital saddle-horse if he is ridden often enough. The groom will be a safe companion for you on your rides. Are you too tired to do some drawing for me to-night?"

"The fortification plans?"

"Yes." His eyes wandered from her face to the night outside. How gray and sad the world was! "You will always love your father, dearie?"

"Love him? Always!"

"Whatever betide, for weal or woe?"

"Whatever betide."

How easy it was for her to say these words!

"And yet, some day, you must leave me, to take up your abode in some other man's heart. My only wish is that it may beat for you as truly as mine does."

She did not reply, but stepped to the window and pressed her brow to the chilled pane. A yellow and purple line marked the path of the vanished sun; the million stars sparkled above; far away she could see the lights of the city. Of what was she thinking, dreaming? Was she dreaming of heroes such as we poets and novelists invent and hang upon the puppet-beam? Ah, the pity of these dreams the young girl has! She dreams of heroes and of god-like men, and of the one that is to come. But, ah! he never comes, he never comes; and the dream fades and dies, and the world becomes real. A man may find his ideal, but a woman, never. To youth, the fields of love; to man, the battle-ground; to old age, a chair in the sunshine and the wreck of dreams!

"The government ought to pay you well if

those plans are successful." She moved away
from the window.

"Yes, the government ought to pay me well.
I should like to make you rich, dearie, and
happy."

"Why, daddy, am I not both? I have more
money than I know what to do with, and I am
happy in having the kindest father." She came
around the table and caressed him, cheek to
cheek. "Money isn't everything. It just makes
me happy to do anything for you."

His arm grew tense around her waist.

"Do you know what was running through my
mind at the embassy last night? I was thinking
how deeply I love this great wide country of
mine. As I looked at the ambassador and his
aides, I was saying to myself, 'You dare not!'
It may have been silly, but I couldn't help it.
We are the greatest people in the world. When
I compared foreign soldiers with our own, how
my heart and pride swelled! No formalities, no
race prejudice, no false pride. I was never introduced to a foreign officer that I did not fear
him, with his weak eyes, his affected manner-
isms, his studied rudeness, not to me, but to the

country I represented. How I made some of them dance! Not for vanity's sake; rather the inborn patriotism of my race. I had only to think of my father, his honorable scars, his contempt for little things, his courage, his steadfastness, his love for his country, which has so honored him with its trust. Oh! I am a patriot; and I shall never, never marry a man whose love for his country does not equal my own." She caught up her father's mutilated hand and kissed it. "And even now this father of mine is planning and planning to safeguard his country."

"But you must not say anything to a soul, my child; it must be a secret till all is ready. I met Karloff to-day at the club. He has promised to dine with us to-morrow night."

"Make him postpone it. I have promised to dine with Nancy Warburton."

"You had better dine with us and spend the evening with your friend. Do you not think him a handsome fellow?"

"He is charming." She touched the bowl of poppies with her fingers and smiled.

"He is very wealthy, too."

Betty offered no comment.

"What did they do to that infernal rascal who

attempted to run away with you and Mrs. Chadwick?"

"They arrested him and locked him up."

"I hope they will keep him there. And what reason did he give the police for attempting to run away with you?"

"He said that he had made a wager with some serving-maids to drive them from the embassy. He claims to have got the wrong number and the wrong carriage."

"A very likely story!"

"Yes, a very likely story!"—and Betty, still smiling, passed on into the music-room, where she took her violin from its case and played some rollicking measures from Offenbach.

. At the same time her father rose and went out on the lawn, where he walked up and down, with a long, quick, nervous stride. From time to time a wailing note from the violin floated out to him, and he would stop and raise his haggard face toward heaven. His face was no longer masked in smiles; it was grief-stricken, self-abhorring. At length he softly crossed the lawn and stood before the music-room window. Ah, no fretting care sat on yonder exquisite face, nor pain, nor trouble; youth, only youth and some pleasant thought which the music had aroused. How like her mother! How like her mother!

Suddenly he smote himself on the brow with a clenched hand. "Wretch! God-forsaken wretch, how have you kept your trust? And how yonder child has stabbed you! How innocently she has stabbed you! My country! . . . My honor! . . . My courage and steadfastness! Mockery!"

XI

THE FIRST RIDE

The next morning Warburton was shown into a neat six-by-eight, just off the carriage-room. There was a cot, running water and a wash-stand, and a boot-blacking apparatus. For the rest, there were a few portraits of fast horses, fighters, and toe-dancers (the adjective qualifying all three!) which the senator's sporting groom had collected and tacked to the walls. For appearance's sake, Mr. James had purchased a cheap trunk. Everything inside was new, too. His silver military brushes, his silver shaving set, and so forth and so forth, were in charge of a safe-deposit storage company, alongside some one's family jewels. The only incriminating things he retained were his signet-ring and his Swiss timepiece.

"Have you had your breakfast, sir?" asked William, the stable-boy.

"Yes, my lad. Now, as Miss Annesley has

153

forgotten it, perhaps you will tell me of just what my duties here will consist."

"You harness, ride and drive, sir, and take care of the metals. I clean the leathers and carriages, exercise the horses and keep their hides shiny. If anything is purchased, sir, we shall have to depend upon your judgment. Are you given to cussing, sir?"

"Cussing?" repeated Warburton.

"Yes, sir. Miss Annesley won't stand for it around the stables. The man before you, sir, could cuss most beautifully; and I think that's why he was fired. At least, it was one reason."

Warburton smoothed his twitching mouth. "Don't you worry, William; it's against my religion to use profane language."

William winked, there was an answering wink, and the two became friends from that moment on.

"I'll bet you didn't say a thing to Pirate yesterday, when he bolted over the wall with you."

"Well, I believe I *did* address a few remarks to Pirate which would not sound well on dress-parade; but so long as it wasn't within hearing distance, William, I suppose it doesn't matter."

"No, sir; I suppose not."

"Now, what kind of a master is the colonel?" asked Warburton, strapping on his English leggings.

"Well, it's hard to say just now. You see, I've been with the family ever since I was six. The colonel used to be the best fellow *I* ever knew. Always looking out for your comfort, never an undeserved harsh word, and always a smile when you pleased him. But he's changed in the last two years."

"How?"

"He doesn't take any interest in the things he used to. He goes about as if he had something on his mind; kind of absent-minded, you know; and forgets to-morrow what he says to-day. He always puts on a good face, though, when Miss Betty is around."

"Ah. What night do I have off?"—of a mind that a question like this would sound eminently professional in William's ears.

"Sunday, possibly; it all depends on Miss Annesley, sir. In Virginia nearly every night was ours. Here it's different." William hurriedly pulled on his rubber boots and gloves, grabbed up the carriage sponges, and vanished.

Warburton sat on the edge of his cot and

laughed silently. All this was very amusing. Had any man, since the beginning of time, found himself in a like position? He doubted it. And he was to be butler besides! It would be something to remember in his old age. Yet, once or twice the pins of his conscience pricked him. He *wasn't* treating Nancy just right. He didn't want her to cry over his gracelessness; he didn't want her to think that he was heartless. But what could he do? He stood too deeply committed.

He was puzzled about one thing, however, and, twist it as he would, he could not solve it with any degree of satisfaction. Why, after what had happened, had she hired him? If she could pass over that episode at the carriage-door and forget it, *he* couldn't. He knew that each time he saw her the memory of that embrace and brotherly salute would rise before his eyes and rob him of some of his assurance—an attribute which was rather well developed in Mr. Robert, though he was loath to admit it. If his actions were a mystery to her, hers were none the less so to him. He made up his mind to move guardedly in whatever he did, to practise control over his mobile features so as to avert any shock or thoughtless sign of interest. He knew that sooner or later the day would come when he would be found out; but this made him not the less eager to court that day.

He shaved himself, and was wiping his face on the towel when Celeste appeared in the doorway. She eyed him, her head inclined roguishly to one side, the exact attitude of a bird that has suddenly met a curious and disturbing specimen of insect life.

"M'sieu Zhames, Mees Annesley rides thees morning. You will pre*pairre* yourself according,"—and she rattled on in her absurd native tongue (every other native tongue *is* absurd to us, you know!)—

> "He is charming and handsome,
> With his uniform and saber;
> And his fine black eyes
> Look love as he rides by! "

while the chef in the kitchen glared furiously at his omelette soufflé, and vowed terrible things to M'sieu Zhames if he looked at Celeste more than twice a day.

"Good morning," said M'sieu Zhames, hanging up his towel. His face glowed as the result of the vigorous rubbing it had received.

"*Bon jour!*"—admiringly.

"Don't give me any of your *bong joors*, Miss,"
—stolidly. "There's only one language for me,
and that's English."

"*Merci!* You Anglaises are *so* conceit'! How
you like *me* to teach you French, eh, M'sieu
Zhames?"

"Not for me,"—shaking his head. She was
very pretty, and under ordinary circumstances
. . . He did not finish the thought, but I will
for him. Under ordinary circumstances, M'sieu
Zhames would have kissed her.

"No teach you French? *Non?* Extraorrdi-
naire!" She tripped away, laughing, while the
chef tugged at his royal and M'sieu Zhames
whistled.

"Hang the witch!" the new groom murmured.
"Her mistress must be very generous, or very
positive of her own charms, to keep a sprite like
this maid about her. I wonder if I'll run into
Karloff?" Karloff! The name chilled him,
somehow. What was Karloff to her? Had he
known that she was to be in Washington for the
winter? What irony, if fate should make him
the groom and Karloff the bridegroom! If Kar-

loff loved her, he could press his suit frankly and openly. And, as matters stood, what chance on earth had he, Warburton? "Chuck was right; I've made a mistake, and I am beginning to regret it the very first morning." He snapped his fingers and proceeded to the right wing, where the horses were.

At nine o'clock he led Jane and Dick out to the porte-cochère and waited. He had not long to loiter, for she came out at once, drawing on her gauntlets and taking in long breaths of the morning air. She nodded briefly, but pleasantly, and came down the steps. Her riding-habit was of the conventional black, and her small, shapely boots were of patent-leather. She wore no hat on her glorious head, which showed her good sense and her scorn for freckles and sunburn. But nature had given her one of those rare complexions upon which the sun and the wind have but trifling effect.

"We shall ride north, James; the roads are better and freer. Jane has a horror of cars."

"Yes, Miss Annesley,"—deferentially. "You will have to teach me the lay of the land hereabouts, as I am rather green."

"I'll see to it that you are made perfectly familiar with the roads. You do not know Washington very well, then?"

"No, Miss. Shall I give you a—er—boot up?" He blushed. He had almost said "leg up".

She assented, and raised her boot, under which he placed his palm, and sprang into the saddle. He mounted in his turn and waited.

"When we ride alone, James, I shall not object to your riding at my side; but when I have guests, always remember to keep five yards to the rear."

"Yes, Miss." If he could have got rid of the idea of Karloff and the possibilities which his name suggested, all this would have appealed to him as exceedingly funny.

"Forward, then!"—and she touched Jane's flank with her crop.

The weather was perfect for riding: no sun, a keen breeze from the northwest, and a dust-settled road. Warburton confessed to me afterward that this first ride with her was one of the most splendid he had ever ridden. Both animals were perfect saddle-horses, such as are to be found only in the South. They started up the

road at a brisk trot, and later broke into a canter
which lasted fully a mile. How beautiful she
was, when at length they slowed down into a
walk! Her cheeks were flaming, her eyes dancing and full of luster, her hair was tumbled
about and tendrils fluttered down her cheeks.
She was Diana: only he hoped that she was not
inclined to celibacy.

What a mistake he had made! He could never
get over this gulf which he himself had thrust
between them. This was no guise in which to
meet a woman of her high breeding. Under his
breath he cursed the impulse that had urged him
to decline to attend the ball at the British embassy. There he would have met her as his own
true self, a soldier, a polished gentleman of the
world, of learning and breeding. Nancy would
have brought them together, calls would have
been exchanged, and he would have defied Karloff. Then he chid himself for the feeling he
had against the Russian. Karloff had a right to
love this girl, a right which far eclipsed his
own. Karloff was Karloff; a handsome fellow,
wealthy, agreeable; while James was not James,
neither was he wealthy nor at present agreeable.
A man can not sigh very well on horseback, and

the long breath which left Warburton's lips made a jerking, hissing sound.

"Have you ever ridden with women before, James?"

"Several times with my major's daughter,"—thoughtlessly.

"Your major's daughter?   Who was your regimental colonel?"

James bit his lips, and under his breath disregarded William's warning about "cussing." "Permit me, Miss Annesley, to decline to answer."

"Did you ride as an attendant?"

"Yes; I was a trooper."

"You speak very good English for a stable-man."

"I have not always been a stable-man."

"I dare say.   I should give a good deal to know what you *have* been.   Come, James, tell me what the trouble was.   I have influence; I might help you."

"I am past help;"—which was true enough, only the real significance of his words passed over her head.   "I thank you for your kindness."

If she was piqued, she made no sign,   "James,

were you once a gentleman, in the sense of being well-born?"

"Miss Annesley, you would not believe me if I told you who I am and what I have been."

"Are you a deserter?"—looking him squarely in the eye. She saw the color as it crept under his tan.

"I have my honorable discharge,"—briefly.

"I shall ask you to let me see it. Have you ever committed a dishonorable act? I have a right to know."

"I have committed one dishonorable act, Miss Annesley. I shall always regret it."

She gave him a penetrating glance. "Very well; keep your secret."

And there was no more questioning on that ride; there was not even casual talk, such as a mistress might make to her servant. There was only the clock-clock of hoofs and the chink of bit metal. Warburton did not know whether he was glad or sorry.

She dismounted without her groom's assistance, which somewhat disappointed that worthy gentleman. If she was angry, to his eye there was no visible evidence of it. As he took the bridles in hand, she addressed him; though in doing so, she did not look at him, but gave her attention to her gauntlets, which she pulled slowly from her aching fingers.

"This afternoon I shall put you in the care of Pierre, the cook. I am giving a small dinner on Monday evening, and I shall have to call on you to serve the courses. Later I shall seek a butler, but for the present you will have to act in that capacity."

He wasn't sure; it might have been a flash of sunlight from behind a cloud. If it *was* a smile, he would have given much to know what had caused it.

He tramped off to the stables. A butler! Well, so be it. He could only reasonably object when she called upon him to act in the capacity of a chambermaid. He wondered why he had no desire to laugh.

XII

Pierre was fierce and fat and forty, but he could cook the most wonderful roasts and ragouts that Warburton ever tasted; and he could take a handful of vegetables and an insignificant bone and make a soup that would have tickled the jaded palate of a Lucullus. Warburton presented himself at the kitchen door.

"Ah!" said Pierre, striking a dramatic pose, a ladle in one hand and a pan in the other. "So you are zee new groom? Good! We make a butler out of you? Bah! Do you know zee difference between a broth and a soup? Eh?"

The new groom gravely admitted that he did.

"Hear to me!"—and Pierre struck his chest with a ladle. "I teach you how to sairve; *I*, Pierre Flageot, will teach a hostler to be a butler! Bah!"

"That is what I am sent here for."

"Hear to me! If zay haf oysters, zay are

placed on zee table before zee guests enter. *V'là?*
Then zee soup. You sairve one deesh at a time.
You do *not* carry all zee deeshes at once. And
you take zee deesh, *so!*"—illustrating. "Then
you wait till zay push aside zee soup deesh. Then
you carry zem away. *V'là?*"

Warburton signified that he understood.

"*I* carve zee meats," went on the amiable
Pierre. "You haf nozzing to do wiz zee meats.
You rest zee deesh on zee flat uf zee hand, *so!*
Always sairve to zee *right* uf zee guest. Vatch
zat zay do not move vhile you sairve. You spill
zee soup, and I keel you! To spill zee soup ees a
crime. Now, take hold uf thees soup deesh."

Warburton took it clumsily by the rim. Pierre
snatched it away with a volley of French oaths.
William said that there was to be no "cussing,"
but Pierre seemed to be an immune and not in-
cluded in this order.

"Idiot! Imbecile! *Non, non! Thees* way.
You would put zee thumb in zee soup. Zare!
You haf catch zat. Come to zee dining-hall. I
show you. I explain."

The new groom was compelled to put forth all
his energies to keep his face straight. If he
laughed, he was lost. If only his old mates could

see him now! The fop of Troop A playing at
butler! Certainly he would have to write Chuck
about it—(which he most certainly never did).
Still, the ordeal in the dining-room was a severe
one. Nothing he attempted was done satisfac-
torily; Pierre, having in mind Celeste's frivolity
and this man's good looks, made the task doubly
hard. He hissed "Idiot!" and "Imbecile!" and
"Jackass!" as many times as there are knives
and forks and spoons at a course dinner. It was
when they came to the wines that Pierre became
mollified. He was forced to acknowledge that
the new groom needed no instructions as to the
varying temperatures of clarets and burgundies.
Warburton longed to get out into the open and
yell. It was very funny. He managed, however,
on third rehearsal, to acquit himself with some
credit. They returned to the kitchen again,
where they found Celeste nibbling crackers and
cheese. She smiled.

"Ha!" The vowel was given a prolonged roll.
"So, Mademoiselle, you haf to come and look on,
eh?"

"Is there any objection, Monsieur?" retorted
Celeste in her native tongue, making handsome
eyes at Warburton, who was greatly amused.

"Ha! if he was hideous, would you be putting on those ribbons I gave you to wear on Sundays?" snarled Pierre.

Warburton followed their French without any difficulty. It was the French of the Parisian, with which he was fairly conversant. But his face remained impassive and his brows only mildly curious.

"I shall throw them away, Monsieur Flageot, if you dare to talk to me like that. He *is* handsome, and you are jealous, and I am glad. You behaved horribly to that coarse Nanon last Sunday. Because she scrubs the steps of the French embassy you consider her above me, *me!*"

"You are crazy!" roared Pierre. "You introduced me to her so that you might make eyes at that abominable valet of the secretary!"

Celeste flounced (whatever means of locomotion that is) abruptly from the kitchen. Pierre turned savagely to his protégé.

"Go! And eef you look at her, idiot, I haf revenge myself. Oh, I am calm! Bah! Go to zee stables, cattle!" And he rattled his pans at a great rate.

Warburton was glad enough to escape.

"I have brought discord into the land, it would seem."

But his trials were not over. The worst ordeal was yet to come. At five, orders were given to harness the coach-horses to the coupé and have them at the steps promptly at eight-thirty. Miss Annesley had signified her intention of making a call in the city. Warburton had not the slightest suspicion of the destination. He didn't care where it was. It would be dark and he would pass unrecognized. He gave the order no more thought. Promptly at eight-thirty he drove up to the steps. A moment later she issued forth, accompanied by a gentleman in evening dress. It was too dark for Warburton to distinguish his features.

"I am very sorry, Count, to leave you; but you understand perfectly. It is an old school friend of mine whom I haven't seen in a long time; one of the best girl friends I have ever known. I promised to dine with her to-night, but I broke that promise and agreed to spend the evening."

"Do not disturb yourself on my account," replied the man in broken English, which was rather pleasant to the ear. "Your excellent father and I can pass the evening very well."

Karloff! Warburton's chin sank into his collar and his hands trembled. This man Karloff had very penetrating eyes, even in the dark.

"But I shall miss the music which I promised myself. Ah, if you only knew how adorable you are when you play the violin! I become lost, I forget the world and its sordidness. I forget everything but that mysterious voice which you alone know how to arouse from that little box of wood. You are a great artist, and if you were before the public, the world would go mad over you—as I have!"

So she played the violin, thought the unhappy man on the box of the coupé.

"Count, you know that is taboo; you must not talk to me like that,"—with a nervous glance at the groom.

"The groom embarrasses you?" The count laughed. "Well, it is only a groom, an animal which does not understand these things."

"Besides, I do not play nearly so well as you would have me believe,"—steering him to safer channels.

"Whatever you undertake, Mademoiselle, becomes at once an art,"—gallantly. "Good night!"—and the count saluted her hand as he helped her into the coupé.

How M'sieu Zhames would have liked to jump down and pommel Monsieur le Comte! Several wicked thoughts surged through our jehu's brain, but to execute any one of them in her presence was impossible.

"Good night, Count. I shall see you at dinner on Monday."

She would, eh? And her new butler would be on duty that same evening? Without a doubt. M'sieu Zhames vowed under his breath that if he got a good chance he would make the count look ridiculous. Not even a king can retain his dignity while a stream of hot soup is trickling down his spinal column. Warburton smiled. He was mentally acting like a school-boy disappointed in love. His own keen sense of the humorous came to his rescue.

"James, to the city, No. — Scott Circle, and hurry." The door closed.

Scott Circle? Warburton's spine wrinkled. Heaven help him, he was driving Miss Annesley to his own brother's house! What the devil was getting into fate, anyhow? He swore softly all

the way to the Connecticut Avenue extension.
He made three mistakes before he struck Sixteenth Street. Reaching Scott Circle finally, he
had no difficulty in recognizing the house. He
drew up at the stepping-stone, alighted and
opened the door.

"I shall be gone perhaps an hour and a half,
James. You may drive around, but return
sharply at ten-thirty." Betty ran up the steps
and rang the bell.

Our jehu did *not* wait to see the door open,
but drove away, lickety-clip. I do not know what
a mile lickety-clip is generally made in, but I
am rather certain that the civil law demands
twenty-five dollars for the same. The gods were
with him this time, and no one called him to a
halt. When he had gone as far away from Scott
Circle as he dared go, his eye was attracted by a
genial cigar sign. He hailed a boy to hold the
horses and went inside. He bought a dozen cigars and lit one. He didn't even take the trouble to see if he could get the cigars for nothing,
there being a penny-in-the-slot machine in one
corner of the shop. I am sure that if he had noticed it, it would have enticed him, for the spirit
of chance was well-grounded in him, as it is in

all Army men. But he hurried out, threw the boy a dime, and drove away. For an hour and twenty minutes he drove and smoked and pondered. So she played the violin! played it wonderfully, as the count had declared. He was passionately fond of music. In London, in Paris, in Berlin, in Vienna, he had been an untiring, unfailing patron of the opera. Some night he resolved to listen at the window, providing the window was open. Yes, a hundred times Chuck was right. Any other girl, and this jest might have passed capitally; but he wanted the respect of this particular woman, and he had carelessly closed the doors to her regard. She might tolerate him, that would be all. She would look upon him as a hobbledehoy.

He approached the curb again in front of the house, and gazed wistfully at the lighted windows. Here was another great opportunity gone. How he longed to dash into the house, confess, and have done with it!

"I wish Chuck was in there. I wish he would come out and kick me good and hearty."

(Chuck would have been delighted to perform the trifling service; and he would not have gone about it with any timidity, either.)

"Hang the horses! I'm going to take a peek in at the side window,"—and he slid cautiously from the box. He stole around the side and stopped at one of the windows. The curtain was not wholly lowered, and he could see into the drawing-room. There they were, all of them; and Miss Annesley was holding the baby, which Mrs. Jack had awakened and brought down stairs. He could see by the diffident manner in which Jack was curling the ends of his mustache that they were comparing the baby with him. "The conceited ass!" muttered the self-appointed outcast; "it doesn't look any more like him than it does like me!" Here Miss Annesley kissed the baby, and Warburton hoped that they hadn't washed its face since he performed the same act.

Mrs. Jack disappeared with the hope of the family, and Nancy got out a bundle of photographs. M'sieu Zhames would have given almost anything he possessed to know what these photographs represented. Crane his neck as he would, he could see nothing. All he could do was to watch. Sometimes they laughed, sometimes they became grave; sometimes they explained, and their guest grew very attentive Once she even leaned forward eagerly. It was

about this time that our jehu chanced to look at
the clock on the mantel, and immediately concluded to vacate the premises. It was half after
ten. He returned to his box forthwith. (I was
going to use the word "alacrity," but I find that
it means "cheerful readiness.") After what
seemed to him an interminable wait, the front
door opened and a flood of light blinded him.
He heard Nancy's voice.

"I'm so sorry, Betty, that I can't dine with
you on Monday. We are going to Arlington.
So sorry."

"I'm not!" murmured the wretch on the box.
"I'm devilish glad! Imagine passing soup to
one's sister! By George, it was a narrow one!
It would have been all over then."

"Well, there will be plenty of times this winter," said Betty. "I shall see you all at the Country Club Sunday afternoon. Good night, every
one. No, no; there's no need of any of you coming to the carriage."

But brother Jack *did* walk to the door with
her; however, he gave not the slightest attention
to the groom, for which *he* was grateful.

"You must all come and spend the evening
with me soon," said Betty, entering the carriage.

"That we shall," said brother Jack, closing the door for her. "Good night."

"Home, James," said the voice within the carriage.

I do not know whether or not he slept soundly that night on his stable cot. He never would confess. But it is my private opinion that he didn't sleep at all, but spent a good part of the night out of doors, smoking very black, strong cigars.

Celeste, however, could have told you that her mistress, as she retired, was in a most amiable frame of mind. Once she laughed.

XIII

Four days passed. I might have used the word "sped," only that verb could not be truthfully applied. Never before in the history of time (so our jehu thought) did four days cast their shadows more slowly across the dial of the hours. From noon till night there was a madding nothing to do but polish bits and buckles and stirrups and ornamental silver. He would have been totally miserable but for the morning rides. These were worth while; for he was riding Pirate, and there was always that expectation of the unexpected. But Pirate behaved himself puzzlingly well. Fortunately for the jehu, these rides were always into the north country. He was continually possessed with fear lest she would make him drive through the shopping district. If he met Nancy, it would be, in the parlance of the day, all off. Nancy would have recognized him in a beard like a Cossack's; and here he was with the boy's face—the face she never would forget.

He was desperately in love. I do not know
what desperately in love is, my own love's course
running smoothly enough; but I can testify that
it was making Mr. Robert thin and appetiteless.
Every morning the impulse came to him to tell
her all; but every morning his courage oozed
like Bob Acres', and his lips became dumb. I
dare say that if she had questioned him he would
have told her all; but for some reason she had
ceased to inquire into his past. Possibly her
young mind was occupied with pleasanter things.

He became an accomplished butler, and served
so well in rehearsals that Pierre could only grum-
ble. One afternoon she superintended the comedy. She found a thousand faults with him, so
many, in fact, that Pierre did not understand
what it meant, and became possessed with the
vague idea that she was hitting him over the
groom's shoulder. He did not like it; and later,
when they were alone, Warburton was distinctly
impressed with Pierre's displeasure.

"You can not please *her,* and you can not
please *me.* Bah! Zat ees vat comes uf teaching
a groom table manners instead uf stable manners.
And you vill smell uf horse! I do *not* understand Mees Annesley; no!"

"May I go now, Miss?"—ACT II.

And there were other humiliations, petty ones. She chid him on having the stirrup too long or too short; the curb chain was rusting; this piece of ornamental silver did not shine like that one; Jane's fetlocks were too long; Pirate's hoofs weren't thoroughly oiled. With dogged patience he tried to remedy all these faults. It was only when they had had a romping run down the road that this spirit fell away from her, and she talked pleasantly.

Twice he ran into Karloff; but that shrewd student of human nature did not consider my hero worth studying; a grave mistake on his part, as he was presently to learn. He was a handsome man, and the only thing he noticed about the groom was his handsome face. He considered it a crime for a servant to be endowed with personal attractions. A servant in the eyes of a Russian noble excites less interest than a breedless dog. Mr. Robert made no complaint; he was very well satisfied to have the count ignore him entirely. Once he met the count in the Turkish room, where, in the capacity of butler, he served liqueur and cigars. There was a certain grim humor in lighting his rival's cigar for him. This service was a test of his ability to pass through a

room without knocking over taborets and chairs.
Another time they met, when Betty and the two
of them took a long ride. Karloff *did* notice how
well the groom rode his mettlesome mount, being himself a soldier and a daring horseman.
Warburton had some trouble. Pirate did not
take to the idea of breathing Jane and Dick's
dust; he wanted to lead these second-raters. Mr.
James' arms ached that afternoon from the effort
he had put forth to restrain Pirate and keep him
in his proper place, five yards to the rear.

Nothing happened Sunday; the day went by
uneventfully. He escaped the ordeal of driving
her to the Chevy Chase Club, William being up
that afternoon.

Then Monday came, and with it Betty's curious
determination to ride Pirate.

"You wish to ride Pirate, Miss?" exclaimed
James, his horror of the idea openly manifest.

"Saddle him for me,"—peremptorily. "I desire to ride him. I find Jane isn't exciting
enough."

"Pardon me, Miss Annesley," he said, "but I
had rather you would not make the attempt."

"You had rather I would not make the attempt?"—slowly repeating the words, making a

knife of each one of them, tipped with the poison of her contempt. "I do not believe I quite understand you."

He bravely met the angry flash of her eyes. There were times when the color of these eyes did not resemble sapphires; rather disks of gunmetal, caused by a sudden dilation of the pupils.

"Yes, Miss, I had rather you would not."

"James, you forget yourself. Saddle Pirate, and take Jane back to the stables. Besides, Jane has a bit of a cold." She slapped her boot with her riding-crop and indolently studied the scurrying clouds overhead; for the day was windy.

Soberly Warburton obeyed. He was hurt and angry, and he knew not what besides. Heavens, if anything should happen to her! His hopes rose a bit. Pirate had shown no temper so far that morning. He docilely permitted his master to put on the side-saddle. But as he came out into the air again, he threw forward his ears, stretched out his long black neck, took in a great breath, and whinnied a hoarse challenge to the elements. William had already saddled Dick, who looked askance at his black rival's small compact heels.

"I am afraid of him," said Warburton, as he

returned. "He will run away with you. I did not wholly subjugate him the other day. He pulls till my arms ache."

Miss Annesley shrugged and patted Pirate on the nose and offered him a lump of sugar. The thirst for freedom and a wild run down the wind lurked in Pirate's far-off gazing eyes, and he ignored the sign of conciliation which his mistress made him.

"I am not afraid of him. Besides, Dick can outrun and outjump him."

This did not reassure Warburton, nor did he know what this comparison meant, being an ordinary mortal.

"With all respect to you, Miss Annesley, I am sorry that you are determined to ride him. He is most emphatically not a lady's horse, and you have never ridden him. Your skirts will irritate him, and if he sees your crop, he'll bolt."

She did not reply, but merely signified her desire to mount. No sooner was she up, however, than she secretly regretted her caprice; but not for a hundred worlds would she have permitted this groom to know. But Pirate, with that rare instinct of the horse, knew that his mistress was not sure of him. He showed the whites of

his eyes and began pawing the gravel. The girl
glanced covertly at her groom and found no color
in his cheeks. Two small muscular lumps appeared at the corners of her jaws. She would
ride Pirate, and nothing should stop her; nothing, nothing. Womanlike, knowing herself to
be in the wrong, she was furious.

And Pirate surprised them both. During the
first mile he behaved himself in the most gentlemanly fashion; and if he shied once or twice,
waltzed a little, it was only because he was full
of life and spirit. They trotted, they cantered,
ran and walked. Warburton, hitherto holding
himself in readiness for whatever might happen,
relaxed the tension of his muscles, and his shoulders sank relievedly. Perhaps, after all, his alarm
had been needless. The trouble with Pirate
might be the infrequency with which he had been
saddled and ridden. But he knew that the girl
would not soon forget his interference. There
would be more humiliations, more bitter pills for
him to swallow. It pleased him, however, to note
the ease with which Dick kept pace with Pirate.

As for the most beautiful person in all the
great world, I am afraid that she was beginning
to feel self-important. Now that her confidence

was fully restored, she never once spoke to, or looked at, her groom. Occasionally from the corner of her eye she could see the white patch on Dick's nose.

"James," she said maliciously and suddenly, "go back five yards. I wish to ride alone."

Warburton, his face burning, fell back. And thus she made her first mistake. The second and final mistake came immediately after. She touched Pirate with her heel, and he broke from a trot into a lively gallop. Dick, without a touch of the boot, kept his distance to a foot. Pirate, no longer seeing Dick at his side, concluded that he had left his rival behind; and the suppressed mischief in his black head began to find an outlet. Steadily he arched his neck; steadily but surely he drew down on the reins. The girl felt the effort and tried to frustrate it. In backing her pull with her right hand, the end of her crop flashed down the side of Pirate's head—the finishing touch. There was a wild leap, a blur of dust, and Mr. Pirate, well named after his freebooting sires, his head down where he wanted it, his feet rolling like a snare-drum, Mr. Pirate ran away, headed for heaven only knew where.

For a brief moment Warburton lost his nerve;

he was struck with horror. If she could not hold her seat, she would be killed or dreadfully hurt, and perhaps disfigured. It seemed rather strange, as he recalled it, that Dick, instead of himself, should have taken the initiative. The noble sorrel, formerly a cavalry horse, shot forward magnificently. Doubtless his horse-sense took in the situation, or else he did not like the thought of yonder proud, supercilious show-horse beating him in a running race. So, a very fast mile was put to the rear.

The girl, appreciating her peril, did as all good horsewomen would have done: locked her knee on the horn and held on. The rush of wind tore the pins from her hair which, like a golden plume, stretched out behind her. (Have you ever read anything like this before? I dare say. But to Warburton and the girl, it never occurred that other persons had gone through like episodes. It was real, and actual, and single, and tragic to them.)

The distance between the two horses began slowly to lessen, and Warburton understood, in a nebulous way, what the girl had meant when she said that Dick could outrun Pirate. If Pirate kept to the road, Dick would bring him

down; but if Pirate took it into his head to vault
a fence! Warburton shuddered. Faster, faster,
over this roll of earth, clattering across this
bridge, around this curve and that angle. Once
the sight of a team drawing a huge grain-wagon
sent a shiver to Warburton's heart. But they
thundered past with a foot to spare. The old
negro on the seat stared after them, his ebony
face drawn with wonder and the whites of his
eyes showing.

Foot by foot, yard by yard, the space lessened,
till Dick's nose was within three feet of Pirate's
flowing tail. Warburton fairly lifted Dick along
with his knees. I only wish I could describe the
race as my jehu told it to me. The description
held me by the throat. I could see the flashing
by of trees and houses and fields; the scampering
of piccaninnies across the road; the horses from
the meadows dashing up to the fences and whin-
nying; the fine stone and dust which Pirate's
rattling heels threw into my jehu's face and eyes;
the old pain throbbing anew in his leg. And when
he finally drew alongside the black brute and saw
the white, set face of the girl he loved, I can
imagine no greater moment but one in his life.
There was no fear on her face, but there was ap-

peal in her eyes as she half turned her head. He leaned across the intervening space and slid his arm around her waist. The two horses came together and twisted his leg cruelly. His jaws snapped.

"Let the stirrup go!" he cried. "Let go, quick!" She heard him. "Your knee from the horn! I can't keep them together any longer. Now!"

Brave and plucky and cool she was. She obeyed him instantly. There was a mighty heave, a terrible straining of the back and the knees, and Pirate was freed of his precious burden. The hardest part of it came now. Dick could not be made to slow down abruptly. He wanted to keep right on after his rival. So, between holding the girl with his right arm and pulling the horse with his left, Warburton saw that he could keep up this terrible effort but a very short time. Her arms were convulsively wound around his neck, and this added to the strain. Not a word did she say; her eyes were closed, as if she expected any moment to be dashed to the earth.

But Dick was only a mortal horse. The fierce run and the double burden began to tell, and shortly his head came up. Warburton stopped him. The girl slid to the ground, and in a moment he was at her side. And just in time. The reaction was too much for her. Dazedly she brushed her hair from her eyes, stared wildly at Warburton, and fainted. He did not catch her with that graceful precision which on the stage is so familiar to us. No. He was lucky to snatch one of her arms, thus preventing her head from striking the road. He dragged her to the side of the highway and rested her head on his shaking knees. Things grew dark for a time. To tell the truth, he himself was very close to that feminine weakness which the old fellows, in their rough and ready plays, used to call "vapours". But he forced his heart to steady itself.

And what do you suppose the rascal did—with nobody but Dick to watch him? Why, he did what any healthy young man in love would have done: pressed his lips to the girl's hair, his eyes filling and half a sob in his parched throat. He dolefully pictured himself a modern Antiochus, dying of love and never confessing it. Then he kissed her hair again; only her hair, for somehow he felt that her lips and cheeks were as yet inviolable to his touch. I should have liked to see the picture they made: the panting horse

a dozen rods away, looking at them inquiringly;
the girl in her dust-covered habit, her hair spread-
ing out like seaweed on a wave, her white face,
her figure showing its graceful lines; my jehu,
his hair matted to his brow, the streaks of dust
and perspiration on his face, the fear and love
and longing in his dark eyes. I recollect a picture called *Love and Honor*, or something like
that. It never appealed to me. It lacked action.
It simply represented a fellow urging a girl to
elope with him. Both of them were immaculately
dressed. But here, on this old highway leading
into Maryland, was something real. A battle
had been fought and won.

Fainting is but transitory; by and by she
opened her eyes, and stared vaguely into the face
above her. I do not know what she saw there;
whatever it was it caused her to struggle to her
feet. There was color enough in her cheeks now;
and there was a question, too, in her eyes. Of
Warburton it asked, "What did you do when I
lay there unconscious?" I'm afraid there was
color in his face, too. Her gaze immediately
roved up the road. There was no Pirate, only a
haze of dust. Doubtless he was still going it,
delighted over the trouble he had managed to

bring about. Warburton knelt at the girl's side and brushed the dust from her skirt. She eyed him curiously. I shan't say that she smiled; I don't know, for I wasn't there.

Meanwhile she made several futile attempts to put up her hair, and as a finality she braided it and let it hang down her back. Suddenly and unaccountably she grew angry—angry at herself, at James, at the rascally horse that had brought her to this pass. Warburton saw something of this emotion in her eyes, and to avoid the storm he walked over to Dick, picked up the reins, and led him back.

"If you will mount Dick, Miss," he said, "I will lead him home. It's about five miles, I should say."

The futility and absurdity of her anger aroused her sense of the ridiculous; and a smile, warm and merry, flashed over her stained face. It surprised her groom.

"Thank you, James. You were right. I ought not to have ridden Pirate. I am punished for my conceit. Five miles? It will be a long walk."

"I shan't mind it in the least," replied James,

inordinately happy; and he helped her to the
saddle and adjusted the left stirrup.

So the journey home began. Strangely enough,
neither seemed to care particularly what had or
might become of Pirate. He disappeared, mentally and physically. One thing dampened the
journey for Warburton. His "game leg" ached
cruelly, and after the second mile (which was
traversed without speech from either of them),
he fell into a slight limp. From her seat above
and behind him, she saw this limp.

"You have hurt yourself?" she asked gently.

"Not to-day, Miss,"—briefly.

"When he ran away with you?"

"No. It's an old trouble."

"While you were a soldier?"

"Yes."

"How?"

He turned in surprise. All these questions
were rather unusual. Nevertheless he answered
her, and truthfully.

"I was shot in the leg by a drunken Indian."

"While on duty?"

"Yes." Unconsciously he was forgetting to
add "Miss", which was the patent of his servility.

'And I do not think that just then she noticed this subtraction from the respect due her.

It was eleven o'clock when they arrived at the gates. She dismounted alone. Warburton was visibly done up.

"Any orders for this afternoon, Miss?"

"I shall want the victoria at three. I have some shopping to do and a call to make. Send William after Pirate. I am very grateful for what you have done."

He made no reply, for he saw her father coming down the steps.

"Betty," said the colonel, pale and worried, "have you been riding Pirate? Where is he, and what in the world has happened?"—noting the dust on her habit and her tangled hair.

She explained: she told the story rather coolly, Warburton thought, but she left out no detail.

"You have James to thank for my safety, father. He was very calm and clear-headed."

Calm and clear-headed! thought Warburton.

The girl then entered the house, humming. Most women would have got out the lavender salts and lain down the rest of the day, considering the routine of a fashionable dinner, which was the chief duty of the evening.

"I am grateful to you, James. My daughter is directly in your care when she rides, and I give you full authority. Never permit her to mount any horse but her own. She is all I have; and if anything should happen to her—"

"Yes, sir; I understand."

The colonel followed his daughter; and War-burton led Dick to the stables, gave his orders to William, and flung himself down on his cot. He was dead tired. And the hour he had dreaded was come! He was to drive her through the shopping district. Well, so be it. If any one exposed him, very good. This groom business was decidedly like work. And there was that confounded dinner-party, and he would have to limp around a table and carry soup plates! And as likely as not he would run into the very last person he expected to see.

Which he did.

XIV

Mr. Robert vows that he will never forgive me for the ten minutes' agony which I gratuitously added to his measure. It came about in this wise. I was on my way down Seventeenth Street that afternoon, and it was in front of a fashionable apartment house that I met him. He was seated on his box, the whip at the proper angle, and his eyes riveted on his pair's ears. It was the first time I had seen him since the day of the episode at the police-station. He was growing thin. He did not see me, and he did not even notice me till I stopped and the sound of my heels on the walk ceased. Arms akimbo, I surveyed him.

"Well?" I began. I admit that the smile I offered him was a deal like that which a cat offers a cornered mouse.

He turned his head. I shall not repeat the word he muttered. It was very improper, though

194

they often refer to it in the Sabbath-schools, always in a hushed breath, however, as though to full-voice it would only fan the flames still higher.

"What have you to say for yourself?" I went on.

"Nothing for myself, but for you, move on and let me alone, or when I get the opportunity, Chuck, I'll punch your head, glasses or no glasses."

"Brother-in-law or no brother-in-law."

"Chuck, will you go on?"—hoarsely. "I mean it."

I saw that he did. "You don't look very happy for a man who has cracked so tremendous a joke."

"Will you go along?"

"Not till I get good and ready, James. I've told too many lies on your account already not to make myself a present of this joyful reunion. Has Miss Annesley any idea of the imposture?"

He did not answer.

"How did you like waiting in Scott Circle the other night?"

Still no answer. I have half an idea that he was making ready to leap from his box. He ran his fingers up and down the lines. I could see that he was mad through and through; but I enjoyed the scene nevertheless. He deserved a little roasting on the gridiron.

"I am given to understand," I continued, "that you act as butler, besides, and pass the soup around the table."

Silence. Then I heard a door close, and saw a look of despair grow on his face. I turned and saw Miss Annesley and Mrs. Chadwick coming down the steps.

"Why, how do you do, Mr. Henderson? Mrs. Chadwick."

"I have already had the pleasure of meeting this famous young orator," purred Mrs. Chadwick, giving me her hand. She was a fashionable, not to say brilliant, *intrigante*. I knew her to have been concerned indirectly with half a dozen big lobby schemes. She was rather wealthy. But she was seen everywhere, and everywhere was admired. She was as completely at home abroad as here in Washington. She was a widow, perhaps thirty-eight, handsome and fascinating, a delightful *raconteur,* and had the remarkable reputation of never indulging in scandal. She was the repository of more secrets than I should care to discover.

I recall one night at a state function when she sat between the French ambassador and that wily Chinaman, Li Hung Chang. She discoursed on wines in French with the ambassador and immediately turned to the Chinaman and recited Confucius in the original Chinese. Where she had ever found time to study Chinese is a mystery to every one. The incident made her quite famous that winter. Brains are always tolerated in Washington, and if properly directed, push a person a good deal further than wealth or pedigree. Washington forgives everything but stupidity.

Not until recently did I learn that at one time Karloff had been very attentive to her. His great knowledge of American politics doubtless came to him through her.

"Where are you bound?" asked Miss Annesley.

"I am on the way to the War Department."

"Plenty of room; jump in and we shall drop you there. James, drive to the War Department."

Ordinarily I should have declined, as I generally prefer to walk; but in this instance it would be superfluous to say that I was delighted to ac-

cept the invitation. I secretly hugged myself as
I thought of the driver.

"How is Miss Warburton?" asked Miss Annesley, as she settled back among the cushions.

"Beautiful as ever," I replied, smiling happily.

"You must meet Miss Warburton, Grace,"—
speaking to Mrs. Chadwick, who looked at me
with polite inquiry. "One of the most charming
girls in the land, and as good as she is beautiful.
Mr. Henderson is the most fortunate of young
men."

"So I admit. She was greatly disappointed
that you did not meet her younger brother."
First shot at the groom.

"I did expect to meet him, but I understand
that he has gone on a hunting expedition. Whom
does he resemble?"

"Neither Nancy nor Jack," I said. "He's a
good-looking beggar, though, only you can't depend upon him for five minutes at a time. Hadn't
seen the family in more than two years. Spends
one night at home, and is off again, no one knows
where. *Some* persons like him, but I like a man
with more stability. Not but what he has his
good points; but he is a born vagabond. His

brother expects to get him a berth at Vienna and
is working rather successfully toward that end."
I wondered how this bit of news affected the
groom.

"A diplomat?" said Mrs. Chadwick. "That is
the life for a young man with brains. Is he a
good linguist?"

"Capital! Speaks French, German, and Span-
ish, besides I don't know how many Indian
sign-languages." *Now* I was patting the groom
on the back. I sat facing the ladies, so it was
impossible to see the expression on his face. I
kept up this banter till we arrived at the Department. I bade the ladies good day. I do not
recollect when I enjoyed ten minutes more thoroughly.

An hour in the shopping district, that is to
say, up and down Pennsylvania Avenue, where
everybody who was anybody was similarly occupied, shopping, nearly took the spine out of our
jehu. Everywhere he imagined he saw Nancy.
And half a dozen times he saw persons whom he
knew, persons he had dined with in New York,
persons he had met abroad. But true to human
nature, they were looking toward higher things

than a groom in livery. When there was no more room for bundles, the women started for Mrs. Chadwick's apartments.

Said Mrs. Chadwick in French: "Where, in the name of uncommon things, did you find such a handsome groom?"

"I *was* rather lucky," replied Miss Annesley in the same tongue. "Don't you see something familiar about him?"

Warburton shuddered.

"Familiar? What do you mean?"

"It is the groom who ran away with us."

"Heavens, no!" Mrs. Chadwick raised her lorgnette. "Whatever possessed you?"

"Mischief, as much as anything."

"But the risk!"

"I am not afraid. There was something about him that appeared very much like a mystery, and you know how I adore mysteries."

"And this is the fellow we saw in the police-court, sitting among those light o' loves?" Mrs. Chadwick could not fully express her surprise.

"I can't analyze the impulse which prompted me to pay his fine and engage him."

"And after that affair at the carriage-door! Where is your pride?"

"To tell the truth, I believe he did make a mistake. Maybe I hired him because I liked his looks." Betty glanced amusedly at the groom, whose neck and ears were red. She laughed.

"You always were an extraordinary child. I do not understand it in the least. I am even worried. He may be a great criminal."

"No, not a great criminal," said Betty, recollecting the ride of that morning; "but a first-class horseman, willing and obedient. I have been forced to make James serve as butler. He has been under the hands of our cook, and I have been watching them. How I have laughed! Of all droll scenes!"

So she had laughed, eh? Warburton's jaws snapped. She had been watching, too?

"I rode Pirate this morning—"

"You rode that horse?" interrupted Mrs. Chadwick.

"Yes, and he ran away with me in fine style. If it hadn't been for the new groom, I shouldn't be here, and the dinner would be a dismal failure, with me in bed with an arm or leg broken. Heavens! I never was so frightened in all my life. We went so fast against the wind that I could scarce breathe. And when it was all over, I fainted like a ninny."

"Fainted! I should have thought you would. *I* should have fallen off the animal and been killed. Betty, you certainly have neither forethought nor discretion. The very idea of your attempting to ride that animal!"

"Well, I am wiser, and none the worse for the scare. . . . James, stop, stop!" Betty cried suddenly.

When this command struck his sense of hearing, James was pretty far away in thought. He was wondering if all this were true. If it was, he must make the best of it; but if it was a dream, he wanted to wake up right away, because it was becoming nightmarish.

"James!" The end of a parasol tickled him in the ribs and he drew up somewhat frightened. What was going to happen now? He was soon to find out. For this was to be the real climax of the day; or, at least, the incident was pregnant with the possibilities of a climax.

"Colonel, surely you are not going to pass us by in this fashion?" cried the girl. They were almost opposite the Army and Navy Club.

"Why, is that you, Miss Betty? Pass you by?

Only when I grow blind!" roared a lion-like voice. "Very glad to see you, Mrs. Chadwick."

That voice, of all the voices he had ever heard! A chill of indescribable terror flew up and down my jehu's spine, and his pores closed up. He looked around cautiously. It was he, he of all men: his regimental colonel, who possessed the most remarkable memory of any Army man west of the Mississippi, and who had often vowed that he knew his subalterns so well that he could al-ways successfully prescribe for their livers!

"I was just about to turn into the club for my mail," declared the colonel. "It was very good of you to stop me. I'll wager you've been speculating in the shops,"—touching the bundles with his cane.

"You win," laughed Betty. "But I'll give you a hundred guesses in which to find out what any one of these packages contains."

"Guessing is a bad business. Whatever these things are, they can add but little to the beauty of those who will wear them; for I presume Mrs. Chadwick has some claim upon these bundles."

"Very adroitly worded," smiled Mrs. Chadwick, who loved a silken phrase.

"We shall see you at dinner to-night?"

"All the battalions of England could not keep me away from that festive board," the colonel vowed. (Another spasm for the groom!) "And how is that good father of yours?"

"As kind and loving as ever."

"I wish you could have seen him in the old days in Virginia," said the colonel, who, like all old men, continually fell back upon the reminiscent. "Handsomest man in the brigade, and a fight made him as happy as a bull-pup. I was with him the day he first met your mother,"— softly. "How she humiliated him because he wore the blue! She was obliged to feed him— fortunes of war; but I could see that she hoped each mouthful would choke him."

"What! My mother wished that?"

Mrs. Chadwick laughed. The groom's chin sank into his collar.

"Wait a moment! She wasn't in love with him then. We were camped on that beautiful Virginian home of yours for nearly a month. You know how courtly he always was and is. Well, to every rebuff he replied with a smile and some trifling favor. She never had to lift her finger about the house. But one thing he was firm in: she should sit at the same table during the meals.

And when Johnston came thundering down that memorable day, and your father was shot in the lungs and fell with a dozen saber cuts besides, you should have seen the change! *He* was the prisoner now, *she* the jailer. In her own white bed she had him placed, and for two months she nursed him. Ah, that was the prettiest love affair the world ever saw."

"And why have you not followed his example?" asked Mrs. Chadwick.

The colonel gazed thoughtfully at his old comrade's daughter, and he saw pity and unbounded respect in her eyes. "They say that for every heart there is a mate, but I do not believe it. Sometimes there are two hearts that seek the same mate. One or the other must win or lose. You will play for me to-night?"

"As often and as long as you please,"—graciously. She was very fond of this upright old soldier, whom she had known since babyhood.

It was now that the colonel casually turned his attention to the groom. He observed him. First, his gray eyebrows arched abruptly in surprise, then sank in puzzlement.

"What is it?" inquired Betty, noting these signs.

"Nothing; nothing of importance," answered the colonel, growing violently red.

It would not be exaggerating to say that if the colonel turned red, his one-time orderly grew purple, only this purple faded quickly into a chalky pallor.

"Well, perhaps I am keeping you," remarked the colonel, soberly. "I shall hold you to your promise about the music."

"We are to have plenty of music. There will be a famous singer and a fine pianist."

"You will play that what-d'-ye-call-it from Schumann I like so well. I shall want you to play that. I want something in the way of memory to take back West with me. Good-by, then, till to-night."

"Good-by. All right, James; home," said the girl.

James relievedly touched his horses.

The colonel remained standing at the curb till the victoria disappeared. Of what he was thinking I don't know; but he finally muttered "James?" in an inquiring way, and made for the club, shaking his head, as if suddenly confronted by a remarkably abstruse problem.

Further on I shall tell you how he solved it.

XV

Show me those invisible, imperceptible steps by which a man's honor first descends; show me the way back to the serene altitude of clean conscience, and I will undertake to enlighten you upon the secret of every great historical event, tragic or otherwise. If you will search history carefully, you will note that the basic cause of all great events, such as revolutions, civil strifes, political assassinations, foreign wars, and race oppressions, lay not in men's honor so much as in some one man's dishonor. A man, having committed a dishonorable act, may reëstablish himself in the eyes of his fellow-beings, but ever and ever he silently mocks himself and dares not look into the mirror of his conscience.

Honor is comparative, as every one will agree. It is only in the highly developed mind that it reaches its superlative state. Either this man becomes impregnable to the assaults of the angel of the pitch robes, or he boldly plunges into the frightful blackness which surrounds her. The great greed of power, the great greed of wealth, the great greed of hate, the great greed of jealousy, and the great greed of love, only these tempt him.

Now, of dishonors, which does man hold in the greatest abhorrence? This question needs no pondering. It may be answered simply. The murderer, the thief, and the rogue—we look upon these callously. But Judas! Treachery to our country! This is the nadir of dishonor; nothing could be blacker. We never stop to look into the causes, nor does history, that most upright and impartial of judges; we brand instantly. Who can tell the truth about Judas Iscariot, and Benedict Arnold, and the host of others? I can almost tolerate a Judas who betrays for a great love. There seems to be a stupendous elimination of self in the man who betrays for those he loves, braving the consequences, the ignominy, the dishonor, the wretchedness; otherwise I should not have undertaken to write this bit of history.

To betray a friend, that is bad; to betray a woman, that is still worse; but to betray one's country!—to commit an act which shall place her at the mercy of her enemies! Ah, the ignoble deaths of the men who were guilty of this crime! And if men have souls, as we are told they have, how the souls of these men must writhe as they look into the minds of living men and behold the horror and contempt in which each traitor's name is held there!

Have you ever thought of the legion of men who have been thrust back from the very foot of this precipice, either by circumstances or by the revolt of conscience? These are the men who reëstablish themselves in the eyes of their fellow-beings, but who for ever silently mock themselves and dare not look into the mirror of their consciences.

In this world motive is everything. A bad thing may be done for a good purpose, or, the other way around. This is the story of a crime, the motive of which was good.

Once upon a time there lived a soldier, a gentleman born, a courtier, a man of fine senses, of high integrity, of tenderness, of courage; he possessed a splendid physical beauty, besides estates, and a comfortable revenue, or rather, he presided over one. Above all this, he was the father of a girl who worshiped him, and not without rea-

son. What mysterious causes should set to work
to ruin this man, to thrust him from light into
darkness? What step led him to attempt to betray his country, even in times of peace, to dishonor his name, a name his honesty had placed
high on the rolls of glory? What defense can
he offer? Well, I shall undertake to defend him;
let yours be the verdict.

Enforced idleness makes a criminal of a poor
man; it urges the man of means to travel. Having seen his native land, it was only natural that
my defendant should desire to see foreign countries. So, accompanied by his child, he went
abroad, visited the famous capitals, and was the
guest of honor at his country's embassies. It
was a delightful period. Both were as happy as
fate ever allows a human being to be. The father
had received his honorable discharge, and till recently had held a responsible position in the War
Department. His knowledge had proved of no
small value to the government, for he was a born
strategist, and his hobby was the coast defenses.
He never beheld a plan that he did not reproduce
it on the back of an envelope, on any handy scrap
of paper, and then pore over it through the night.
He had committed to memory the smallest de-

tails, the ammunition supplies of each fort, the number of guns, the garrison, the pregnable and impregnable sides. He knew the resource of each, too; that is to say, how quickly aid could be secured, the nearest transportation routes, what forage might be had. He had even submitted plans for a siege gun.

One day, in the course of their travels, the father and daughter stopped at Monte Carlo. Who hasn't heard of that city of fever? Who that has seen it can easily forget its gay harbor, its beautiful walks, its crowds, its music, its hotels, its white temple of fortune? Now, my defendant had hitherto ignored the principality of Monaco. The tales of terror which had reached his ears did not prepossess him in its favor. But his daughter had friends there, and she wanted to see them. There would be dances on the private yacht, and dinners, and teas, and fireworks. On the third night of his arrival he was joined by the owner of the yacht, a millionaire banker whose son was doing the honors as host. I believe that there was a musicale on board that night, and as the banker wasn't particularly fond of this sort of entertainment, he inveigled his soldier friend to accompany him on a sight-seeing trip. At midnight they entered the temple of fortune. At first the soldier demurred; but the banker told him that he hadn't seen Monte Carlo unless he saw the wheel go around. So, laughing, they entered the halls.

The passion for gaming is born in us all, man and woman alike, and is conceded by wise analysts to be the most furious of all passions and the most lasting. In some, happily, the serpent sleeps for ever, the fire is for ever banked. But it needs only the opportunity to rouse the dull ember into flame, to stir the venom of the serpent. It seems a simple thing to toss a coin on the roulette boards. Sometimes the act is done contemptuously, sometimes indifferently, sometimes in the spirit of fun and curiosity; but the result is always the same.

The banker played for a while, won and lost, lost and won. The soldier put his hand into a pocket and drew forth a five-franc piece. He placed it on a number. The angel in the pitch robes is always lying in wait for man to make his first bad step; so she urged fortune to let this man win. It is an unwritten law, high up on Olympus, that the gods must give to the gods; only the prayers of the mortals go unanswered.

So my defendant won. He laughed like a boy

who had played marbles for "keeps" and had taken away his opponent's agates. His mind was perfectly innocent of any wrong-doing. That night he won a thousand francs. His real first bad step was in hiding the escapade from his daughter. The following night he won again. Then he dallied about the flame till one night the lust of his forebears shone forth from his eyes. The venom of the serpent spread, the ember grew into a flame. His daughter, legitimately enjoying herself with the young people, knew nothing nor dreamed. Indeed, he never entered the temple till after he had kissed her good night.

He lost. He lost twice, thrice, in succession. One morning he woke up to the fact that he was several thousand dollars on the wrong side of the book. If the money had been his own, he would have stopped, and gone his way, cured. But it was money which he held in trust. He *must* replace it. The angel in the pitch robes stood at his side; she even laid a hand on his shoulder and urged him to win back what he had lost. Then indeed he could laugh, go his way, and gamble no more. This was excellent advice. That winter he lost something like fifteen thousand. Then began the progress of de-

cline. The following summer his losses were
even greater than before. He began to mortgage
the estates, for his authority over his daughter's
property was absolute. He dabbled in stocks; a
sudden fall in gold, and he realized that his
daughter was nearly penniless. Ah, had he been
alone, had the money been his, he would have
faced poverty with all the courage of a brave
man. But the girl, the girl! She must never
know, she must never want for those luxuries to
which she was accustomed. For her sake he
must make one more effort. He *must* win, must,
must! He raised more money on the property.
He became irritable, nervous, to which were added sudden bursts of tenderness which the girl
could not very well understand.

The summer preceding the action of this tale
saw them at Dieppe. At one time he had recov-
ered something between sixty and seventy thousand of his losses. Ah, had he stopped then, confessed to his daughter, all would have gone well.
But, no; he must win the entire sum. He lost,
lost, lost. The crash came in August. But a
corner of the vast Virginian estates was left, and
this did not amount to twenty thousand. Five
francs carelessly tossed upon a roulette table had

ruined and dishonored him. The angel of the pitch robes had fairly enveloped him now. The thought that he had gambled uselessly his daughter's legacy, the legacy which her mother had left confidingly in his care, filled his soul with the bitterness of gall. And she continued the merry round of happiness, purchasing expensive garments, jewelry, furs, the little things which women love; gave dinners and teas and dances, considered herself an heiress, and thought the world a very pleasant place to live in. Every laugh from her was a thorn to him, the light of happiness in her eyes was a reproach, for he knew that she was dancing toward the precipice which he had digged for her.

Struggling futilely among these nettles of despair, he took the final step. His ruin became definitive. His evil goddess saw to it that an opportunity should present itself. (How simple all this reads! As I read it over it does not seem credible. Think of a man who has reached the height of his ambition, has dwelt there serenely, and then falls in this silly, inexcusable fashion! Well, that is human nature, the human part of it. Only here and there do we fall grandly.)

One starlit night he met a distinguished young

diplomat, rich and handsome. He played some, but to pass away the time rather than to coquet with fortune. He was lucky. The man who plays for the mere fun of it is generally lucky. He asks no favors from fortune; he does not pay any attention to her, and, woman-like, she is piqued. He won heavily this night; my soldier lost correspondingly heavily. The diplomat pressed a loan upon his new-found friend, who, with his usual luck, lost it.

The diplomat was presented to the daughter. They owned to mutual acquaintance in Paris and Washington. The three attended the concert. The girl returned to the hotel bubbling with happiness and the echoes of enchanting melodies, for she was an accomplished musician. She retired and left the two men to their coffee and cigars. The conversation took several turns, and at length stopped at diplomacy.

"It has always puzzled me," said the soldier, "how Russia finds out all she does."

"That is easily explained. Russia has the wisdom of the serpent. Here is a man who possesses a secret which Russia must have. They study him. If he is gallant, one day he meets a fascinating woman; if he is greedy, he turns to find a bowl of gold at his elbow; if he seeks power, Russia points out the shortest road."

"But her knowledge of foreign army and naval strength?"

"Money does all that. Russia possesses an accurate knowledge of every fort, ship and gun England boasts of; France, Germany, and Japan. We have never taken it into our heads to investigate America. Till recently your country as a foe to Russian interests had dropped below the horizon. And now Russia finds that she must proceed to do what she has done to all other countries; that is, duplicate her rival's fortification plans, her total military and naval strength; and so forth, and so on. The United States is not an enemy, but there are possibilities of her becoming so. Some day she must wrest Cuba from Spain, and then she may become a recognized quantity in the Pacific."

"The Pacific?"

"Even so. Having taken Cuba, the United States, to protect her western coast, will be forced to occupy the Philippines; and having taken that archipelago, she becomes a menace to Russian territorial expansion in the far East. I do not always speak so frankly. But I wish you to see

the necessity of knowing all about your coast defenses."

"It can not be done!"—spiritedly. So far the
American had only gambled.

"It can and will be done," smiling. "Despite
the watchfulness of your officials, despite your
secret service, despite all obstacles, Russia will
quietly gain the required information. She possesses a key to every lock."

"And what might this key be?"—with tolerant
irony.

"Gold."

"But if the United States found out what
Russia was doing, there might be war."

"Nothing of the kind. Russia would simply
deny all knowledge. The man whom she se-
lected to do the work would be discredited, ban-
ished, perhaps sent to Siberia to rot in the mines.
No, there would be no war. Russia would weigh
all these possibilities in selecting her arm. She
would choose a man of high intellect, rich, well-
known in social circles, a linguist, a man acquainted with all histories and all phases of life,
a diplomat, perhaps young and pleasing. You
will say, why does he accept so base a task?
When a Russian noble takes his oath in the pres-

ence of his czar, he becomes simply an arm; he
no longer thinks, his master thinks for him. He
only acts. So long as he offers his services without remuneration, his honor remains untouched,
unsullied. A paid spy is the basest of all crea-
tures."

"Count, take care that I do not warn my country of Russia's purpose. You are telling me very
strange things." The American eyed his companion sharply.

"Warn the United States? I tell you, it will
not matter. All Russia would need would be a
dissatisfied clerk. What could he not do with
half a million francs?" The diplomat blew a
cloud of smoke through his nostrils and filliped
the end of his cigarette.

"A hundred thousand dollars?"

The diplomat glanced amusedly at his American friend. "I suppose that sounds small enough
to you rich Americans. But to a clerk it reads
wealth."

The American was silent. A terrible thought
flashed through his brain, a thought that he re-
pulsed almost immediately.

"Of course, I am only speculating; nothing
has been done as yet."

"Then something *is* going to be done?" asked the American, clearing his voice.

"One day or another. If we can not find the clerk, we shall look higher. We should consider a million francs well invested. America is rapidly becoming a great power. But let us drop' the subject and turn to something more agreeable to us both. Your daughter is charming. I honestly confess to you that I have not met her equal in any country. Pardon my presumption, but may I ask if she is engaged to be married?"

"Not to my knowledge,"—vastly surprised and at the same time pleased.

"Are you averse to foreign alliances?" The diplomat dipped the end of a fresh-lighted cigar into his coffee.

"My dear Count, I am not averse to foreign alliances, but I rather suspect that my daughter is. This aversion might be overcome, however."

What a vista was opened to this wretched father! If only she might marry riches, how easily he might confess what he had done, how easily all this despair and terror might be dispersed! And here was a man who was known in the great world, rich, young and handsome.

The other gazed dreamily at the ceiling; from

there his gaze traveled about the coffee-room, with its gathering of coffee-drinkers, and at length came back to his *vis-à-vis*.

"You will return to Washington?" he asked.

"I shall live there for the winter; that is, I expect to."

"Doubtless we shall see each other this winter, then,"—and the count threw away his cigar, bade his companion good night, and went to his room.

How adroitly he had sown the seed! At that period he had no positive idea upon what kind of ground he had cast it. But he took that chance which all far-sighted men take, and then waited. There was little he had not learned about this handsome American with the beautiful daughter. How he had learned will always remain dark to me. My own opinion is that he had been studying him during his tenure of office in Washington, and, with that patience which is making Russia so formidable, waited for this opportunity.

I shall give the Russian all the justice of impartiality. When he saw the girl, he rather shrank from the affair. But he had gone too far, he had promised too much; to withdraw now meant his own defeat, his government's anger, his political oblivion. And there was a zest in this life of his. He could no more resist the call of intrigue than a gambler can resist the croupier's, "Make your game, gentlemen!" I believe that he loved the girl the moment he set eyes upon her. Her beauty and bearing distinguished her from the other women he had met, and her personality was so engaging that her conquest of him was complete and spontaneous. How to win this girl and at the same time ruin her father was an embarrassing problem. The plan which finally came to him he repelled again and again, but at length he surrendered. To get the parent in his power and then to coerce the girl in case she refused him! To my knowledge this affair was the first dishonorable act of a very honorable man. But love makes fools and rogues of us all.

You will question my right to call this diplomat an honest man. As I have said elsewhere, honor is comparative. Besides, a diplomat generally falls into the habit of lying successfully to himself.

When the American returned to the world, his cigar was out and his coffee was stale and cold.

"A million francs!" he murmured. "Two hundred thousand!"

The seed had fallen on fruitful ground.

XVI

THE PREVIOUS AFFAIR

Mrs. Chadwick had completed her toilet and now stood smiling in a most friendly fashion at the reflection in the long oval mirror. She addressed this reflection in melodious tones.

"Madam, you are really handsome; and let no false modesty whisper in your ear that you are not. Few women in Washington have such clear skin, such firm flesh, such color. Thirty-eight? It is nothing. It is but the half-way post; one has left youth behind, but one has not reached old age. Time must be very tolerant, for he has given you a careful selection. There were no years of storm and poverty, of violent passions; and if I have truly loved, it has been you, only you. You are too wise and worldly to love any one but yourself. And yet, once you stood on the precipice of dark eyes, pale skin, and melancholy wrinkles. And even now, if he were to speak . . . Enough! Enough of this folly.

I have something to accomplish to-night." She
glided from the boudoir into the small but luxurious drawing-room which had often been graced
by the most notable men and women in the country.

Karloff threw aside the book of poems by De
Banville, rose, and went forward to meet her.

"Madam,"—bending and brushing her hand
with his lips, "Madam, you grow handsomer
every day. If I were forty, now, I should fear
for your single blessedness."

"Or, if I were two-and-twenty, instead of
eight-and-thirty,"—beginning to draw on her
long white gloves. There was a challenge in her
smile.

"Well, yes; if you were two-and-twenty."

"There was a time, not so long ago," she said,
drawing his gaze as a magnet draws a needle,
"when the disparity in years was of no matter."

The count laughed. "That was three years
ago; and, if my memory serves me, you smiled."

"Perhaps I was first to smile; that is all."

"I observe a mental reservation,"—owlishly.

"I will put it plainly, then. I preferred to
smile over your protestations rather than see you

laugh over the possibility and the folly of my loving you."

"Then it was possible?"—with interest.

"Everything is possible . . . and often absurd."

"How do you know that I was not truly in love with you?"—narrowing his eyes.

"It is not explanatory; it can be given only one name—instinct, which in women and animals is more fully developed than in man. Besides, at that time you had not learned all about Colonel Annesley, whose guests we are to be this evening. Whoever would have imagined a Karloff accepting the hospitalities of an Annesley? Count, hath not thy rose a canker?"

"Madam!" Karloff was frowning.

"Count, you look like a paladin when you scowl; but scowling never induces anything but wrinkles. That is why we women frown so seldom. We smile. But let us return to your query. Supposing I had accepted your declarations seriously; supposing you had offered me marriage in that burst of gratitude; supposing I *had* committed the folly of becoming a countess: what a position I should be in to-day!"

"I do not understand,"—perplexedly.

"No?"—shrugging. She held forth a gloved arm. "Have you forgotten how gallantly you used to button my gloves?"

"A thousand pardons! My mind was occupied with the mystery of your long supposition." He took the arm gracefully and proceeded to slip the pearl buttons through their holes. (Have you ever buttoned the gloves of a handsome woman? I have. And there is a subtile thrill about the proceeding which I can not quite define. Perhaps it is the nearness of physical beauty; perhaps it is the delicate scent of flowers; perhaps it is the touch of the cool, firm flesh; perhaps it is just romance.) The gaze which she bent upon his dark head was emotional; yet there was not the slightest tremor of arm or fingers. It is possible that she desired him to observe the steadiness of her nerves. "What did you mean?" he asked.

"What did I mean?"—vaguely. Her thought had been elsewhere.

"By that supposition."

"Oh! I mean that my position, had I married you, would have been rather anomalous to-day." She extended the other arm. "You are in love."

"In love?" He looked up quickly.

"Decidedly; and I had always doubted your capacity for that sentiment."

"And pray tell me, with whom am I in love?"

"Come, Count, you and I know each other too well to waste time in beating about the bushes. I do not blame you for loving her; only, I say, it must not be."

"Must not be?" The count's voice rose a key.

"Yes, must not be. You must give them up— the idea and the girl. What! You, who contrive the father's dishonor, would aspire to the daughter's hand? It is not equable. Love her honorably, or not at all. The course you are following is base and wholly unworthy of you."

He dropped the arm abruptly and strode across the room, stopping by a window. He did not wish her to see his face at that particular instant. Some men would have demanded indignantly to know how she had learned these things; not so the count.

"There is time to retrieve. Go to the colonel frankly, pay his debts out of your own pockets, then tell the girl that you love her. Before you tell her, her father will have acquainted her with

his sin and your generosity. She will marry you
out of gratitude."

Karloff spun on his heels. His expression was
wholly new. His eyes were burning; he stretched
and crumpled his gloves.

"Yes, you are right, you are right! I have
been trying to convince myself that I was a machine where the father was concerned and wholly
a man in regard to the girl. You have put it
before me in a bold manner. Good God, yes! I
find that I am wholly a man. How smoothly all
this would have gone to the end had she not
crossed my path! I *am* base, I, who have always considered myself an honorable man. And
now it is too late, too late!"

"Too late? What do you mean? Have you
dared to ask her to be your wife?" Had Karloff
held her arm at this moment, he would have
comprehended many things.

"No, no! My word has gone forth to my
government; there is a wall behind me, and I can
not go back. To stop means worse than death.
My property will be confiscated and my name obliterated, my body rot slowly in the frozen north.
Oh, I know my country; one does not gain her
gratitude by failure. I must have those plans,

and nowhere could I obtain such perfect ones."

"Then you will give her up?" There was a broken note.

The count smiled. To her it was a smile scarce less than a snarl.

"Give her up? Yes, as a mother gives up her child, as a lioness her cub. She *has* refused me, but nevertheless she shall be my wife. Oh, I am well-versed in human nature. She loves her father, and I know what sacrifices she would make to save his honor. To-night!—" But his lips suddenly closed.

"Well, to-night? Why do you not go on?" Mrs. Chadwick was pale. Her gloved hands were clenched. A spasm of some sort seemed to hold her in its shaking grasp.

"Nothing, nothing! In heaven's name, why have you stirred me so?" he cried.

"Supposing, after all, I loved you?"

He retreated. "Madam, your suppositions are becoming intolerable and impossible."

"Nothing is impossible. Supposing I loved you as violently and passionately as you love this girl?"

"Madam,"—hastily and with gentleness, "do not say anything which may cause me to blush

for you; say nothing you may regret to-morrow."

"I am a woman of circumspection. My suppositions are merely argumentative. Do you realize, Count, that I could force you to marry me?"

Karloff's astonishment could not be equaled.
"Force me to marry you?"

"Is the thought so distasteful, then?"

"You are mad to-night!"

"Not so. In whatever manner you have succeeded in this country, your debt of gratitude is
owing to me. I do not recall this fact as a reproach; I make the statement to bear me on in
what I have to submit to your discerning intelligence. I doubt if there is another woman, here
or abroad, who knows you so well as I. Your
personal honor is beyond impeachment, but
Russia is making vast efforts to speckle it. She
will succeed. Yes, I could force you to marry
me. With a word I could tumble your house of
cards. I am a worldly woman, and not without
wit and address. I possess every one of your
letters, most of all have I treasured the extravagant ones. To some you signed your name. If
you have kept mine, you will observe that my
given name might mean any one of a thousand

women who are named 'Grace.' Shall you marry
me? Shall I tumble your house of cards? I
could go to Colonel Annesley and say to him that
if he delivers these plans to you, I shall denounce
him to the secret service officers. I might cause
his utter financial ruin, but his name would de-
scend to his daughter untarnished."

"You would not dare!" the count interrupted.

"What? And you know me so well? I have
not given you my word to reveal nothing. You
confided in my rare quality of silence; you confided in me because you had proved me. Man is
not infallible, even when he is named Karloff."
She lifted from a vase her flowers, from which
she shook the water. "Laws have been passed
or annulled; laws have died at the executive desk.
Who told you that this was to be, or that, long
before it came to pass? In all the successful in-
trigues of Russia in this country, whom have you
to thank? Me. Ordinarily a woman does not do
these things as a pastime. There must be some
strong motive behind. You asked me why I have
stirred you so. Perhaps it is because I am neither
two-and-twenty nor you two-score. It is these
little barbs that remain in a woman's heart. Well,
I do not love you well enough to marry you, but

I love you too well to permit you to marry Miss Annesley."

"That has the sound of war. I *did* love you that night,"—not without a certain nobility.

"How easily you say 'that night'! Surely there was wisdom in that smile of mine. And I nearly tumbled into the pit! I must have looked exceedingly well . . . *that night!*"—drily.

"You are very bitter to-night. Had you taken me at my word, I never should have looked at Miss Annesley. And had I ceased to love you, not even you would have known it."

"Is it possible?"—ironically.

"It is. I have too much pride to permit a woman to see that I have made a mistake."

"Then you consider in the present instance that you have not made a mistake? You are frank."

"At least I have not made a mistake which I can not rectify. Madam, let us not be enemies. As you say, I owe you too much. What is it you desire?"—with forced amiability.

"Deprive Colonel Annesley of his honor, that, as you say, is inevitable; but I love that girl as I would a child of my own, and I will not see her caught in a net of this sort, or wedded to a man whose government robs him of his manhood and individuality."

"Do not forget that I hold my country first and, foremost,"—proudly.

"Love has no country, nor laws, nor galling chains of incertitude. Love is magnificent only in that it gives all without question. You love this girl with reservations. You shall not have her. You shall not have even me, who love you after a fashion, for I could never look upon you as a husband; in my eyes you would always be an accomplice."

"It is war, then?"—curtly.

"War? Oh, no; we merely sever our diplomatic relations," she purred.

"Madam, listen to me. I shall make one more attempt to win this girl honorably. For you are right: love to be love must be magnificent. If she accepts me, for her sake I will become an outcast, a man without a country. If she refuses me, I shall go on to the end. Speak to the colonel, Madam; it is too late. Like myself, he has gone too far. Why did you open the way for me as you did? I should have been satisfied with a discontented clerk. You threw this girl across my path, indirectly, it is true; but nevertheless the fault is yours."

"I recognize it. At that time I did not realize how much you were to me."

"You are a strange woman. I do not understand you."

"Incompatibility. Come, the carriage is waiting. Let us be gone."

"You have spoilt the evening for me," said the count, as he threw her cloak across her shoulders.

"On the contrary, I have added a peculiar zest. Now, let us go and appear before the world, and smile, and laugh, and eat, and gossip. Let the heart throb with a dull pain, if it will; the mask is ours to do with as we may."

They were, in my opinion, two very unusual persons.

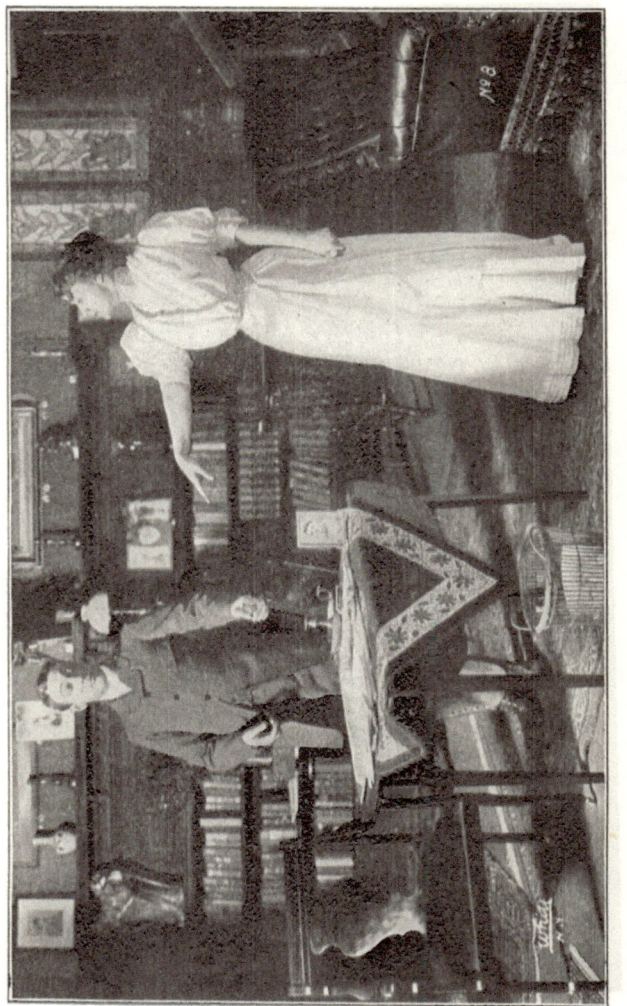

" Lay the rose on the table." —ACT II.

XVII

"Ha!"

Monsieur Pierre, having uttered this ejacula-
tion, stepped back and rested his fat hands on his
fat hips. As he surveyed the impromptu butler,
a shade of perplexity spread over his oily face.
He smoothed his imperial and frowned. This
groom certainly *looked* right, but there was
something lacking in his make-up, that indefinable something which is always found in the true
servant—servility. There was no humility here,
no hypocritical meekness, no suavity; there was
nothing smug or self-satisfied. In truth, there
was something grimly earnest, which was not to
be understood readily. Monsieur Pierre, having
always busied himself with soups and curries and
roasts and sauces, was not a profound analyst;
yet his instinctive shrewdness at once told him
that this fellow was no servant, nor could he ever
be made into one. Though voluble enough in his
kitchen, Monsieur Pierre lacked expression when

confronted by any problem outside of it. Here
was the regulation swallow-tail coat and trousers
of green, the striped red vest, and the polished
brass buttons; but the man inside was too much
for him.

"*Diable!* you *luke* right. But, no, I can not
explain. Eet ees on zee tongue, but eet rayfuse.
Ha! I haf eet! You lack vot zay call zee real.
You make me t'ink uf zee sairvant on zee stage,
somet'ing bettair off; eh?" This was as near as
monsieur ever got to the truth of things.

During this speculative inventory, Warburton's
face was gravely set; indeed, it pictured his exact feelings. He *was* grave. He even wanted
Pierre's approval. He was about to pass through
a very trying ordeal; he might not even pass
through it. There was no deceiving his colonel's
eyes, hang him! Whatever had induced fate to
force this old Argus-eyed soldier upon the scene?
He glanced into the kitchen mirror. He instantly saw the salient flaw in his dress. It was the
cravat. Tie it as he would, it never approached
the likeness of the conventional cravat of the
waiter. It still remained a polished cravat, a
worldly cravat, the cravat seen in ball-rooms,
drawing-rooms, in the theater stalls and boxes,

anywhere but in the servants' hall. Oh, for
the ready-made cravat that hitched to the collar-
button! And then there was that servant's low
turned-down collar, glossy as celluloid. He felt
as diffident in his bare throat as a débutante feels
in her first décolleté ball-gown, not very well
covered up, as it were. And, heaven and earth,
how appallingly large his hands had grown, how
clumsy his feet! Would the colonel expose him?
Would he keep silent? This remained to be
found out: wherein lay the terror of suspense.

"Remem*bair*," went on Monsieur Pierre, after
a pause, feeling that he had a duty to fulfil and
a responsibility to shift to other shoulders than
his own, "remem*bair*, eef you spill zee soup, I
keel you. You carry zee tureen in, zen you deesh
out zee soup, and sairve. Zee oystaires should
be on zee table t'ree minutes before zee guests
haf arrive'. Now, can you make zee American
cocktail?"

"I can,"—with a ghost of a smile.

"Make heem,"—with a pompous wave of the
hand toward the favorite ingredients.

"What kind?"

"Vot kind! Eez zare more cocktails, zen?"

"Only two that are proper, the manhattan and the martini."

"Make zee martini; I know heem."

"But cocktails ought not be mixed before serving."

"I say, make zee one cocktail,"—coldly and skeptically. "I test heem."

Warburton made one. Monsieur sipped it slowly, making a wry face, for, true Gaul that he was, only two kinds of stimulants appealed to his palate, liqueurs and wines. He found it as good as any he had ever tasted.

"Ver' good,"—softening. "Zare ees, zen, one t'ing zat all zee Americans can make, zee cocktail? I am educate'; I learn. Now, leaf me till eight. Keep zee collect head;"—and Monsieur Pierre turned his attention to his partridges.

James went out of doors to get a breath of fresh air and to collect his thoughts, which were wool-gathering, whatever that may mean. They needed collecting, these thoughts of his, and labeling, for they were at all points of the compass, and he was at a loss upon which to draw for support. Here he was, in a devil of a fix, and no possible way of escaping except by absolutely bolting; and he vowed that he wouldn't bolt, not if he stood the chance of being exposed fifty times over. He had danced; he was going to pay the fiddler like a man. He had never run away from anything, and he wasn't going to begin now.

At the worst, they could only laugh at him; but his secret would be his no longer. Ass that he had been! How to tell this girl that he loved her? How to appear to her as his natural self? What a chance he had wilfully thrown away! He might have been a guest to-night; he might have sat next to her, turned the pages of her music, and perhaps sighed love in her ear, all of which would have been very proper and conventional. Ah, if he only knew what was going on behind those Mediterranean eyes of hers, those heavenly sapphires. Had she any suspicion? No, it could not be possible; she had humiliated him too often, to suspect the imposture. Alackaday!

Had any one else applied the disreputable terms he applied to himself there would have been a battle royal. When he became out of breath, he reëntered the house to have a final look at the table before the ordeal began.

Covers had been laid for twelve; immaculate

linen, beautiful silver, and sparkling cut-glass. He wondered how much the girl was worth, and thought of his own miserable forty-five hundred the year. True, his capital could at any time be converted into cash, some seventy-five thousand,' but it would be no longer the goose with the golden egg. A great bowl of roses stood on a glass center-piece. As he leaned toward them to inhale their perfume he heard a sound. He turned.

She stood framed in a doorway, a picture such as artists conjure up to fit in sunlit corners of gloomy studios: beauty, youth, radiance, luster, happiness. To his ardent eyes she was supremely beautiful. How wildly his heart beat! This was the first time he had seen her in all her glory. His emotion was so strong that he did not observe that she was biting her nether lip.

"Is everything well, James?" she asked, meaning the possibilities of service and not the cardiac intranquillity of the servant.

"Very well, Miss Annesley,"—with a sudden bold scrutiny.

Whatever it was she saw in his eyes it had the effect of making hers turn aside. To bridge the awkwardness of the moment, he rearranged a napkin; and she remarked his hands. They were tanned, but they were elegantly shaped and scrupulously well taken care of—the hands of a gentleman born, of an aristocrat. He could feel her gaze penetrate like acid. He grew visibly nervous.

"You haven't the hand of a servant, James," —quietly.

He started, and knocked a fork to the floor.

"They are too clumsy," she went on maliciously.

"I am not a butler, Miss; I am a groom. I promise to do the very best I can." Wrath mingled with the shame on his face.

"A man who can do what you did this morning ought not to be afraid of a dinner-table."

"There is some difference between a dinner-table and a horse, Miss." He stooped to recover the fork while she touched her lips with her handkerchief. The situation was becoming unendurable. He knew that, for some reason, she was quietly laughing at him.

"Never put back on the table a fork or piece of silver that has fallen to the floor," she advised. "Procure a clean one."

"Yes, Miss." Why, in heaven's name, didn't she go and leave him in peace?

"And be very careful not to spill a drop of the burgundy. It is seventy-eight, and a particular favorite of my father's."

Seventy-eight! As if he hadn't had many a bottle of that superb vintage during the past ten months! The glands in his teeth opened at the memory of that taste.

"James, we have been in the habit of paying off the servants on this day of the month. Pay-day comes especially happy this time. It will put good feeling into all, and make the service vastly more expeditious."

She counted out four ten-dollar notes from a roll in her hand and signified him to approach. He took the money, coolly counted it, and put it in his vest-pocket.

"Thank you, Miss."

I do not say that she looked disappointed, but I assert that she was slightly disconcerted. She never knew the effort he had put forth to subdue the desire to tear the money into shreds, throw it at her feet and leave the house.

"When the gentlemen wish for cigars or cig-arettes, you will find them in the usual place, the lower drawer in the sideboard." With a swish she was gone.

He took the money out and studied it. No, he wouldn't tear it up; rather he would put it among his keepsakes.

I shall leave Mr. Robert, or M'sieu Zhames, to recover his tranquillity, and describe to you the character and quality of the guests. There was the affable military attaché of the British embassy, there was a celebrated American countess, a famous dramatist and his musical wife, Warburton's late commanding colonel, Mrs. Chadwick, Count Karloff, one of the notable grand opera prima-donnas, who would not sing in opera till February, a cabinet officer and his wife, Colonel Annesley and his daughter. You will note the cosmopolitan character of these distinguished persons. Perhaps in no other city in America could they be brought together at an informal dinner such as this one was. There was no question of precedence or any such nonsense. Everybody knew everybody else, with one exception. Colonel Raleigh was a comparative stranger. But he was a likable old fellow, full of stories of the wild, free West, an excellent listener besides, who always stopped a goodly distance on the

right side of what is known in polite circles as
the bore's dead-line. Warburton held for him a
deep affection, martinet though he was, for he
was singularly just and merciful.

They had either drunk the cocktail or had set
it aside untouched, and had emptied the oyster
shells, when the ordeal of the soup began. Very
few of those seated gave any attention to my butler. The first thing he did was to drop the silver
ladle. Only the girl saw this mishap. She
laughed; and Raleigh believed that he had told
his story in an exceptionally taking manner. My
butler quietly procured another ladle, and proceeded coolly enough. I must confess, however,
that his coolness was the result of a physical effort. The soup quivered and trembled outrage-
ously, and more than once he felt the heat of the
liquid on his thumb. This moment his face was
pale, that moment it was red. But, as I remarked, few observed him. Why should they?
Everybody had something to say to everybody
else; and a butler was only a machine anyway.
Yet, three persons occasionally looked in his direction: his late colonel, Mrs. Chadwick, and the
girl; each from a different angle of vision. There
was a scowl on the colonel's face, puzzlement on

Mrs. Chadwick's, and I don't know what the girl's represented, not having been there with my discerning eyes.

Once the American countess raised her lorgnette and murmured: "What a handsome butler!"

Karloff, who sat next to her, twisted his mustache and shrugged. He had seen handsome peasants before. They did not interest him. He glanced across the table at the girl, and was much annoyed that she, too, was gazing at the butler, who had successfully completed the distribution of the soup and who now stood with folded arms by the sideboard. (How I should have liked to see him!)

When the butler took away the soup-plates, Colonel Raleigh turned to his host.

"George, where the deuce did you pick up that butler?"

Annesley looked vaguely across the table at his old comrade. He had been far away in thought. He had eaten nothing.

"What?" he asked.

"I asked you where the deuce you got that butler of yours."

"Oh, Betty found him somewhere. Our own

butler is away on a vacation. I had not noticed him. Why?"

"Well, if he doesn't look like a cub lieutenant of mine, I was born without recollection of faces."

"An orderly of yours, a lieutenant, did you say?" asked Betty, with smoldering fires in her eyes.

"Yes."

"That is strange," she mused.

"Yes; very strange. He was a daredevil, if there ever was one."

"Ah!"

"Yes; best bump of location in the regiment, and the steadiest nerve,"—dropping his voice.

The girl leaned on her lovely arms and observed him interestedly.

"A whole company got lost in a snowstorm one winter. You know that on the prairie a snowstorm means that only a compass can tell you where you are; and there wasn't one in the troop,—a bad piece of carelessness on the captain's part. Well, this cub said *he'd* find the way back, and the captain wisely let him take the boys in hand."

"Go on," said the girl.

"Interested, eh?"

"I am a soldier's daughter, and I love the recital of brave deeds."

"Well, he did it. Four hours later they were being thawed out in the barracks kitchens. Another hour and not one of them would have lived to tell the tale. The whisky they poured into my cub—"

"Did he drink?" she interrupted.

"Drink? Why, the next day he was going to lick the men who had poured the stuff down his throat. A toddy once in a while; that was all he ever took. And how he loved a fight! He had the tenacity of a bulldog; once he set his mind on getting something, he never let up till he got it."

The girl trifled thoughtfully with a rose.

"Was he ever in any Indian fights?" she asked, casually.

"Only scraps and the like. He went into the reservation alone one day and arrested a chief who had murdered a sheep-herder. It was a volunteer job, and nine men out of ten would never have left the reservation alive. He was certainly a cool hand."

"I dare say,"—smiling. She wanted to ask him if he had ever been hurt, this daredevil of a lieutenant, but she could not bring the question to her lips. "What did you say his name was?"—innocently.

"Warburton, Robert Warburton."

Here the butler came in with the birds. The girl's eyes followed him, hither and thither, her lips hidden behind the rose.

XVIII

CAUGHT!

Karloff came around to music. The dramatist's wife should play Tosti's *Ave Maria,* Miss Annesley should play the obligato on the violin and the prima-donna should sing; but just at present the dramatist should tell them all about his new military play which was to be produced in December.

"Count, I beg to decline," laughed the dramatist. "I should hardly dare to tell my plot before two such military experts as we have here. I should be told to write the play all over again, and now it is too late."

Whenever Betty's glance fell on her father's face, the gladness in her own was somewhat dimmed. What was making that loved face so care-worn, the mind so listless, the attitude so weary? But she was young; the spirits of youth never flow long in one direction. The repartee, brilliant and at the same time with every sting withdrawn, flashed up and down the table like so many fireflies on a wet lawn in July, and drew her irresistibly.

As the courses came and passed, so the conversation became less and less general; and by the time the ices were served the colonel had engaged his host, and the others divided into twos. Then coffee, liqueurs and cigars, when the ladies rose and trailed into the little Turkish room, where the "distinguished-looking butler" supplied them with the amber juice.

A dinner is a function where everybody talks and nobody eats. Some have eaten before they come, some wish they had, and others dare not eat for fear of losing some of the gossip. I may be wrong, but I believe that half of these listless appetites are due to the natural confusion of forks.

After the liqueurs my butler concluded that his labor was done, and he offered up a short prayer of thankfulness and relief. Heavens, what mad, fantastic impulses had seized him while he was passing the soup! Supposing he *had* spilled the hot liquid down Karloff's back, or poured out a glass of burgundy for himself and drained it before them all, or slapped his late

colonel on the back and asked him the state of
his liver? It was maddening, and he marveled
at his escape. There hadn't been a real mishap.
The colonel had only scowled at him; he was
safe. He passed secretly from the house and
hung around the bow-window which let out on
the low balcony. The window was open, and
occasionally he could hear a voice from beyond
the room, which was dark.

It was one of those nights, those mild November nights, to which the novelists of the old ré-
gime used to devote a whole page; the silvery
pallor on the landscape, the moon-mists, the
round, white, inevitable moon, the stirring
breezes, the murmur of the few remaining leaves,
and all that. But these busy days we have not
the time to read nor the inclination to describe.

Suddenly upon the stillness of the night the
splendor of a human voice broke forth; the
prima-donna was trying her voice. A violin
wailed a note. A hand ran up and down the keys
of the piano. Warburton held his breath and
waited. He had heard Tosti's *Ave Maria* many
times, but he never will forget the manner in
which it was sung that night. The songstress
was care-free and among persons she knew

and liked, and she put her soul into that magnificent and mysterious throat of hers. And throbbing all through the song was the vibrant, loving voice of the violin. And when the human tones died away and the instruments ceased to speak, Warburton felt himself swallowing rapidly. Then came Schumann's *Träumerei* on the strings, Handel's *Largo,* Grieg's *Papillon,* and a *ballade* by Chaminade. Then again sang the primadonna; old folksy songs, sketches from the operas, grand and light, *Faust, The Barber of Seville, La Fille de Madame Angot.* In all his days Warburton had never heard such music. Doubtless he *had*—even better; only at this period he was in love. The imagination of love's young dream is the most stretchable thing I know of. Seriously, however, he was a very good judge of music, and I am convinced that what he heard was out of the ordinary.

But I must guide my story into the channel proper.

During the music Karloff and Colonel Annesley drifted into the latter's study. What passed between them I gathered from bits recently dropped by Warburton.

"Good God, Karloff, what a net you have sprung about me!" said the colonel, despairingly.

"My dear Colonel, you have only to step out of it. It is the eleventh hour; it is not too late." But Karloff watched the colonel eagerly.

"How in God's name can I step out of it?"

"Simply reimburse me for that twenty thousand I advanced to you in good faith, and nothing more need be said." The count's Slavonic eyes were half-lidded.

"To give you back that amount will leave me a beggar, an absolute beggar, without a roof to shelter me. I am too old for the service, and besides, I am physically incapacitated. If you should force me, I could not meet my note save by selling the house my child was born in. Have you discounted it?"

"No. Why should I present it at the bank? It does not mature till next Monday, and I am in no need of money."

"What a wretch I am!"

Karloff raised his shoulders resignedly.

"My daughter!"

"Or my ducats," whimsically quoted the count. "Come, Colonel; do not waste time in useless re-

trospection.   He stumbles who looks back.   I
have been thinking of your daughter.   I love her,
deeply, eternally."

"You love her?"

"Yes.   I love her because she appeals to all
that is young and good in me; because she repre-
sents the highest type of womanhood.   With her
as my wife, why, I should be willing to renounce
my country, and your indebtedness would be
crossed out of existence with one stroke of the
pen."

The colonel's haggard face grew light with
sudden hopefulness.

"I have been," the count went on, studying the
ash of his cigar, "till this night what the world
and my own conscience consider an honorable
man.   I have never wronged a man or woman
personally.   What I have done on the order of
duty does not agitate my conscience.   I am simply a machine.   The moral responsibility rests
with my czar.   When I saw your daughter, I
deeply regretted that you were her father."

The colonel grew rigid in his chair.

"Do not misunderstand me.   Before I saw her,
you were but the key to what I desired.   As her
father the matter took on a personal side.   I

could not very conscientiously make love to your daughter and at the same time—" Karloff left the sentence incomplete.

"And Betty?"—in half a whisper.

"Has refused me,"—quietly. "But I have not given her up; no, I have not given her up."

"What do you mean to do?"

Karloff got up and walked about the room. "Make her my wife,"—simply. He stooped and studied the titles of some of the books in the cases. He turned to find that the colonel had risen and was facing him with flaming eyes.

"I demand to know how you intend to accomplish this end," the colonel said. "My daughter shall not be dragged into this trap."

"To-morrow night I will explain everything; to-night, nothing,"—imperturbably.

"Karloff, to-night I stand a ruined and dishonored man. My head, once held so proudly before my fellow-men, is bowed with shame. The country I have fought and bled for I have in part betrayed. But not for my gain, not for my gain. No, no! Thank God that I can say that! Personal greed has not tainted me. Alone, I should have gone serenely into some poor house and eked out an existence on my half-pay. But this

child of mine, whom I love doubly, for her mother's sake and her own,—I would gladly cut off
both arms to spare her a single pain, to keep her
in the luxury which she still believes rightfully
to be hers. When the fever of gaming possessed
me, I should have told her. I did not; therein
lies my mistake, the mistake which has brought
me to this horrible end. Virginius sacrificed his
child to save her; I will sacrifice my honor to
save mine from poverty. Force her to wed a
man she does not love? No. To-morrow night
we shall complete this disgraceful bargain. The
plans are all finished but one. Now leave me;
I wish to be alone."

"Sir, it is my deep regret—"

"Go; there is nothing more to be said."

Karloff withdrew. He went soberly. There
was nothing sneering nor contemptuous in his attitude. Indeed, there was a frown of pity on his
face. He recognized that circumstances had
dragged down a noble man; that chance had
tricked him of his honor. How he hated his own
evil plan! He squared his shoulders, determined
once more to put it to the touch to win or lose it
all.

He found her at the bow-window, staring up

at the moon. As I remarked, this room was dark, and she did not instantly recognize him.

"I am moon-gazing," she said.

"Let me sigh for it with you. Perhaps together we may bring it down." There was something very pleasing in the quality of his tone.

"Ah, it is you, Count? I could not see. But let us not sigh for the moon; it would be useless. Does any one get his own wish-moon? Does it not always hang so high, so far away?"

"The music has affected you?"

"As it always does. When I hear a voice like madam's, I grow sad, and a pity for the great world surges over me."

"Pity is the invisible embrace which enfolds all animate things. There is pity for the wretched, for the fool, for the innocent knave, for those who are criminals by their own folly; pity for those who love without reward; pity that embraces . . . even me."

Silence.

"Has it ever occurred to you that there are two beings in each of us; that between these two there is a continual conflict, and that the victor finally prints the victory on the face? For what lines and haggards a man's face but the victory

of the evil that is in him? For what makes the
aged ruddy and smooth of face and clear of eye
but the victory of the good that is in him? It is
so. I still love you; I still have the courage to
ask you to be my wife. Shall there be faces haggard or ruddy, lined or smooth?"

She stepped inside. She did not comprehend
all he said, and his face was in the shadow—that
is to say, unreadable.

"I am sorry, very, very sorry."

"How easily you say that!"

"No, not easily; if only you knew how hard
it comes, for I know that it inflicts a hurt,"—gently. "Ah, Count, why indeed do I not love
you?"—impulsively, for at that time she held
him in genuine regard. "You represent all that
a woman could desire in a man."

"You could learn,"—with an eager step toward her.

"You do not believe that; you know that you
do not. Love has nothing to learn; the heart
speaks, and that is all. My heart does not speak
when I see you, and I shall never marry a man to
whom it does not. You ask for something which
I can not give, and each time you ask you only
add to the pain."

"This is finality?"

"It is."

"Eh, well; then I must continue on to the end."

She interpreted this as a plaint of his coming loneliness.

"Here!" she said. She held in her hands two red roses. She thrust one toward him. "That is all I may give you."

For a moment he hesitated. There were thorns, invisible and stinging.

"Take it!"

He accepted it, kissed it gravely, and hid it.

"This is the bitterest moment in my life, and doubly bitter because I love you."

When the portière fell behind him, she locked her hands, grieving that all she could give him was an ephemeral flower. How many men had turned from her in this wise, even as she began to depend upon them for their friendships! The dark room oppressed her and she stepped out once more into the silver of moonshine. Have you ever beheld a lovely woman fondle a lovely rose? She drew it, pendent on its slender stem, slowly across her lips, her eyes shining mistily with waking dreams. She breathed in the perfume, then cupped the flower in the palm of her

hand and pressed it again and again to her lips.
A long white arm stretched outward and upward
toward the moon, and when it withdrew the hand
was empty.

Warburton, hidden behind the vines, waited
until she was gone, and then hunted in the grass
for the precious flower. On his hands and knees
he groped. The dew did not matter. And when
at last he found it, not all the treasures of the
fabled Ophir would have tempted him to part
with it. It would be a souvenir for his later
days.

As he rose from his knees he was confronted
by a broad-shouldered, elderly man in evening
clothes. The end of a cigar burned brightly between his teeth.

"I'll take that flower, young man, if you
please."

Warburton's surprise was too great for sudden
recovery.

"It is mine, Colonel," he stammered.

The colonel filliped away his cigar and caught
my butler roughly by the arm.

"Warburton, what the devil does this mean—
a lieutenant of mine peddling soup around a gentleman's table?"

XIX

"OH, MISTER BUTLER!"

Warburton had never lacked that rare and peculiar gift of immediately adapting himself to circumstances. To lie now would be folly, worse than useless. He had addressed this man at his side by his military title. He stood committed. He saw that he must throw himself wholly on the colonel's mercy and his sense of the humorous. He pointed toward the stables and drew the colonel after him; but the colonel held back.

"That rose first; I insist upon having that rose till you have given me a satisfactory account of yourself."

Warburton reluctantly surrendered his treasure. Force of habit is a peculiar one. The colonel had no real authority to demand the rose; but Warburton would no more have thought of disobeying than of running away.

"You will give it back to me?"

"That remains to be seen. Go on; I am ready

261

to follow you. And I do not want any dragging story, either." The colonel spoke impatiently.

Warburton led him into his room and turned on the light. The colonel seated himself on the edge of the cot and lighted a fresh cigar.

"Well, sir, out with it. I am waiting."

Warburton took several turns about the room. "I don't know how the deuce to begin, Colonel. It began with a joke that turned out wrong."

"Indeed?"—sarcastically. "Let   me   hear about this joke."

M'sieu Zhames dallied no longer, but plunged boldly into his narrative. Sometimes the colonel stared at him as if he beheld a species of lunatic absolutely new to him, sometimes he laughed silently, sometimes he frowned.

"That's all," said Zhames; and he stood watching the colonel with dread in his eyes.

"Well, of all the damn fools!"

"Sir?"

"Of all the jackasses!"

Warburton bit his lip angrily.

The colonel swung the rose to and fro. "Yes, sir, a damn fool!"

"I dare say that I am, sir. But I have gone

too far to back out now. Will you give me back
that rose, Colonel?"

"What do you mean by her?"—coldly.

"I love her with all my heart,"—hotly. "I
want her for my comrade, my wife, my companion, my partner in all I have or do. I love her,
and I don't care a hang who knows it."

"Not so loud, my friend; not so loud."

"Oh, I do not care who hears,"—discour-
agedly.

"This beats the very devil! You've got me all
balled up. Is Betty Annesley a girl of the kind
we read about in the papers as eloping with her
groom? What earthly chance had you in this
guise, I should like to know?"

"I only wanted to be near her; I did not look
ahead."

"Well, I should say not! How long were you
hidden behind that trellis?"

"A year, so it seemed to me."

"Any lunatics among your ancestors?"

Warburton shook his head, smiling wanly.

"I can't make it out," declared the colonel.
"A graduate of West Point, the fop of Troop A,
the hero of a hundred ball-rooms, disguised as a
hostler and serving soup!"

"Always keep the motive in mind, Colonel; you were young yourself once."

The colonel thought of the girl's mother. Yes, he had been young once, but not quite so young as this cub of his.

"What chance do you suppose you have against the handsome Russian?"

"She has rejected him,"—thoughtlessly.

"Ha!"—frowning; "so you were eavesdropping?"

"Wait a moment, Colonel. You know that I am very fond of music. I was listening to the music. It had ceased, and I was waiting for it to begin again, when I heard voices."

"Why did you not leave then?"

"And be observed? I dared not."

The colonel chewed the end of his cigar in silence.

"And now may I have that rose, sir?"—quietly.

The colonel observed him warily. He knew that quiet tone. It said that if he refused to give up the rose he would have to fight for it, and probably get licked into the bargain.

"I've a notion you might attempt to take it by force in case I refused."

"I surrendered it peacefully enough, sir."

"So you did. Here." The colonel tossed the flower across the room and Warburton caught it.

"I should like to know, sir, if you are going to expose me. It's no more than I deserve."

The colonel studied the lithographs on the walls. "Your selection?"—with a wave of the hand.

"No, sir. I should like to know what you are going to do. It would relieve my mind. As a matter of fact, I confess that I am growing weary of the mask." Warburton waited.

"You make a very respectable butler, though," —musingly.

"Shall you expose me, sir?"—persistently.

"No, lad. I should not want it to get about that a former officer of mine could possibly make such an ass of himself. You have slept all night in jail, you have groomed horses, you have worn a livery which no gentleman with any self-respect would wear, and all to no purpose whatever. Why, in the name of the infernal regions, didn't you meet her in a formal way? There would have been plenty of opportunities."

Warburton shrugged; so did the colonel, who

stood up and shook the wrinkles from his trousers.

"Shall you be long in Washington, sir?" asked Warburton, politely.

"In a hurry to get rid of me, eh?"—with a grim smile. "Well, perhaps in a few days."

"Good night."

The colonel stopped at the threshold, and his face melted suddenly into a warm, humorous smile. He stretched out a hand which Warburton grasped most gratefully. His colonel had been playing with him.

"Come back to the Army, lad; the East is no place for a man of your kidney. Scrape up a commission, and I'll see to it that you get back into the regiment. Life is real out in the great West. People smile too much here; they don't laugh often enough. Smiles have a hundred meanings, laughter but one. Smiles are the hiding places for lies, and sneers, and mockeries, and scandals. Come back to the West; we all want you, the service and I. When I saw you this afternoon I knew you instantly, only I was worried as to what devilment you were up to. Win this girl, if you can; she's worth any kind

of struggle, God bless her! Win her and bring
her out West, too."

Warburton wrung the hand in his till the old
fellow signified that his fingers were beginning
to ache.

"Do you suppose she suspects anything?" ventured Warburton.

"No. She may be a trifle puzzled, though. I
saw her watching your hands at the table. She
has eyes and can readily see that such hands as
yours were never made to carry soup-plates. For
the life of me, I had a time of it, swallowing my
laughter. I longed for a vacant lot to yell in. It
would have been a positive relief. The fop of
Troop A peddling soup! Oh, I shall have to
tell the boys. You used more pipe-clay than any
other man in the regiment. Don't scowl. Never
mind; you've had your joke; I must have mine.
Don't let that Russian fellow get the inside track.
Keep her on American soil. I like him and I
don't like him; and for all your tomfoolery and
mischief, there is good stuff in you—stuff that
any woman might be proud of. If you hadn't
adopted this disguise, I could have helped you
out a bit by cracking up some of your exploits.

Well, they will be inquiring for me. Good night and good luck. If you should need me, a note will find me at the Army and Navy Club." And the genial old warrior, shaking with silent laughter, went back to the house.

Warburton remained standing. He was lost in a dream. All at once he pressed the rose to his lips and kissed it shamelessly, kissed it uncountable times. Two or three leaves, not withstanding this violent treatment, fluttered to the floor. He picked them up: any one of those velvet leaves might have been the recipient of *her* kisses, the rosary of love. He was in love, such a love that comes but once to any man, not passing, uncertain, but lasting. He knew that it was all useless. He had digged with his own hands the abyss between himself and this girl. But there was a secret gladness: to love was something. (For my part, I believe that the glory lies, not in being loved, but in loving.)

I do not know how long he stood there, but it must have been at least ten minutes. Then the door opened, and Monsieur Pierre lurched or rolled (I can't quite explain or describe the method of his entrance) into the room, his face red with anger, and a million thousand thunders on the tip of his Gallic tongue.

"So! You haf leaf *me* to clear zee table, eh? Not by a damn! *I,* clear zee table? *I?* I t'ink not. I *cook,* nozzing else. To zee dining-room, or I haf you discharge'!"

"All right, Peter, old boy!" cried Warburton, the gloom lifting from his face. This Pierre was a very funny fellow.

"Pe*taire!* You haf zee insolence to call me Pe*taire?* Why, I haf you keeked out in zee morning, lackey!"

"Cook!"—mockingly.

Pierre was literally dumfounded. Such disrespect he had never before witnessed. It was frightful. He opened his mouth to issue a volley of French oaths, when Zhames's hand stopped him.

"Look here, Peter, you broil your partridges and flavor your soups, but keep out of the stables, or, in your own words, I *keel* you or *keek* you out. You tell the scullery maid to clear off the table. I'm off duty for the rest of the night. Now, then, *allons! Marche!*"

And M'sieu Zhames gently but firmly and

steadily pushed the scandalized Pierre out of the room and closed the door in his face. I shan't repeat what Pierre said, much less what he thought.

Let me read a thought from the mind of each of my principals, the final thought before retiring that night.

Karloff (on leaving Mrs. Chadwick): Dishonor against dishonor; so it must be. I can not live without that girl.

Mrs. Chadwick: (when Karloff had gone): He has lost, but I have not won.

Annesley: So one step leads to another, and the labyrinth of dishonor has no end.

The Colonel: What the deuce will love put next into the young mind?

Pierre (to Celeste): I haf heem discharge'!

Celeste (to Pierre): He ees handsome!

Warburton (sighing in the *doloroso*): How I love her!

The Girl (standing before her mirror and smiling happily): Oh, Mister Butler! Why?

XX

THE EPISODE OF THE STOVE-PIPE

In the morning Monsieur Pierre faithfully reported to his mistress the groom's extraordinary insolence and impudence of the night before. The girl struggled with and conquered her desire to laugh; for monsieur was somewhat grotesque in his rage.

"Frightful, Mademoiselle, most frightful! He call me Pe*taire* most disrrrespectful way, and eject me from zee stables. I can not call heem out; he ees a groom and knows nozzing uf zee *amende honorable.*"

Mademoiselle summoned M'sieu Zhames. She desired to make the comedy complete in all its phases.

"James, whenever you are called upon to act in the capacity of butler, you must clear the table after the guests leave it. This is imperative. I do not wish the scullery girl to handle the porcelain save in the tubs. Do you understand?"

271

"Yes, Miss. There were no orders to that effect last night, however." He was angry.

Monsieur Pierre puffed up like the lady-frog
in Æsop's fables.

"And listen, Pierre," she said, collapsing the
bubble of the chef's conceit, "you must give no
orders to James. I will do that. I do not wish
any tale-bearing or quarreling among my servants. I insist upon this. Observe me carefully,
Pierre, and you, James."

James *did* observe her carefully, so carefully,
indeed, that her gaze was forced to wander to
the humiliated countenance of Monsieur Pierre.

"James, you must not look at me like that.
There is something in your eyes; I can't explain
what it is, but it somehow lacks the respect due
me." This command was spoken coldly and
sharply.

"Respect?" He drew back a step. "I disre-
spectful to you, Miss Annesley? Oh, you wrong
me. There can not be any one more respectful
to you than I am." The sincerity of his tones
could not be denied. In fact, he was almost too
sincere.

"Nevertheless, I wish you to regard what I
have said. Now, you two shake hands."

The groom and the chef shook hands. I am ashamed to say that James squeezed Monsieur Pierre's flabby hand out of active service for several hours that followed. Beads of agony sparkled on Monsieur Pierre's expansive brow as he turned to enter the kitchen.

"Shall we ride to-day, Miss?" he asked, inwardly amused.

"No, *I* shall not ride this morning."—calmly.

James bowed meekly under the rebuke. What did he care? Did he not possess a rose which had known the pressure of her lips, her warm, red lips?

"You may go," she said.

James went. James whistled on the way, too.

Would that it had been my good fortune to have witnessed the episode of that afternoon! My jehu, when he hears it related these days, smiles a sickly grin. I do not believe that he ever laughed heartily over it. At three o'clock, while Warburton was reading the morning paper, interested especially in the Army news of the day, he heard Pierre's voice wailing.

"What's the fat fool want now?" James grumbled to William.

"Oh, he's always yelling for help. They've coddled him so long in the family that he acts like a ten-year-old kid. I stole a kiss from Celeste one day, and I will be shot if he didn't start to blubber."

"You stole a kiss, eh?" said James, admiringly.

"Only just for the sport of making him crazy, that was all." But William's red visage belied his indifferent tone. "You'd better go and see what he wants. My hands are all harness grease."

Warburton concluded to follow William's advice. He flung down his paper and strode out to the rear porch, where he saw Pierre gesticulating wildly.

"What's the matter? What do you want?"— churlishly.

"Frightful! Zee stove-pipe ees vat you call *bust!*"

James laughed.

"I can not rrreach eet. I can not cook till eet ees fix'. You are tall, eh?"—affably.

"All right; I'll help you fix it."

Grumbling, James went into the kitchen, mounted a chair, and began banging away at the pipe, very much after the fashion of Bunner's "Culpepper Ferguson." The pipe acted piggish-ly. James grew determined. One end slipped in and then the other slipped out, half a dozen times. James lost patience and became angry; and in his anger he overreached himself. The chair slid back. He tried to balance himself and, in the mad effort to maintain a perpendicular position, made a frantic clutch at the pipe. Ruin and de-vastation! Down came the pipe, and with it a peck of greasy soot.

Monsieur Pierre yelled with terror and de-spair. The pies on the rear end of the stove were lost for ever. Mademoiselle Celeste screamed with laughter, whether at the sight of the pies or M'sieu Zhames, is more than I can say.

James rose to his feet, the cuss-words of a corporal rumbled behind his lips. He sent an energetic kick toward Pierre, who succeeded in eluding it.

Pierre's eyes were full of tears. What a kitchen! What a kitchen! Soot, soot, every-where, on the floor, on the tables, on the walls, in the air!

"Zee pipe!" he burst forth; "zee pipe! You haf zee house full of gas!"

James, blinking and sneezing, boiling with rage and chagrin, remounted the chair and finally succeeded in joining the two lengths. Nothing happened this time. But the door to the forward rooms opened, and Miss Annesley looked in upon the scene.

"Merciful heavens!" she gasped, "what has happened?"

"Zee stove-pipe bust, Mees," explained Pierre. The girl gave Warburton one look, balled her handkerchief against her mouth, and fled. This didn't add to his amiability. He left the kitchen in a downright savage mood. He had appeared before her positively ridiculous, laughable. A woman never can love a man, nor entertain tender regard for him at whom she has laughed. And the girl had laughed, and doubtless was still laughing. (However, I do not offer his opinion as infallible.)

He stood in the roadway, looking around for some inanimate thing upon which he might vent his anger, when the sound of hoofs coming toward him distracted him. He glanced over his shoulder . . . and his knees all but gave way under him. Caught! The rider was none other than his sister Nancy! It was all over now, for a certainty. He knew it; he had about one minute to live. She was too near, so he dared not fly. Then a brilliant inspiration came to him. He quickly passed his hand over his face. The disguise was complete. Vidocq's wonderful eye could not have penetrated to the flesh.

"James!" Miss Annesley was standing on the veranda. "Take charge of the horse. Nancy, dear, I am so glad to see you!"

James was anything but glad.

"Betty, good gracious, whatever is the matter with this fellow? Has he the black plague? Ugh!" She slid from the saddle unaided.

James stolidly took the reins.

"The kitchen stove-pipe fell down," Betty replied, "and James stood in the immediate vicinity of it."

The two girls laughed joyously, but James did not even smile. He had half a notion to kiss Nancy, as he had planned to do that memorable night of the ball at the British embassy. But even as the notion came to him, Nancy had climbed up the steps and was out of harm's way.

"James," said Miss Annesley, "go and wash your face at once."

"Yes, Miss."

At the sound of his voice Nancy turned swiftly; but the groom had presented his back and
was leading the horse to the stables.

Nancy would never tell me the substance of
her conversation with Miss Annesley that afternoon, but I am conceited enough to believe that
a certain absent gentleman was the main topic.
When she left, it was William who led out the
horse. He explained that James was still engaged with soap and water and pumice-stone.
Miss Annesley's laughter rang out heartily, and
Nancy could not help joining her.

"And have you heard from that younger
brother of yours?" Betty asked, as her friend
settled herself in the saddle.

"Not a line, Betty, not a line; and I had set
my heart on your meeting him. I do not know
where he is, or when he will be back."

"Perhaps he is in quest of adventures."

"He is in Canada, hunting caribou."

"You don't tell me!"

"What a handsome girl you are, Betty!"—admiringly.

"What a handsome girl you are, Nancy!"
mimicked the girl on the veranda. "If your

brother is only half as handsome, I do not know whatever will become of this heart of mine when we finally meet." She smiled and drolly placed her hands on her heart. "Don't look so disappointed, Nan; perhaps we may yet meet. I have an idea that he will prove interesting and entertaining;"—and she laughed again.

"Whoa, Dandy! What *are* you laughing at?" demanded Nancy.

"I was thinking of James and his soap and water and pumice-stone. That was all, dear. Saturday afternoon, then, we shall ride to the club and have tea. Good-by, and remember me to the baby."

"Good-by!"—and Nancy cantered away.

What a blissful thing the lack of prescience is, sometimes!

When James had scraped the soot from his face and neck and hands, and had sudsed it from his hair, James observed, with some concern, that Pirate was coughing at a great rate. His fierce run against the wind the day before had given him a cold. So James hunted about for the handy veterinarian.

"Where do you keep your books here?" he asked William. "Pirate's got a cold."

"In the house library. You just go in and get it. We always do that at home. You'll find it on the lower shelf, to the right as you enter the door."

It was half after four when James, having taken a final look at his hands and nails, proceeded to follow William's instructions. He found no one about. Outside the kitchen the lower part of the house was deserted. To reach the library he had to pass through the music-room. He saw the violin-case on the piano, and at once unconsciously pursed his lips into a noiseless whistle. He passed on into the library. He had never been in any of these rooms in the daytime. It was not very light, even now.

The first thing that caught his attention was a movable drawing-board, on which lay an uncompleted drawing. At one side stood a glass, into which were thrust numerous pens and brushes. Near this lay a small ball of crumpled cambric, such as women insist upon carrying in their street-car purses, a delicate, dainty, useless thing. So she drew pictures, too, he thought. Was there anything this beautiful creature could not do? Everything seemed to suggest her presence. An indefinable feminine perfume still lingered on the air, speaking eloquently of her.

Curiosity impelled him to step forward and examine her work. He approached with all the stealth of a gentlemanly burglar. He expected to see some trees and hills and mayhap a brook, or some cows standing in a stream, cr some children picking daisies. He had a sister, and was reasonably familiar with the kind of subjects chosen by the lady-amateur.

A fortification plan!

He bent close to it. Here was the sea, here was the land, here the number of soldiers, cannon, rounds of ammunition, resources in the matter of procuring aid, the telegraph, the railways, everything was here on this pale, waxen cloth, everything but a name. He stared at it, bewildered. He couldn't understand what a plan of this sort was doing outside the War Department. Instantly he became a soldier; he forgot that he was masquerading as a groom; he forgot everything but this mute thing staring up into his face. Underneath, on a little shelf, he saw a stack of worn envelopes. He looked at them. Rough drafts of plans. Governor's Island! Fortress

Monroe! What did it mean? What *could*
it mean? He searched and found plans, plans,
plans of harbors, plans of coast defenses, plans
of ships building, plans of full naval and
military strength; everything, everything! He
straightened. How his breath pained him!
. . . And all this was the handiwork of the
woman he loved! Good God, what was going
on in this house? What right had such things
as these to be in a private home? For what purpose had they been drawn? so accurately repro-
duced? For what purpose?

Oh, whatever the purpose was, *she* was innocent; upon this conviction he would willingly
stake his soul. Innocent, innocent! ticked the
clock over the mantel. Yes, she was innocent.
Else, how could she laugh in that light-hearted
fashion? How could the song tremble on her
lips? How could her eyes shine so bright and
merry? . . . Karloff, Annesley! Karloff
the Russian, Annesley the American; the one a secret agent of his country, the other a former
trusted official! No, no! He could not entertain so base a thought against the father of the
girl he loved. Had he not admired his clean
record, his personal bravery, his fearless hon-

" A Saint Bernard dog might have done as much." —ACT III.

esty? And yet, that absent-mindedness, this care-worn countenance, these must mean something. The purpose, to find out the purpose of these plans!

He took the handkerchief and hid it in his breast, and quietly stole away. . . . A handkerchief, a rose, and a kiss; yes, that was all that would ever be his.

Pirate nearly coughed his head off that night; but, it being William's night off, nobody paid any particular attention to that justly indignant animal.

XXI

On a Wednesday morning, clear and cold: not
a cloud floated across the sky, nor did there rise
above the horizon one of those clouds (portentous
forerunners of evil!) to which novelists refer as
being "no larger than a man's hand". Heaven
knew right well that the blight of evil was approaching fast enough, but there was no visible
indication on her face that glorious November
morning. Doubtless you are familiar with history and have read all about what great person-
ages did just before calamity swooped down on
them. The Trojans laughed at the wooden
horse; I don't know how many Roman banquet-
ers never reached the desert because the enemy
had not paid any singular regard to courtesies
in making the attack; men and women danced
on the eve of Waterloo—"On with the dance, let
joy be unconfined"; *my* heroine simply went
shopping. It doesn't sound at all romantic; very
prosaic, in fact.

284

She declared her intention of making a tour
of the shops and of dropping into Mrs. Chadwick's on the way home. She ordered James to
bring around the pair and the coupé. James was
an example of docile obedience. As she came
down the steps, she was a thing of beauty and
a joy for ever. She wore one of those jackets
to which several gray-squirrel families had con-
tributed their hides, a hat whose existence was
due to the negligence of a certain rare bird, and
many silk-worms had spun the fabric of her
gown. Had any one called her attention to all
this, there isn't any doubt that she would have
been shocked. Only here and there are women
who see what a true Moloch fashion is; this ten-
der-souled girl saw only a handsome habit which
pleased the eye. Health bloomed in her cheeks,
health shone from her eyes, her step had all the
elasticity of youth.

"Good morning, James," she said pleasantly.

James touched his hat. What was it, he wondered. Somehow her eyes looked unfamiliar to
him. Had I been there I could have read the
secret easily enough. Sometimes the pure pools
of the forests are stirred and become impenetra-
ble; but by and by the commotion subsides,

and the water clears. So it is with the human soul. There had been doubt hitherto in this girl's eyes; now, the doubt was gone.

To him, soberly watchful, her smile meant much; it was the patent of her innocence of any wrong thought. All night he had tossed on his cot, thinking, thinking! What should he do? What*ever* should he do? That some wrong was on the way he hadn't the least doubt. Should he confront the colonel and demand an explanation, a demand he knew he had a perfect right to make? If this should be evil, and the shame of it fall on this lovely being? . . . No, no! He must stand aside, he must turn a deaf ear to duty, the voice of love spoke too loud. His own assurance of her innocence made him desire to fall at her feet and worship. After all, it *was* none of his affair. Had he not played at this comedy, this thing would have gone on, and he would have been in ignorance of its very existence. So, why should he meddle? Yet that monotonous query kept beating on his brain: What *was* this thing?

He saw that he must wait. Yesterday he had feared nothing save his own exposure. Comedy had frolicked in her grinning mask. And here was Tragedy stalking in upon the scene.

The girl named a dozen shops which she desired to honor with her custom and presence, and stepped into the coupé. William closed the door, and James touched up the pair and drove off toward the city. He was perfectly indifferent to any possible exposure. In truth, he forgot everything, absolutely and positively everything, but the girl and the fortification plans she had been drawing.

Scarce a half a dozen bundles were the result of the tour among the shops.

"Mrs. Chadwick's, James."

The call lasted half an hour.

As a story-teller I am supposed to be everywhere, to follow the footsteps of each and all of my characters, and with a fidelity and a perspicacity nothing short of the marvelous. So I take the liberty of imagining the pith of the conversation between the woman and the girl.

The Woman: How long, dear, have we known each other?

The Girl: Since I left school, I believe. Where *did* you get that stunning morning gown?

The Woman (smiling in spite of the serious purpose she has in view): Never mind the gown, my child; I have something of greater importance to talk about.

The Girl: Is there anything more important to talk about among women?

The Woman: Yes. There is age.

The Girl: But, mercy, we do not talk about that!

The Woman: I am going to establish a precedent, then. I am forty, or at least, I am on the verge of it.

The Girl (warningly): Take care! If we should ever become enemies! If I should ever become treacherous!

The Woman: The world very well knows that I am older than I look. That is why it takes such interest in my age.

The Girl: The question is, how *do* you preserve it?

The Woman: Well, then, I am forty, while you stand on the threshold of the adorable golden twenties. (Walks over to picture taken eighteen years before and contemplates it.) Ah, to be twenty again; to start anew, possessing my present learning and wisdom, and knowledge of the world; to avoid the pits into which I so carelessly stumbled! But no!

The Girl: Mercy! what have you to wish for? Are not princes and ambassadors your friends; have you not health and wealth and beauty? You wish for something, you who are so handsome and brilliant!

The Woman: Blinds, my dear Betty, only blinds; for that is all beauty and wealth and wit are. Who sees behind sees scars of many wounds. You are without a mother, I am without a child. (Sits down beside the girl and takes her hand in hers.) Will you let me be a mother to you for just this morning? How can any man help loving you! (impulsively.)

The Girl: How foolish you are, Grace!

The Woman: Ah, to blush like that!

The Girl: You are very embarrassing this morning. I believe you are even sentimental. Well, my handsome mother for just this morning, what is it you have to say to me? (jestingly.)

The Woman: I do not know just how to begin. Listen. If ever trouble should befall you, if ever misfortune should entangle you, will you promise to come to me?

The Girl: Misfortune?   What is on your mind, Grace?

The Woman: Promise!

The Girl: I promise.   (Laughs.)

The Woman: I am rich.   Promise that if poverty should ever come to you, you will come to me.

The Girl (puzzled) :   I do not understand you at all!

The Woman: Promise!

The Girl: I promise; but—

The Woman: Thank you, Betty.

The Girl (growing serious) :   What is all this about, Grace?   You look so earnest.

The Woman: Some day you will understand. Will you answer me one question, as a daughter would answer her mother?

The Girl (gravely) :   Yes.

The Woman: Would you marry a title for the title's sake?

The Girl (indignantly) :   I?

The Woman: Yes; would you?

The Girl: I shall marry the man I love, and if not him, nobody.   I mean, of course, *when* I love.

The Woman: Blushing again? My dear, is Karloff anything to you?

The Girl: Karloff? Mercy, no. He is handsome and fascinating and rich, but I could not love him. It would be easier to love—to love my groom outside.

(They both smile.)

The Woman (grave once more): That is all I wished to know, dear. Karloff is not worthy of you.

The Girl (sitting very erect): I do not understand. Is he not honorable?

The Woman (hesitating): I have known him for seven years; I have always found him honorable.

The Girl: Why, then, should he not be worthy of me?

The Woman (lightly): Is any man?

The Girl: You are parrying my question. If I am to be your daughter, there must be no fencing.

The Woman (rising and going over to the portrait again): There are some things that a mother may not tell even to her daughter.

The Girl (determinedly): Grace, you have

said too much or too little. I do not love Karloff, I never could love him; but I like him, and liking him, I feel called upon to defend him.

The Woman (surprised into showing her dismay): You defend him? You!

The Girl: And why not? That is what I wish to know: why not?

The Woman: My dear, you do not love him. That is all I wished to know. Karloff is a brilliant, handsome man, a gentleman; his sense of honor, such as it is, would do credit to many another man; but behind all this there is a power which makes him helpless, makes him a puppet, and robs him of certain worthy impulses. I have read somewhere that corporations have no souls; neither have governments. Ask me nothing more, Betty, for I shall answer no more questions.

The Girl: I do not think you are treating me fairly.

The Woman: At this moment I would willingly share with you half of all I possess in the world.

The Girl: But all this mystery!

The Woman: As I have said, some day you will understand. Treat Karloff as you have always treated him, politely and pleasantly. And I beg of you never to repeat our conversation.

The Girl (to whom illumination suddenly comes; rises quickly and goes over to the woman; takes her by the shoulders, and the two stare into each other's eyes, the one searchingly, the other fearfully): Grace!

The Woman: I am a poor foolish woman, Betty, for all my worldliness and wisdom; but I love you (softly), and that is why I appear weak before you. The blind envy those who see, the deaf those who hear; what one does not want another can not have. Karloff loves you, but you do not love him.

(The girl kisses the woman gravely on the cheek, and without a word, makes her departure.)

The Woman (as she hears the carriage roll away): Poor girl! Poor, happy, unconscious, motherless child! If only I had the power to stay the blow! . . . Who can it be, then, that she loves?

The Girl (in her carriage): Poor thing! She adores Karloff, and I never suspected it! I shall begin to hate him.

How well women read each other!

James had never parted with his rose and his handkerchief. They were always with him, no matter what livery he wore. After luncheon, William said that Miss Annesley desired to see him in the study. So James spruced up and duly presented himself at the study door.

"You sent for me, Miss?"—his hat in his hand, his attitude deferential and attentive.

She was engaged upon some fancy work, the name of which no man knows, and if he were told, could not possibly remember for longer than ten minutes. She laid this on the reading-table, stood up and brushed the threads from the little two-by-four cambric apron.

"James, on Monday night I dropped a rose on the lawn. (Finds thread on her sleeve.) In the morning when I looked for it (brushes the apron again), it was gone. Did you find it?" She made a little ball of the straggling threads and dropped it into the waste-basket. A woman who has the support of beauty can always force a man to lower his gaze. James looked at his boots. His heart gave one great bound toward his throat, then sank what seemed to be fathoms deep in his breast. This was a thunderbolt out

of heaven itself. Had she seen him, then? For
a space he was tempted to utter a falsehood; but
there was that in her eyes which warned him of
the uselessness of such an expedient. Yet, to
give up that rose would be like giving up some
part of his being. She repeated the question:
"I ask you if you found it."

"Yes, Miss Annesley."

"Do you still possess it?"

"Yes, Miss."

"And why did you pick it up?"

"It was fresh and beautiful; and I believed
that some lady at the dinner had worn it."

"And so you picked it up? Where did you
find it?"

"Outside the bow-window, Miss."

"When?"

He thought for a moment. "In the morning,
Miss."

"Take care, James; it was not yet eleven
o'clock, at night."

"I admit what I said was not true, Miss. As
you say, it was not yet eleven." James was pale.
So she had thrown it away, confident that this
moment would arrive. This humiliation was pre-

meditated. Patience, he said inwardly; this would be the last opportunity she should have to humiliate him.

"Have you the flower on your person?"

"Yes, Miss."

"Did you know that it was mine?"

He was silent.

"Did you know that it was mine?"—mercilessly.

"Yes; but I believed that you had deliberately thrown it away. I saw no harm in taking it."

"But there *was harm.*"

"I bow to your superior judgment, Miss,"—ironically.

She deemed it wisest to pass over this experimental irony. "Give the flower back to me. It is not proper that a servant should have in his keeping a rose which was once mine, even if I had thrown it away or discarded it."

Carefully he drew forth the crumpled flower. He looked at her, then at the rose, hoping against hope that she might relent. He hesitated till he saw an impatient movement of the extended hand. He surrendered.

"Thank you. That is all. You may go."

She tossed the withered flower into the waste-basket.

"Pardon me, but before I go I have to announce that I shall resign my position next Monday. The money which has been advanced to me, deducting that which is due me, together with the amount of my fine at the police-court, I shall be pleased to return to you on the morning of my departure."

Miss Annesley's lips fell apart, and her brows arched. She was very much surprised.

"You wish to leave my service?"—as if it were quite impossible that such a thing should occur to him.

"Yes, Miss."

"You are dissatisfied with your position?"—icily.

"It is not that, Miss. As a groom I am perfectly satisfied. The trouble lies in the fact that I have too many other things to do. It is very distasteful for me to act in the capacity of butler. My temper is not equable enough for that position." He bowed.

"Very well. I trust that you will not regret your decision." She sat down and coolly resumed her work.

"It is not possible that I shall regret it."

"You may go."

He bowed again, one corner of his mouth twisted. Then he took himself off to the stables. He was certainly in what they call a towering rage.

If I were not a seer of the first degree, a narrator of the penetrative order, I should be vastly puzzled over this singular action on her part.

XXII

When a dramatist submits his *scenario,* he always accompanies it with drawings, crude or otherwise, of the various set-scenes and curtains known as drops. To the uninitiated these scrawls would look impossible; but to the stage-manager's keen, imaginative eye a whole picture is represented in these few pothooks. Each object on the stage is labeled alphabetically; thus A may represent a sofa, B a window, C a table, and so forth and so on. I am not a dramatist; I am not writing an acting drama; so I find that a diagram of the library in Senator Blank's house is neither imperative nor advisable.

It is half after eight; the curtain rises; the music of a violin is heard coming from the music-room; Colonel Annesley is discovered sitting in front of the wood fire, his chin sunk on his breast, his hands hanging listlessly on each side of the chair, his face deeply lined. From time to time he looks at the clock. I can imagine no sorrier picture than that of this loving, tender-hearted, wretched old man as he sits there, waiting for Karloff and the ignominious end. Fortune gone with the winds, poverty leering into his face, shame drawing her red finger across his brow, honor in sackcloth and ashes!

And but two short years ago there had not been in all the wide land a more contented man than himself, a man with a conscience freer. God! Even yet he could hear the rolling, whirring ivory ball as it spun the circle that fatal night at Monte Carlo. Man does not recall the intermediate steps of his fall, only the first step and the last. In his waking hours the colonel always heard the sound of it, and it rattled through his troubled dreams. He could not understand how everything had gone as it had. It seemed impossible that in two years he had dissipated a fortune, sullied his honor, beggared his child. It was all so like a horrible dream. If only he might wake; if only God would be so merciful as to permit him to wake! He hid his face. There is no hell save conscience makes it.

The music laughed and sighed and laughed.

It was the music of love and youth; joyous, rollicking, pulsing music.

The colonel sprang to his feet suddenly, his
hands at his throat. He was suffocating. The
veins gnarled on his neck and brow. There was
in his heart a pain as of many knives. His arms
fell: of what use was it to struggle? He was
caught, trapped in a net of his own contriving.

Softly he crossed the room and stood by the
portière beyond which was the music-room. She
was happy, happy in her youth and ignorance;
she could play all those sprightly measures, her
spirit as light and conscience-free; she could sing,
she could laugh, she could dance. And all the
while his heart was breaking, breaking!

"How shall I face her mother?" he groaned.

The longing which always seizes the guilty to
confess and relieve the mind came over him. If
only he dared rush in there, throw himself at her
feet, and stammer forth his wretched tale! She
was of his flesh, of his blood; when she knew she
would not wholly condemn him . . . No,
no! He could not. She honored and trusted
him now; she had placed him on so high a pedes-
tal that it was utterly impossible for him to disil-

lusion her young mind, to see for ever and ever the mute reproach in her honest eyes, to feel that though his arm encircled her she was beyond his reach. . . . God knew that he could not tell this child of the black gulf he had digged for himself and her.

Sometimes there came to him the thought to put an end to this maddening grief, by violence to period this miserable existence. But always he cast from him the horrible thought. He was not a coward, and the cowardice of suicide was abhorrent to him. Poverty he might leave her, but not the legacy of a suicide. If only it might be God's kindly will to let him die, once this abominable bargain was consummated! Death is the seal of silence; it locks alike the lips of the living and the dead. And she might live in ignorance, till the end of her days, without knowing that her wealth was the price of her father's dishonor.

A mist blurred his sight; he could not see. He steadied himself, and with an effort regained his chair noiselessly. And how often he had smiled at the drama on the stage, with its absurdities, its tawdriness, its impossibilities! Alas, what did they on the stage that was half so weak as he had done: ruined himself without motive or reason!

The bell sang its buzzing note; there was the sound of crunching wheels on the driveway; the music ceased abruptly. Silence. A door opened and closed. A moment or so later Karloff, preceded by the girl, came into the study. She was grave because she remembered Mrs. Chadwick. He was grave also; he had various reasons for being so.

"Father, the count tells me that he has an engagement with you," she said. She wondered if this appointment in any way concerned her.

"It is true, my child. Leave us, and give orders that we are not to be disturbed."

She scrutinized him sharply. How strangely hollow his voice sounded! Was he ill?

"Father, you are not well. Count, you must promise me not to keep him long, however important this interview may be. He is ill and needs rest,"—and her loving eyes caressed each line of care in her parent's furrowed cheeks.

Annesley smiled reassuringly. It took all the strength of his will, all that remained of a high order of courage, to create this smile. He wanted to cry out to her that it was a lie, a mockery. Behind that smile his teeth grated.

"I shall not keep him long, Mademoiselle," said the count. He spoke gently, but he studiously avoided her eyes.

She hesitated for a moment on the threshold; she knew not why. Her lips even formed words, but she did not speak. What was it? Something oppressed her. Her gaze wandered indecisively from her father to the count, from the count to her father.

"When you are through," she finally said, "bring your cigars into the music-room."

"With the greatest pleasure, Mademoiselle," replied the count. "And play, if you so desire; our business is such that your music will be as a pleasure added."

Her father nodded; but he could not force another smile to his lips. The brass rings of the portière rattled, and she was gone. But she left behind a peculiar tableau, a tableau such as is formed by those who stand upon ice which is about to sink and engulf them.

The two men stood perfectly still. I doubt not that each experienced the same sensation, that the same thought occurred to each mind, though it came from different avenues: love and shame. The heart of the little clock on the mantel beat tick-tock, tick-tock; a log crackled and fell between the irons, sending up a shower of evanescent sparks; one of the long windows giving out upon the veranda creaked mysteriously.

Karloff was first to break the spell. He made a gesture which was eloquent of his distaste of the situation.

"Let us terminate this as quickly as possible," he said.

"Yes, let us have done with it before I lose my courage," replied the colonel, his voice thin and quavering. He wiped his forehead with his handkerchief. His hand shone white and his nails darkly blue.

The count stepped over to the table, reached into the inner pocket of his coat, and extracted a packet. In this packet was the enormous sum of one hundred and eighty thousand dollars in notes of one thousand denomination; that is to say, one hundred and eighty slips of paper redeemable in gold by the government which had issued them. On top of this packet lay the colonel's note for twenty thousand dollars.

(It is true that Karloff never accepted money from his government in payment for his services; but it is equally true that for every penny he laid out he was reimbursed by Russia.)

Karloff placed the packet on the table, first taking off the note, which he carelessly tossed beside the bank-notes.

"You will observe that I have not bothered with having your note discounted. I have fulfilled my part of the bargain; fulfil yours." The count thrust his trembling hands into his trousers pockets. He desired to hide this embarrassing sign from his accomplice.

Annesley went to a small safe which stood at the left of the fireplace and returned with a packet somewhat bulkier than the count's. He dropped it beside the money, shudderingly, as though he had touched a poisonous viper.

"My honor," he said simply. "I had never expected to sell it so cheap."

There was a pause, during which neither man's gaze swerved from the other's. There was not the slightest, not even the remotest, fear of treachery; each man knew with whom he was dealing; yet there they stood, as if fascinated.

" I am simply Miss Annesly's servant."—ACT III.

One would have thought that the colonel would
have counted his money, or Karloff his plans;
they did neither. Perhaps the colonel wanted
Karloff to touch the plans first, before he touched
the money; perhaps Karloff had the same desire,
only the other way around.

The colonel spoke.

"I believe that is all," he said quietly. The
knowledge that the deed was done and that there
was no retreat gave back to him a particle of his
former coolness and strength of mind. It had
been the thought of committing the crime that
had unnerved him. Now that his bridges were
burned, a strange, unnatural calm settled on him.

The count evidently was not done. He moistened his lips. There was a dryness in his throat.

"It is not too late," he said; "I have not yet
touched them."

"We shall not indulge in moralizing, if you
please," interrupted the colonel, with savage
irony. "The moment for that has gone by."

"Very well." Karloff's shoulders settled; his
jaws became aggressively angular; some spirit
of his predatory forebears touched his face here
and there, hardening it. "I wish to speak in regard to your daughter."

"Enough! Take my honor and be gone!" The colonel's voice was loud and rasping.

Karloff rested his hands on the table and inclined his body toward the colonel.

"Listen to me," he began. "There is in every man the making and the capacity of a great rascal. Time and opportunity alone are needed —and a motive. The other night I told you that I could not give up your daughter. Well, I have not given her up. She must be my wife."

"Must?" The colonel clenched his hands.

"Must. To-night I am going to prove myself a great rascal—with a great motive. What is Russia to me? Nothing. What is your dishonor or my own? Less than nothing. There is only one thing, and that is my love for your daughter." He struck the table and the flame of the student-lamp rose violently. "She must be mine, mine! I have tried to win her as an honorable man tries to win the woman he loves; now she must be won by an act of rascality. Heaven nor hell shall force me to give her up. Yes, I love her; and I lower myself to your level to gain her."

"To my level! Take care; I am still a man, with a man's strength," cried the colonel.

Karloff swept his hand across his forehead. "I have lied to myself long enough, and to you. I can see now that I have been working solely toward one end. My country is not to be considered, neither is yours. Do you realize that you stand wholly and completely in my power?" He ran his tongue across his lips, which burned with fever.

"What do you mean?"—hoarsely.

"I mean, your daughter must become my wife, or I shall notify your government that you have attempted to betray it."

"You dishonorable wretch!" The colonel balled his fists and protruded his nether lip. Only the table stood between them.

"That term or another, it does not matter. The fact remains that you have sold to me the fortification plans of your country; and though it be in times of peace, you are none the less guilty and culpable. Your daughter shall be my wife."

"I had rather strangle her with these hands!" —passionately.

"Well, why should I not have her for my wife? Who loves her more than I? I am rich; from hour to hour, from day to day, what shall I not

plan to make her happy? I love her with all the
fire and violence of my race and blood. I can not
help it. I will not, can not, live without her!
Good God, yes! I recognize the villainy of my
actions. But I am mad to-night."

"So I perceive." The colonel gazed wildly
about the walls for a weapon. There was not
even the usual ornamental dagger.

A window again stirred mysteriously. A few
drops of rain plashed on the glass and zigzagged
down to the sash.

"Sooner or later your daughter must know.
Request her presence. It rests with her, not with
you, as to what course I must follow." Karloff
was extraordinarily pale, and his dark eyes, re-
flecting the dancing flames, sparkled like rubies.

He saw the birth of horror in the elder's eyes,
saw it grow and grow. He saw the colonel's
lips move spasmodically, but utter no sound.
What was it he saw over his (the count's) shoulders and beyond? Instinctively he turned, and
what he saw chilled the heat of his blood.

There stood the girl, her white dress marble-
white against the dark wine of the portière, an
edge of which one hand clutched convulsively.
Was it Medusa's beauty or her magic that turned

men into stone? My recollection is at fault. At any rate, so long as she remained motionless, neither man had the power to stir. She held herself perfectly erect; every fiber in her young body was tense. Her beauty became weirdly powerful, masked as it was with horror, doubt, shame, and reproach. She had heard; little or much was of no consequence. In the heat of their variant passions, the men's voices had risen to a pitch that penetrated beyond the room.

Karloff was first to recover, and he took an involuntary step toward her; but she waved him back disdainfully.

"Do not come near me. I loathe you!" The voice was low, but every note was strained and unmusical.

He winced. His face could not have stung or burned more hotly had she struck him with her hand.

"Mademoiselle!"

She ignored him. "Father, what does this mean?"

"Agony!" The colonel fell back into his chair, pressing his hands over his eyes.

"I will tell you what it means!" cried Karloff, a rage possessing him. He had made a mistake.

He had misjudged both the father and the child. He could force her into his arms, but he would always carry a burden of hate. "It means that this night you stand in the presence of a dishonored parent, a man who has squandered your inheritance over gambling tables, and who, to recover these misused sums, has sold to me the principal fortification plans of his country. That is what it means, Mademoiselle."

She grasped the portière for support.

"Father, is this thing true?" Her voice fell to a terror-stricken whisper.

"Oh, it is true enough," said Karloff. "God knows that it is true enough. But it rests with you to save him. Become my wife, and yonder fire shall swallow his dishonor—and mine. Refuse, and I shall expose him. After all, love is a primitive state, and with it we go back to the beginning; before it honor or dishonor is nothing. To-night there is nothing, nothing in the world save my love for you, and the chance that has given me the power to force you to be mine. What a fury and a tempest love produces! It makes an honorable man of the knave, a rascal of the man of honor; it has toppled thrones, destroyed nations, obliterated races.

ʙ ∴ ∴ Well, I have become a rascal. Mademoiselle, you must become my wife." He lifted his handsome head resolutely.

Without giving him so much as a glance, she swept past him and sank on her knees at her father's side, taking his hands by the wrists and pressing them down from his face.

"Father, tell him he lies! Tell him he lies!" Ah, the entreaty, the love, the anxiety, the terror that blended her tones!

He strove to look away.

"Father, you are all I have," she cried brokenly. "Look at me! Look at me and tell him that he lies! . . . You will not look at me? God have mercy on me, it is true, then!" She rose and spread her arms toward heaven to entreat God to witness her despair. "I did not think or know that such base things were done. . . . That these loving hands should have helped to encompass my father's dishonor, his degradation! . . . For money! What is money? You knew, father, that what was mine was likewise yours. Why did you not tell me? I should have laughed; we should have begun all over again; I could have earned a living with my music; we should have been honest and happy. And now! . . . And I drew those plans with a heart full of love and happiness! Oh, it is not that you gambled, that you have foolishly wasted a fortune; it is not these that hurt here,"—pressing her heart. "It is the knowledge that you, my father, should let *me* draw those horrible things. It hurts! Ah, how it hurts!" A sob choked her. She knelt again at her parent's side and flung her arms around the unhappy, wretched man. "Father, you have committed a crime to shield a foolish act. I know, I know! What you have done you did for my sake, to give me back what you thought was my own. Oh, how well I know that you had no thought of yourself; it was all for me, and I thank God for that. But something has died here, something here in my heart. I have been so happy! . . . too happy! My poor father!" She laid her head against his breast.

"My heart is broken! Would to God that I might die!" Annesley threw one arm across the back of the chair and turned his face to his sleeve.

Karloff, a thousand arrows of regret and shame and pity quivering in his heart, viewed the scene moodily, doggedly. No, he could not go back; there was indeed a wall behind him: pride.

"Well, Mademoiselle?"

She turned, still on her knees.

"You say that if I do not marry you, you will ruin my father, expose him?"

"Yes,"—thinly.

"Listen. I am a proud woman, yet will I beg you not to do this horrible thing—force me into your arms. Take everything, take all that is left; you can not be so utterly base as to threaten such a wrong. See!"—extending her lovely arms, "I am on my knees to you!"

"My daughter!" cried the father.

"Do not interrupt me, father; he will relent; he is not wholly without pity."

"No, no! No, no!" Karloff exclaimed, turning his head aside and repelling with his hands, as if he would stamp out the fires of pity which, at the sound of her voice, had burst anew in his heart. "I *will* not give you up!"

She drew her sleeve across her eyes and stood up. All at once she wheeled upon him like a lioness protecting its young. In her wrath she was as magnificent as the wife of Æneas at the funeral pyre of that great captain.

"She knew! That was why she asked me all those questions; that is why she exacted those promises! Mrs. Chadwick knew and dared not tell me! And I trusted you as a friend, as a gentleman, as a man of honor!" Her laughter rang out wildly. "And for these favors you bring dishonor! Shame! Shame! Your wife? Have you thought well of what you are about to do?"

"So well," he declared, "that I shall proceed to the end, to the very end." How beautiful she was! And a mad desire urged him to spring to her, crush her in his arms, and force upon her lips a thousand mad kisses!

"Have you weighed well the consequences?"

"Upon love's most delicate scales."

"Have you calculated what manner of woman I am?"—with subdued fierceness.

"To me you are the woman of all women."

"Do you think that I am a faint-hearted girl? You are making a mistake. I am a woman with a woman's mind, and a thousand years would not alter my utter contempt of you. Force me to marry you, and as there is a God above us to witness, every moment of suffering you now inflict upon me and mine, I shall give back a day, a long, bitter, galling day. Do you think that it will be wise to call me countess?" Her scorn was superb.

"I am waiting for your answer. Will you be my wife, or shall I be forced to make my villainy definitive?"

"Permit me to take upon these shoulders the burden of answering that question," said a voice from the window.

Warburton, dressed in his stable clothes and leggings, hatless and drenched with rain, stepped into the room from the veranda and quickly crossed the intervening space. Before any one of the tragic group could recover from the surprise caused by his unexpected appearance, he had picked up the packet of plans and had dropped it into the fire. Then he leaned with his back against the mantel and faced them, or rather Karloff, of whom he was not quite sure.

XXIII

Tick-tock, tick-tock went the voice of the little
friend of eternity on the mantel-piece; the waxen
sheets (to which so much care and labor had been
given) writhed and unfolded, curled and crackled, and blackened on the logs; the cold wind
and rain blew in through the opened window;
the lamp flared and flickered inside its green
shade; a legion of heroes peered out from the
book-cases, no doubt much astonished at the
sight of this ordinary hero of mine and his mean,
ordinary clothes. I have in my mind's eye the
picture of good D'Artagnan's frank contempt,
Athos' magnificent disdain, the righteous (I had
almost said honest!) horror of the ultra-fashion-
able Aramis, and the supercilious indignation of
the bourgeois Porthos. What! this a hero?
Where, then, was his rapier, his glittering bal-
dric, his laces, his dancing plumes, his fine air?
Several times in the course of this narrative

318

I have expressed my regret in not being an active witness of this or that scene, a regret which, as I am drawing most of these pictures from hearsay, is perfectly natural. What must have been the varying expressions on each face! Warburton, who, though there was tumult in his breast, coolly waited for Karloff to make the next move; Annesley, who saw his terrible secret in the possession of a man whom he supposed to be a stable-man; Karloff, who saw his house of cards vanish in the dartling tongues of flame, and recognized the futility of his villainy; the girl . . . Ah, who shall describe the dozen shadowy emotions which crossed and recrossed her face?

From Warburton's dramatic entrance upon the scene to Karloff's first movement, scarce a minute had passed, though to the girl and her father an eternity seemed to come and go. Karloff was a brave man. Upon the instant of his recovery, he sprang toward Warburton, silently and with predetermination: he must regain some fragment of those plans. He would not, could not, suffer total defeat before this girl's eyes; his blood rebelled against the thought. He expected the groom to strike him, but James simply caught him by the arms and thrust him back.

"No, Count; no, no; they shall burn to the
veriest crisp!"

"Stand aside, lackey!" cried Karloff, a sob of
rage strangling him. Again he rushed upon
Warburton, his clenched hand uplifted. Warburton did not even raise his hands this time.
So they stood, their faces within a hand's span
of each other, the one smiling coldly, the other
in the attitude of striking a blow. Karloff's hand
fell unexpectedly, but not on the man in front of
him. "Good God, no! a gentleman does not
strike a lackey! Stand aside, stand aside!"

"They shall burn, Count,"—quietly; "they
shall burn, because I am physically the stronger."
Warburton turned quickly and with the toe of
his boot shifted the glowing packet and renewed
the flames. "I never realized till to-night that I
loved my country half so well. Lackey? Yes,
for the present."

He had not yet looked at the girl.

"Ah!" Karloff cried, intelligence lighting his
face. "You are no lackey!"—subduing his voice.

James smiled. "You are quite remarkable."

"Who are you? I demand to know!"

"First and foremost, I am a citizen of the
United States; I have been a soldier besides. It

was my common right to destroy these plans, which indirectly menaced my country's safety. These,"—pointing to the bank-notes, "are yours, I believe. Nothing further requires your presence here."

"Yes, yes; I remember now! Fool that I have been!" Karloff struck his forehead in helpless rage. "I never observed you closely till now. I recall. The secret service: Europe, New York, Washington; you have known it all along. Spy!"

"That is an epithet which easily rebounds. Spy? Why, yes; I do for my country what you do for yours."

"The name, the name! I can not recollect the name! The beard is gone, but that does not matter,"—excitedly.

Warburton breathed easier. While he did not want the girl to know who he was just then, he was glad that Karloff's memory had taken his thought away from the grate and its valuable but rapidly disappearing fuel.

"Father! Father, what is it?" cried the girl, her voice keyed to agony. "Father!"

The two men turned about. Annesley had fainted in his chair. Both Warburton and Karloff mechanically started forward to offer aid, but she repelled their approach.

"Do not come near me; you have done enough. Father, dear!" She slapped the colonel's wrists and unloosed his collar.

The antagonists, forgetting their own battle, stood silently watching hers. Warburton's mind was first to clear, and without a moment's hesitation he darted from the room and immediately returned with a glass of water. He held it out to the girl. Their glances clashed; a thousand mute, angry questions in her eyes, a thousand mute, humble answers in his. She accepted the glass, and her hand trembled as she dipped her fingers into the cool depths and flecked the drops into the unconscious man's face.

Meanwhile Karloff stood with folded arms, staring melancholically into the grate, where his dreams had disappeared in smoke.

By and by the colonel sighed and opened his eyes. For a time he did not know where he was, and his gaze wandered mistily from face to face. Then recollection came back to him, recollection bristling with thorns. He struggled to his feet and faced Warburton. The girl put her arms around him to steady him, but he gently disengaged himself.

"Are you from the secret service, sir? If so, I am ready to accompany you wherever you say. I, who have left my blood on many a battleground, was about to commit a treasonable act. Allow me first to straighten up my affairs, then you may do with me as you please. I am guilty of a crime; I have the courage to pay the penalty." His calm was extraordinary, and even Karloff looked at him with a sparkle of admiration.

As a plummet plunges into the sea, so the girl's look plunged into Warburton's soul; and had he been an officer of the law, he knew that he would have utterly disregarded his duty.

"I am not a secret service man, sir," he replied unevenly. "If I were,"—pointing to the grate, "your plans would not have fed the fire."

"Who are you, then, and what do you in my house in this guise?"—proudly.

"I am your head stable-man—for the present. It was all by chance. I came into this room yesterday to get a book on veterinary surgery. I accidentally saw a plan. I have been a soldier. I knew that such a thing had no rightful place in this house. . . . I was coming across the lawn, when I looked into the window. . . . It is not for me to judge you, sir. My duty lay in destroying those plans before they harmed any one."

"No, it is not for you to judge me," said the colonel. "I have gambled away my daughter's fortune. To keep her in ignorance of the fact and to return to her the amount I had wrongfully used, I consented to sell to Russia the coast fortification plans of my country, such as I could draw from memory. No, it is not for you to judge me; only God has the right to do that."

"I am only a groom," said Warburton, simply. "What I have heard I shall forget."

Ah, had he but looked at the girl's face then!

A change came over Karloff's countenance; his shoulders drooped; the melancholy fire died out of his face and eyes. With an air of resignation and a clear sense of the proportion of things, he reached out and took up the note upon which Annesley had scrawled his signature.

Warburton, always alert, seized the count's wrist. He saw the name of a bank and the sum of five figures.

"What is this?" he demanded.

"It is mine," replied the count, haughtily. Warburton released him.

"He speaks truly," said the colonel. "It is his."

"The hour of madness is past," the Russian began, slowly and musically. The tone was musing. He seemed oblivious of his surroundings and that three pairs of curious eyes were leveled in his direction. He studied the note, creased it, drew it through his fingers, smoothed it and caressed it. "And I should have done exactly as I threatened. There is, then, a Providence which watches jealously over the innocent? And I was a skeptic! . . . Two hundred thousand dollars,"—picking up the packet of banknotes and balancing it on his hand. "Well, it is a sum large enough to tempt any man. How the plans and schemes of men crumble to the touch! Ambition is but the pursuit of mirages. : . . Mademoiselle, you will never know what the ignominy of this moment has cost me—nor how well I love you. I come of a race of men who pursue their heart's desire through fire and water. Obstacles are nothing; the end is everything. In Europe I should have won, in honor or in dishonor. But this American people, I do not quite understand them; and that is why I have played the villain to no purpose."

He paused, and a sad, bitter smile played over his face.

"Mademoiselle," he continued, "henceforth, wherever I may go, your face and the sound of your voice shall abide with me. I do not ask you to forget, but I ask you to forgive." Again he paused.

She uttered no sound.

"Well, one does not forget nor forgive these things in so short a time. And, after all, it was your own father's folly. Fate threw him across my path at a critical moment—but I had reckoned without you. Your father is a brave man, for he had the courage to offer himself to the law; I have the courage to give you up. I, too, am a soldier; I recognize the value of retreat." To Warburton he said: "A groom, a hostler, to upset such plans as these! I do not know who you are, sir, nor how to account for your timely and peculiar appearance. But I fully recognize the falseness of your presence here. Eh, well, this is what comes of race prejudice, the senseless battle which has always been and always will be waged between the noble and the peasant. Had I observed you at the proper time, our positions might relatively have been changed. Useless retrospection!" To Arnesley: "Sir, we are equally culpable. Here is this note of yours. I might, as a small contribution toward righting the comparative wrong which I have done you, I might cast it into the fire. But between gentlemen, situated as we are, the act would be as useless as it would be impossible. I might destroy the note, but you would refuse to accept such generosity at my hands,—which is well."

"What you say is perfectly true." The colonel drew his daughter closer to him.

"So," went on the count, putting the note in his pocket, "to-morrow I shall have my ducats."

"My bank will discount the note," said the colonel, with a proud look; "my indebtedness shall be paid in full."

"As I have not the slightest doubt. Mademoiselle, fortune ignores you but temporarily; misfortune has brushed only the hem of your garment, as it were. Do not let the fear of poverty alarm you,"—lightly. "I prophesy a great public future for you. And when you play that *Largo* of Handel's, to a breathless audience, who knows that I may not be hidden behind the curtain of some stall, drinking in the heavenly sound made by that loving bow? . . . . Romance enters every human being's life; like love and hate, it is primitive. But to every book fate writes *finis*."

He thrust the bank-notes carelessly into his coat pocket, and walked slowly toward the hallway. At the threshold he stopped and looked back. The girl could not resist the magnetism of his dark eyes. She was momentarily fascinated, and her heart beat painfully.

"If only I might go with the memory of your forgiveness," he said.

"I forgive you."

"Thank you." Then Karloff resolutely proceeded; the portière fell behind him. Shortly after she heard the sound of closing doors, the rattle of a carriage, and then all became still. Thus the handsome barbarian passed from the scene.

The colonel resumed his chair, his arm propped on a knee and his head bowed in his hand. Quickly the girl fell to her knees, hid her face on his breast, and regardless of the groom's presence, silently wept.

"My poor child!" faltered the colonel. "God could not have intended to give you so wretched a father. Poverty and dishonor, poverty and dishonor; I who love you so well have brought you these!"

Warburton, biting his trembling lips, tiptoed cautiously to the window, opened it and stepped outside. He raised his fevered face gratefully to the icy rain. A great and noble plan had come to him.

As Mrs. Chadwick said, love is magnificent only when it gives all without question.

XXIV

A FINE LOVER

Karloff remained in seclusion till the following Tuesday; after that day he was seen no more
in Washington. From time to time some news
of him filters through the diplomatic circles of
half a dozen capitals to Washington. The latest
I heard of him, he was at Port Arthur. It was
evident that Russia valued his personal address
too highly to exile him because of his failure in
Washington. Had he threatened or gone about
noisily, we should all have forgotten him completely. As it is, the memory of him to-day is
as vivid as his actual presence. Thus, I give him
what dramatists call an agreeable exit.

I was in the Baltimore and Potomac station
the morning after that unforgetable night at
Senator Blank's house. I had gone there to see
about the departure of night trains, preparatory
to making a flying trip to New York, and was
leaving the station when a gloved hand touched
me on the arm. The hand belonged to Mrs.

Chadwick. She was dressed in the conventional traveling gray, and but for the dark lines under her eyes she would have made a picture for any man to admire. She looked tired, very tired, as women look who have not slept well.

"Good morning, Mr. Orator," she said, saluting me with a smile.

"You are going away?" I asked, shaking her hand cordially.

"'Way, 'way, away! I am leaving for Nice, where I expect to spend the winter. I had intended to remain in Washington till the holidays; but I plead guilty to a roving disposition, and I frequently change my mind."

"Woman's most charming prerogative," said I, gallantly.

What a mask the human countenance is! How little I dreamed that I was jesting with a woman whose heart was breaking, and numbed with a terrible pain!

Her maid came up to announce that everything was ready for her reception in the state-room, and that the train was about to draw out of the station. Mrs. Chadwick and I bade each other good-by. Two years passed before I saw her again.

At eleven o'clock I returned to my rooms to pack a case and have the thing off my mind. Tramping restlessly up and down before my bachelor apartment house I discerned M'sieu Zhames. His face was pale and troubled, but the angle of his jaw told me that he had determined upon something or other.

"Ha!" I said railingly. He wore a decently respectable suit of ready-made clothes. "Lost your job and want me to give you a recommendation?"

"I want a few words with you, Chuck, and no fooling. Don't say that you can't spare the time. You've simply *got* to."

"With whom am I to talk, James, the groom, or Warburton, the gentleman?"

"You are to talk with the man whose sister you are to marry."

I became curious, naturally. "No police affair?"

"No, it's not the police. I can very well go to a lawyer, but I desire absolute secrecy. Let us go up to your rooms at once."

I led the way. I was beginning to desire to know what all this meant.

"Has anybody recognized you?" I asked, unlocking the door to my apartment.

"No; and I shouldn't care a hang if they had."

"Oho!"

Warburton flung himself into a chair and lighted a cigar. He puffed it rapidly, while I got together my shaving and toilet sets.

"Start her up," said I.

"Chuck, when my father died he left nearly a quarter of a million in five per cents; that is to say, Jack, Nancy and I were given a yearly income of about forty-five hundred. Nancy's portion and mine are still in bonds which do not mature till 1900. Jack has made several bad investments, and about half of his is gone; but his wife has plenty, so his losses do not trouble him. Now, I have been rather frugal during the past seven years. I have lived entirely upon my Army pay. I must have something like twenty-five thousand lying in the bank in New York. On Monday, between three and four o'clock, Colonel Annesley will become practically a beggar, a pauper."

"What?" My shaving-mug slipped from my hand and crashed to the floor, where it lay in a hundred pieces.

"Yes. He and his daughter will not have a roof of their own: all gone, every stick and stone. Don't ask me any questions; only do as I ask of you." He took out his check-book and filled out two blanks. These he handed to me. "The large one I want you to place in the Union bank, to the credit of Colonel Annesley."

I looked at the check. "Twenty thousand dollars?" I gasped.

"The Union bank has this day discounted the colonel's note. It falls due on Monday. In order to meet it, he will have to sell what is left of the Virginian estate and his fine horses. The interest will be inconsiderable."

"What—" I began, but he interrupted me.

"I shall not answer a single question. The check for three thousand is for the purchase of the horses, which will be put on sale Saturday morning. They are easily worth this amount. Through whatever agency you please, buy these horses for me, but not in my name. As for the note, cash my check first and present the currency for the note. No one will know anything about it then. You can not trace money."

"Good Lord, Bob, you are crazy! You are giving away a fortune," I remonstrated.

"It is my own, and my capital remains un-touched."

"Have you told her that you love her? Does she know who you are?" I was very much ex-cited.

"No,"—sadly, "I haven't told her that I love her. She does not know who I am. What is more, I never want her to know. I have thrown my arms roughly around her, thinking her to be Nancy, and have kissed her. Some reparation is due her. On Monday I shall pack up quietly and return to the West."

"Annesley beggared? What in heaven's name does this all mean?" I was confounded.

"Some day, Chuck, when you have entered the family properly as my sister's husband, perhaps I may confide in you. At present the secret isn't mine. Let it suffice that through peculiar cir-cumstances, the father of the girl I love is ruined. I am not doing this for any theatrical play, grati-tude and all that rot,"—with half a smile. "I admire and respect Colonel Annesley; I love his daughter, hopelessly enough. I have never been of much use to any one. Other persons' troubles never worried me to any extent; I was happy-go-lucky, careless and thoughtless. True, I never passed a beggar without dropping a coin into his cup. But often this act was the result of a good dinner and a special vintage. The twenty thousand will keep the colonel's home, the house his child was born in and her mother before her. I am doing this crazy thing, as you call it, because it is going to make me rather happy. I shall disappear Monday. They may or they may not suspect who has come to their aid. They may even trace the thing to you; but you will be honor-bound to reveal nothing. When you have taken up the note, mail it to Annesley. You will find Count Karloff's name on it."

"Karloff?" I was in utter darkness.

"Yes. Annesley borrowed twenty thousand of him on a three months' note. Both men are well known at the Union bank, Karloff having a temporary large deposit there, and Annesley always having done his banking at the same place. Karloff, for reasons which I can not tell you, did not turn in the note till this morning. You will take it up this afternoon."

"Annesley, whom I believed to be a millionaire, penniless; Karloff one of his creditors? Bob, I do not think that you are treating me fairly. I can't go into this thing blind."

"If you will not do it under these conditions,
I shall have to find some one who will,"—resolutely.

I looked at the checks and then at him. . . .
Twenty-three thousand dollars! It was more
than I ever before held in my hand at one time.
And he was giving it away as carelessly as I
should have given away a dime. Then the big-
ness of the act, the absolute disinterestedness of
it, came to me suddenly.

"Bob, you are the finest lover in all the world!
And if Miss Annesley ever knows who you are,
she isn't a woman if she does not fall immediately in love with you." I slapped him on the
shoulder. I was something of a lover myself,
and I could understand.

"She will never know. I don't want her to
know. That is why I am going away. I want
to do a good deed, and be left in the dark to en-
joy it. That is all. After doing this, I could
never look her in the eyes as Robert Warburton.
I shall dine with the folks on Sunday. I shall
confess all only to Nancy, who has always been
the only confidante I have ever had among the
women."

There was a pause. I could bring no words

to my lips. Finally I stammered out: "Nancy knows. I told her everything last night. I broke my word with you, Bob, but I could not help it. She was crying again over what she thinks to be your heartlessness. I *had* to tell her."

"What did she say?"—rising abruptly.

"She laughed, and I do not know when I have seen her look so happy. There'll be a double wedding yet, my boy." I was full of enthusiasm.

"I wish I could believe you, Chuck; I wish I could. I'm rather glad you told Nan. I love her, and I don't want her to worry about me." He gripped my hand. "You will do just as I ask?"

"To the very letter. Will you have a little Scotch to perk you up a bit? You look rather seedy."

"No,"—smiling dryly. "If she smelt liquor on my breath I should lose my position. Goodby, then, till Sunday."

I did not go to New York that night. I forgot all about going. Instead, I went to Nancy, to whom I still go whenever I am in trouble or in doubt.

XXV

Friday morning.

Miss Annesley possessed more than the ordinary amount of force and power of will. Though the knowledge of it was not patent to her, she was a philosopher. She always submitted gracefully to the inevitable. She was religious, too, feeling assured that God would provide. She did not go about the house, moaning and weeping; she simply studied all sides of the calamity, and looked around to see what could be saved. There were moments when she was even cheerful. There were no new lines in her face; her eyes were bright and eager. All persons of genuine talent look the world confidently in the face; they know exactly what they can accomplish. As Karloff had advised her, she did not trouble herself about the future. Her violin would support her and her father, perhaps in comfortable circumstances. The knowledge of this gave her a

339

silent happiness, that kind which leaves upon the face a serene and beautiful calm.

At this moment she stood on the veranda, her hand shading her eyes. She was studying the sky. The afternoon would be clear; the last ride should be a memorable one. The last ride! Tears blurred her eyes and there was a smothering sensation in her throat. The last ride! After to-day Jane would have a new, strange mistress. If only she might go to this possible mistress and tell her how much she loved the animal, to obtain from her the promise that she would be kind to it always. How mysteriously the human heart spreads its tendrils around the objects of its love! What is there in the loving of a dog or a horse that, losing one or the other, an emptiness is created? Perhaps it is because the heart goes out wholly without distrust to the faithful, to the undeceiving, to the dumb but loving beast, which, for all its strength, is so helpless.

She dropped her hand and spoke to James, who was waiting near by for her orders.

"James, you will have Pierre fill a saddle-hamper; two plates, two knives and forks, and so forth. We shall ride in the north country this

afternoon. It will be your last ride. To-morrow the horses will be sold." How bravely she
said it!

"Yes, Miss Annesley." Whom were they going to meet in the north country? "At what hour
shall I bring the horses around?"

"At three."

She entered the house and directed her steps
to the study. She found her father arranging the
morning's mail. She drew up a chair beside him,
and ran through her own letters. An invitation
to lunch with Mrs. Secretary-of-State; she
tossed it into the waste-basket. A dinner-dance
at the Country Club, a ball at the Brazilian lega-
tion, a tea at the German embassy, a box party
at some coming play, an informal dinner at the
executive mansion; one by one they fluttered into
the basket. A bill for winter furs, a bill from the
dressmaker, one from the milliner, one from the
glover, and one from the florist; these she laid
aside, reckoning their sum-total, and frowning.
How could she have been so extravagant? She
chanced to look at her father. He was staring
rather stupidly at a slip of paper which he held
in his trembling fingers.

"What is it?" she asked, vaguely troubled.

"I do not understand," he said, extending the paper for her inspection.

Neither did she at first.

"Karloff has not done this," went on her father, "for it shows that he has had it discounted at the bank. It is canceled; it is paid. I did not have twenty thousand in the bank; I did not have even a quarter of that amount to my credit. There has been some mistake. Our real estate agent expects to realize on the home not earlier than Monday morning. In case it was not sold then, he was to take up the note personally. This is not his work, or I should have been notified." Then, with a burst of grief: "Betty, my poor Betty! How can you forgive me? How can I forgive myself?"

"Father, I am brave. Let us forget. It will be better so."

She kissed his hand and drew it lovingly across her cheek. Then she rose and moved toward the light. She studied the note carefully. There was nothing on it save Karloff's writing and her father's and the red imprint of the bank's cancelation. Out of the window and beyond she saw James leading the horses to the watering trough.

Her face suddenly grew crimson with shame, and as suddenly as it came the color faded. She folded the note and absently tucked it into the bosom of her dress. Then, as if struck by some strange thought, her figure grew tense and rigid against the blue background of the sky. The glow which stole over her features this time had no shame in it, and her eyes shone like the waters of sunlit seas. It must never be; no it must never be.

"We shall make inquiries at the bank," she said. "And do not be downcast, father, the worst is over. What mistakes you have made are forgotten. The future looks bright to me."

"Through innocent young eyes the future is ever bright; but as we age we find most of the sunshine on either side, and we stand in the shadow between. Brave heart, I glory in your courage. God will provide for you; He will not let my shadow fall on you. Yours shall be the joy of living, mine shall be the pain. God bless you! I wonder how I shall ever meet your mother's accusing eyes?"

"Father, you *must* not dwell upon this any longer; for my sake you must not. When everything is paid there will be a little left, enough till

I and my violin find something to do. After all,
the world's applause must be a fine thing. I can
even now see the criticisms in the great newspapers. 'A former young society woman, well-
known in the fashionable circles of Washington,
made her *début* as a concert player last night.
She is a stunning young person.' 'A young queen
of the diplomatic circles, here and abroad, appeared in public as a violinist last night. She is
a member of the most exclusive sets, and society
was out to do her homage.' 'One of Washington's brilliant young horsewomen,' and so forth.
Away down at the bottom of the column, somewhere, they will add that I play the violin rather
well for an amateur." In all her trial, this was
the one bitter expression, and she was sorry for
it the moment it escaped her.

Happily her father was not listening. He was
wholly absorbed in the mystery of the canceled
note.

She had mounted Jane and was gathering up
the reins, while James strapped on the saddle-
hamper. This done, he climbed into the saddle
and signified by touching his cap that all was
ready. So they rode forth in the sweet fresh-

ness of that November afternoon. A steady wind was blowing, the compact white clouds sailed swiftly across the brilliant heavens, the leaves whispered and fluttered, hither and thither, wherever the wind listed; it was the day of days. It was the last ride, and fate owed them the compensation of a beautiful afternoon.

The last ride! Warburton's mouth drooped. Never again to ride with her! How the thought tightened his heart! What a tug it was going to be to give her up! But so it must be. He could never face her gratitude. He must disappear, like the good fairies in the story-books. If he left now, and she found out what he had done, she would always think kindly of him, even tenderly. At twilight, when she took out her violin and played soft measures, perhaps a thought or two would be given to him. After what had happened—this contemptible masquerading and the crisis through which her father had just passed —it would be impossible for her to love him. She would always regard him with suspicion, as a witness of her innocent shame.

He recalled the two wooden plates in the hamper. Whom was she going to meet? Ah, well, what mattered it? After to-day the abyss of eternity would yawn between them. How he loved her! How he adored the exquisite profile, the warm-tinted skin, the shining hair! . . . And he had lost her! Ah, that last ride!

The girl was holding her head high because her heart was full. No more to ride on a bright morning, with the wind rushing past her, bringing the odor of the grasses, of the flowers, of the earth to tingle her nostrils; no more to follow the hounds on a winter's day, with the pack baying beyond the hedges, the gay, red-coated riders sweeping down the field; no more to wander through the halls of her mother's birthplace and her own! Like a breath on a mirror, all was gone. Why? What had *she* done to be flung down ruthlessly? She, who had been brought up in idleness and luxury, must turn her hands to a living! Without being worldly, she knew the world. Once she appeared upon the stage, she would lose caste among her kind. True, they would tolerate her, but no longer would her voice be heard or her word have weight.

Soon she would be tossed about on the whirlpool and swallowed up. Then would come the haggling with managers, long and tiresome journeys, gloomy hotels and indifferent fare, curious

"Go home, Colonel—and stay home !"—ACT III.

people who desired to see the one-time fashionable belle; her portraits would be lithographed and hung in shop-windows, in questionable resorts, and the privacy so loved by gentlewomen gone; and perhaps there would be insults. And she was only on the threshold of the twenties, the radiant, blooming twenties!

During the long ride (for they covered something like seven miles) not a word was spoken. The girl was biding her time; the man had nothing to voice. They were going through the woods, when they came upon a clearing through which a narrow brook loitered or sallied down the incline. She reined in and raised her crop. He was puzzled. So far as he could see, he and the girl were alone. The third person, for whom, he reasoned, he had brought the second plate, was nowhere in sight.

A flat boulder lay at the side of the stream, and she nodded toward it. Warburton emptied the hamper and spread the cloth on the stone. Then he laid out the salad, the sandwiches, the olives, the almonds, and two silver telescope-cups. All this time not a single word from either; Warburton, busied with his task, did not lift his eyes to her.

The girl had laid her face against Jane's nose, and two lonely tears trailed slowly down her velvety cheeks. Presently he was compelled to look at her and speak.

"Everything is ready, Miss." He spoke huskily. The sight of her tears gave him an indescribable agony.

She dropped the bridle-reins, brushed her eyes, and the sunshine of a smile broke through the troubled clouds.

"Mr. Warburton," she said gently, "let us not play any more. I am too sad. Let us hang up the masks, for the comedy is done."

XXVI

THE CASTLE OF ROMANCE

How silent the forest was! The brook no longer murmured, the rustle of the leaves was without sound. A spar of sunshine, filtering through the ragged limbs of the trees, fell aslant her, and she stood in an aureola. As for my hero, a species of paralysis had stricken him motionless and dumb. It was all so unexpected, all so sudden, that he had the sensation of being whirled away from reality and bundled unceremoniously into the unreal. . . . She knew, and had known! A leaf brushed his face, but he was senseless to the touch of it. All he had the power to do was to stare at her. . . . She knew, and had known!

Dick stepped into the brook and began to paw the water, and the intermission of speech and action came to an end.

"You—and you knew?" What a strange sound his voice had in his own ears!

349

"Yes. From the very beginning I knew you to be a gentleman in masquerade; that is to say, when I saw you in the police-court. The absence of the beard confused me at first, but presently I recognized the gentleman whom I had noticed on board the ship."

So she had noticed him!

"That night you believed me to be your sister Nancy. But I did not know this till lately. And the night I visited her she exhibited some photographs. Among these was a portrait of you without a beard."

Warburton started. And the thought that this might be the case had never trickled through his thick skull! How she must have laughed at him secretly!

She continued: "Even then I was not sure. But when Colonel Raleigh declared that you resembled a former lieutenant of his, then I knew." She ceased. She turned to her horse as if to gather the courage to go on; but Jane had her nose hidden in the stream, and was oblivious of her mistress' need.

He waited dully for her to resume, for he supposed that she had not yet done.

"I have humiliated you in a hundred ways,

and for this I want you to forgive me. I sent
the butler away for the very purpose of making
you serve in his stead. But you were so good
about it all, with never a murmur of rebellion,
that I grew ashamed of my part in the comedy.
But now—" Her eyes closed and her body
swayed; but she clenched her hands, and the
faintness passed away. "But for you, my poor
father would have been dishonored, and I should
have been forced into the arms of a man whom I
despise. Whenever I have humiliated you, you
have returned the gift of a kind deed. You will
forgive me?"

"Forgive you? There is nothing for me to
forgive on my side, much on yours. It is you
who should forgive me. What you have done I
have deserved." His tongue was thick and dry.
How much did she know?

"No, not wholly deserved it." She fumbled
with the buttons of her waist; her eyes were so
full that she could not see. She produced an ob-
long slip of paper.

When he saw it, a breath as of ice enveloped
him. The thing she held out toward him was
the canceled note. For a while he did me the
honor to believe that I had betrayed him.

"I understand the kind and generous impulse which prompted this deed. Oh, I admire it, and I say to you, God bless you! But don't you see how impossible it is? It can not be; no, no! My father and I are proud. What we owe we shall pay. Poverty, to be accepted without plaint, must be without debts of gratitude. But it was noble and great of you; and I knew that you intended to run away without ever letting any one know."

"Who told you?"

"No one. I guessed it."

And he might have denied all knowledge of it!

"Won't you—won't you let it be as it is? I have never done anything worth while before, and this has made me happy. Won't you let me do this? Only you need know. I am going away on Monday, and it will be years before I see Washington again. No one need ever know."

"It is impossible!"

"Why?"

She looked away. In her mind's eye she could see this man leading a troop through a snowstorm. How the wind roared! How the snow whirled and eddied about them, or suddenly blotted them from sight! But, on and on, resolutely, courageously, hopefully, he led them on to safety. . . . He was speaking, and the picture dissolved.

"Won't you let it remain just as it is?" he pleaded.

Her head moved negatively, and once more she extended the note. He took it and slowly tore it into shreds. With it he was tearing up the dream and tossing it down the winds.

"The money will be placed to your credit at the bank on Monday. We can not accept such a gift from any one. You would nct, I know. But always shall I treasure the impulse. It will give me courage in the future—when I am fighting alone."

"What are you going to do?"

"I? I am going to appear before the public,"—with assumed lightness; "I and my violin."

He struck his hands together. "The stage?"—horrified.

"I must live,"—calmly.

"But a servant to public caprice? It ought not

to be! I realize that I can not force you to accept my gift, but this ·I shall do: I shall buy in the horses and give them back to you."

"You mustn't. I shall have no place to put them. Oh!"—with a gesture full of despair and unshed tears, "why have you done all this? Why this mean masquerade, this submitting to the humiliations I have contrived for you, this act of generosity? Why?"

Perhaps she knew the answers to her own questions, but, womanlike, wanted to be told.

And at that moment, though I am not sure, I believe Warburton's guarding angel gave him some secret advice.

"You ask me why I have played the fool in the motley?"—finding the strength of his voice. "Why I have submitted in silence to your just humiliations? Why I have acted what you term generously? Do you mean to tell me that you have not guessed the riddle?"

She turned her delicate head aside and switched the grasses with her riding-crop.

"Well,"—flinging aside his cap, which he had been holding in his hand, "I will tell you. I wanted to be near you. I wanted to be, what

you made me, your servant. It is the one great
happiness that I have known. I have done all
these things because—because, God help me,
I love you! Yes, I love you, with every beat
of my heart!"—lifting his head proudly. Upon
his face love had put the hallowed seal. "Do not
turn your head away, for my love is honest. I
ask nothing, nothing; I expect nothing. I know
that it is hopeless. What woman could love a
man who has made himself ridiculous in her
eyes, as I have made myself in yours?"—bit-
terly.

"No, not ridiculous; never that!" she interrupted, her face still averted.

He strode toward her hastily, and for a moment her heart almost ceased to beat. But all
he did was to kneel at her feet and kiss the hem
of her riding-skirt. He rose hurriedly.

"God bless you, and good-by!" He knew that
if he remained he would lose all control, crush
her madly in his arms, and hurt her lips with his
despairing kisses. He had not gone a dozen
paces, when he heard her call pathetically. He
stopped.

"Mr. Warburton, surely you are not going to
leave me here alone with the horses?"

"Pardon me, I did not think! I am confused!"
he blundered.

"You are modest, too." Why is it that, at the
moment a man succumbs to his embarrassment,
a woman rises above hers? "Come nearer,"—a
command which he obeyed with some hesitation.
"You have been a groom, a butler, all for the
purpose of telling me that you love me. Listen.
Love is like a pillar based upon a dream: one by
one we lay the stones of beauty, of courage, of
faith, of honor, of steadfastness. We wake, and
how the beautiful pillar tumbles about our ears!
What right have you to build up your pillar upon
a dream of me? What do you know of the real
woman—for I have all the faults and vanities of
the sex; what do you know of me? How do you
know that I am not selfish? that I am constant?
that I am worthy a man's loving?"

"Love is not like Justice, with a pair of scales
to weigh this or that. I do not ask *why* I love
you; the knowledge is all I need. And you are
not selfish, inconstant, and God knows' that you
are worth loving. As I said, I ask for nothing."

"On the other hand," she continued, as if she
had not heard his interpolation, "I know you
thoroughly. I have had evidence of your cour-

age, your steadfastness, your unselfishness. Do not misunderstand me. I am proud that you love me. This love of yours, which asks for no reward, only the right to confess, ought to make any good woman happy, whether she loved or not. And you would have gone away without telling me, even!"

"Yes." He dug into the earth with his riding-boot. If only she knew how she was crucifying him!

"Why were you going away without telling me?"

He was dumb.

Her arms and eyes, uplifted, appealed to heaven. "What shall I say? How shall I make him understand?" she murmured. "You love me, and you ask for nothing? Is it because in spirit my father has committed a crime?"—growing tall and darting a proud glance at him.

"Good heaven, do not believe that!" he cried.

"What *am* I to believe?"—tapping the ground with her boot so that the spur jingled.

A pause.

"Mr. Warburton, do you know what a woman loves in a man? I will tell you the secret. She loves courage, constancy, and honor, purpose that surmounts obstacles; she loves pursuit; she loves the hour of surrender. Every woman builds a castle of romance and waits for Prince Charming to enter, and once he does, there must be a game of hide and seek. Perhaps I have built my castle of romance, too. I wait for Prince Charming, and—a man comes, dressed as a groom. There has been a game of hide and seek, but somehow he has tripped. Will you not ask me if I love you?"

"No, no! I understand. I do not want your gratitude. You are meeting generosity with generosity. I do not want your gratitude,"—brokenly. "I want your love, every thought of your mind, every beat of your heart. Can you give me these, honestly?"

She drew off a glove. Her hand became lost in her bosom. When she drew it forth she extended it, palm upward. Upon it lay a faded, withered rose. Once more she turned her face away.

He was at her side, and the hand and rose were crushed between his two hands.

"Can you give what I ask? Your love, your thoughts, your heart-beats?"

It was her turn to remain dumb.

"Can you?" He drew her toward him perhaps roughly, being unconscious of his strength and the nervous energy which the sight of the rose had called into being.

"Can we give those things which are—already —given?"

Only Warburton and the angels, or rather the angels and Warburton, to get at the chronological order of things, heard her, so low had grown her voice.

You may tell any kind of secret to a horse; the animal will never betray you. Warburton would never tell me what followed; and I am too sensible to hang around the horses in hopes of catching them in the act of talking over the affair among themselves. But I can easily imagine this bit of equine dialogue:

Jane: Did you ever see such foolishness?

Dick: Never! And with all this good grass about!

Whatever *did* follow caused the girl to murmur: "This is the lover I love; this is the lover I have been waiting for in my castle of romance.

I am glad that I have lost all worldly things; I am glad, glad! When did you first learn that you loved me?"

(Old, very old; thousands of years old, and will grow to be many thousand years older. But from woman's lips it is the sweetest question man ever heard.)

"At the *Gare du Nord*, in Paris; the first time I saw you."

"And you followed me across the ocean?"— wonderingly.

"And when did you first learn that you loved me?" he asked.

(Oh, the trite phrases of lovers' litany.)

"When I saw you in the police-court. Mercy! what a scandal! I am to marry my butler!"

Jane: They are laughing!

Dick: That is better than weeping. Besides, they will probably walk us home. (Wise animal!)

He was not only wise but prophetic. The lovers *did* walk the horses home. Hand in hand they came back along the road, through the flame and flush of the ripening year. The god of light burned in the far west, blending the brown earth with his crimson radiance, while the purple shadows of the approaching dusk grew larger and larger. The man turned.

"What a beautiful world it is!" he said.

"I begin to find it so," replied the girl, looking not at the world, but at him.

THE END

Postscript:

I believe they sent William back for the saddle-hamper and my jehu's cap.